DATE DUE

Owens
No. Co. B. 2-Mark
PB 2011

TEXAS SHERIFF

TEXAS SHERIFF

EUGENE CUNNINGHAM

THORNDIKE
CHIVERS

This Large Print edition is published by Thorndike Press, Waterville, Maine, USA and by AudioGO Ltd, Bath, England.
Thorndike Press, a part of Gale, Cengage Learning.

LIBRARY OF CONGRESS CATALOGING-IN-PUBLICATION DATA

Cunningham, Eugene, 1896–1957.
  Texas sheriff / by Eugene Cunningham.
    p. cm. — (Thorndike Press large print Western)
  ISBN-13: 978-1-4104-3226-1 (hardcover)
  ISBN-10: 1-4104-3226-2 (hardcover)
  1. Sheriffs—Fiction. 2. Women gamblers—Fiction. 3. Texas—Fiction.
4. Large type books. I. Title.
PS3553.U4733T48 2010
813'.54—dc22   2010037045

BRITISH LIBRARY CATALOGUING-IN-PUBLICATION DATA AVAILABLE
Published in 2010 in the U.S. by arrangement with Golden West Literacy Agency.
Published in 2011 in the U.K. by arrangement with Golden West Literacy Agency.

U.K. Hardcover: 978 1 408 49383 0 (Chivers Large Print)
U.K. Softcover: 978 1 408 49384 7 (Camden Large Print)

Printed in the United States of America
1 2 3 4 5 6 7 14 13 12 11 10

TEXAS SHERIFF

CHAPTER I

Curt Thompson rode up Gurney's sandy main street through the April dusk. He was halfway to the corral when a man walked out to the edge of a plank sidewalk and called his name. Curt pulled in. Mechanically, his hand slipped up and under his goatskin jacket, to cuddle a pistol's butt.

"Well?" he answered. "What do you want?"

The cowboy came on out to stand at Curt's stirrup and look up. Curt recognized him as one of Jim Moore's riders.

"The big augerin's on at the court house, Sheriff," he said. "Jim sent me out a-huntin' for you."

"I reckon," Curt nodded. "Who's there?"

"Tom Card, and the old man, of course, and Wolf Montague, and the Howard boys. And — quite a slew of other outfits."

"All right, I'll drift in pretty soon. Not that my being late is apt to delay those gentlemen any," Curt said grimly.

As he put his horse in the sheriff's corral and walked across the dusty width of several lots, his tight mouth lifted a little — and unpleasantly — at the corners. The sheriff's office was on the ground floor of the big 'dobe building that served the county as court house. When he came in, the room was crowded with cowmen, merchants and a sprinkling of men of various local enterprises, including Harrel, who was president of the Gurney bank. The small, square, 'dobe-walled room was hot. The smoke of pipe and cigar and cigarette made a gray, rippling canopy against the ceiling.

Curt spoke briefly and generally to the gathering. In the normal course of things, Smoky Cole would have presided over this council of war, but Smoky — though still officially sheriff of the county — was on furlough down El Paso–way, recovering from old wounds. Curt Thompson saw that grizzled old Moore of the JM, lean, saturnine dean of the Territory's cowmen, had become by tacit consent of all the chairman of this meeting.

And on a soapbox beside Moore was Tom Card, owner of the Palace Saloon. Card was best-dressed man of the crowd. He sat bolt upright with heavy, handsome, white face impassive, and steady, round blue eyes alert, as always. Curt knew that the gambler's blank-seeming stare missed no smallest detail, no slightest movement, in that place.

"Come in, Curt," Moore said drawlingly. "Come on in, I reckon you're to take a hand in this squabble."

Curt nodded inscrutably. He worked his way into a quiet and dusky corner. There he leaned against the wall. Moore looked frowningly after him for a moment. Then he took up again what he had evidently been saying before Curt's entrance.

"— It's been going on, now, for five months. Worse than it was during Frenchy Leonard's time. And it's certainly time something was figured out to snub this gang. They've been running along without a lick being hit back at 'em. First crack, they stuck up the bullion stage coming from The Points. Then the Wagon Wheel outfit lost three-four hundred head of good steers. Then Rawlin's bank was busted into up at Faith — right under the nose of the Governor. Next, I lost fifty horses slicker than a whistle — why, you'd think the damn' ground had opened up and swallowed 'em. And then, last week, the bullion stage is stuck up again!"

Redder and redder his harsh features had

become, as he enumerated the incidents in the Territory's latest crime-wave. Now, he glared around at the grim faces of his neighbors — owners and managers of every important outfit in the Territory or prominent business men of the region. Energetically, they nodded agreement with their spokesman.

"By Gemini!" he snarled. "It's certainly time something was *done!* It's a gang and a smart'n' — no denying that! Five months this here business has been going on. If something ain't done they'll be stealing the shells out of our belts and the shoes off our horses and the grub off our knives! This-here sheriff's office has got to land 'em!"

Tom Card moved his big body a trifle on his soapbox. He made a slight gesture with his cigar, so that the huge diamond he wore on the little finger of his right hand twinkled in the lamplight. His round, blue eyes went briefly to that dusky corner of the office where Curt Thompson leaned, silent and moveless.

"Of course," said Card in his deep, smooth voice, "the sheriff's office has been somewhat demoralized since Cole's injuries forced him to give up active work. I think that no blame attaches to anyone. But I do agree with Jim Moore that something

10

should be done — right now. Normally, the county could rock along with Cole on leave of absence. But, it seems to me that this condition which we met tonight to discuss — this new, mysterious gang's systematic activities — calls for immediate and forceful action. We can't wait for Cole to recover and return. We need a thoroughly capable sheriff — and we need him now!"

He looked around him, somewhat obviously avoiding any glance toward Curt Thompson's corner, now. There were nods of agreement from Bob Allister, from Wolf Montague, from the Howard brothers — from virtually every man there, cowman and merchant and banker.

"No," continued Card, squinting thoughtfully against the smoke of his cigar, "my idea is that — for the present, anyway — it would not be fair to Cole to declare his office vacant and elect a successor. We are all agreed that Cole is an excellent man; that if he were able to take the trail of this gang, today, their career would be short. But we need a shooting sheriff — today! So it seems to me that the thing to do is to choose an outstanding man and appoint him chief deputy, to carry on the office during Cole's absence, and to get this gang."

He turned on the soapbox, so that he

faced Sam Bain. The owner of the Lazy B outfit was a tall, dark young man of exceedingly handsome features. Automatically, the others glanced at him and Bain tried to look as if he were unaware of their attention.

"I have an opinion to offer, regarding the choice of a man," Card went on smoothly. "I rather pride myself on a certain ability to size a man and I *hope* that you'll agree with me when I nominate —"

"Momentito!" Curt Thompson's soft but arresting drawl checked Card. "Not so fast. Not — so — fast."

He came lounging out into the center of the room, a smallish figure moving with a jaguar's lazy ease of muscles. He was only twenty-four, but deep-tanned face and violet-blue eyes alike owned an odd maturity. Now, his eyes were twinkling and a little smile lifted the corners of his tight mouth. But the expression of neither eyes nor mouth was particularly good-humored. He pushed back the Stetson upon reddish hair, then stood rocking upon high bootheels with thumbs hooked in the waistband of his overalls. Deliberately, he looked them over.

"Things *are* in sorry shape, up and down the whole Territory," he drawled. "Jim Moore is right — dead right! A man could might' near think that Frenchy Leonard and

12

Tim Fenelon and the whole gang we downed two years back had come up from under the grass roots to ride high, wide and handsome again. A stage stuck up over here. A string of horses or a bunch of cows just leaving us somewhere else."

His shrewd eyes went wandering from face to face. He lifted one slender, muscular shoulder in a small movement.

"But the difference is, now, that the gang is not out in the open. It's not putting a brand onto its jobs. We're not finding a thing to say who is what! It was different when Frenchy was swinging the long rope. Everybody knew that it was Frenchy. And, the only reason he rode so long was that the people of the Territory just flopped down and crawled on their bellies — until Lit Taylor came smoking it from over on the Diamond. Lit was different from the people in the Territory. He didn't give a little bitty damn about Frenchy, or his gunplay, or his gang."

Slowly, the violet-blue eyes came to rest upon Tom Card's blank gambler-face. He shook his head; clicked tongue reprovingly against teeth.

"And now — goodness me! Everybody wants action. Everybody's yelling for scalps. You want the sheriff's office to *do* something. Yes, sir! You want this — this *trackless bunch* roped and hog-tied and beefed. And you want all this done *pronto* — no later than early yesterday morning."

Tom Card looked steadily at Curt, who smiled softly at the gambler — in the fashion he reserved for men he did not like. Then he went on, drawlingly, like a man only thinking aloud.

"All this talk about the sheriff's office . . . Why, the gentlemen are talking about *me!* They must be — for with Smoky gone, I'm the sheriff's office. Then, if I'm being talked about, I ought to have a right to talk back, a little bit. That's only fair."

"Go ahead and talk, then," Jim Moore grunted in not unfriendly tone. "Nobody's stopping you — nor ever did that *I* know about!"

"Thanks!" Curt nodded. "I appreciate the chance, Jim. Well — the truth is, you-all are doing a lot of beefing about what I'm not doing. But, you — all of you — know as much about this gang as I do. And not one of you — not all of you put together — can go out and collect this gang! Now, I'm just a common kind of chief deputy. I don't claim to be a ring-tailed whizzer. Least of all do I claim to be a detective. But, if I stick around as acting sheriff, *I'll get this gang!*

14

Why? Because it's my job — *that's* why!"

Once more, he looked around from face to face.

"I don't think I'm claiming too much when I say, the chances are I'll get 'em quicker than a new man could. I think I will, because I've already seen trouble in the Territory, from behind this star I'm wearing. I've seen that trouble through the smoke! I know more about this kind of work than — Sam Bain over there. I mention Sam because we all know that he's the candidate Tom Card wants to put in over my head."

Men's heads turned to Card. But he never let his emotions show in his expression. Now, he merely regarded Curt Thompson's daredevil face steadily. Curt lifted a mouth-corner sardonically, shrugged and continued in the lazy drawl that had not altered since beginning the longest speech of his life.

"Now, here's the way she lies: If you-all are certain you can't win your race with the horse you're riding — then shift your hull! But, if you put Sam Bain in as chief deputy, I pack my warbags and rattle my hocks! I won't work with Bain. I'm free to say that I don't like Bain a little bit. I can go further: I wouldn't *trust* Bain as far's I could throw an elephant by the tail — a real sizable elephant. And you-all know this is poor

15

elephant country! Taking it all around, I reckon that I just have got no time for the man. And that goes any way Sam Bain elects to play her."

Bain began to get up. A quick flush dyed his dark skin cherry-red. Curt Thompson, still with the little humorless smile at lip-corners, slightly hunched his shoulders and waited. He wore no visible weapon, but that deceived nobody there. They knew that beneath the short jacket of tanned goatskin was a trick vest that carried two cunningly slung holsters. They knew, also, that Curt Thompson was good at the deadly cross-arm draw. How good, none was sure. But — They waited tensely.

Then Tom Card touched the knee of the Lazy B owner. Bain sat back sullenly, with glint of white teeth beneath his small, black mustache. Before there was heard more than muttered comment among the men there, the door of the sheriff's office swung open. A lithe, gray-eyed cowboy stood framed in it for an instant, a slender, efficient-looking youngster, who wrinkled his nose in a sniff of distaste as a wave of stale tobacco smoke rolled into his face:

"For the Lord's sake! Why'n't you hairpins let a little fresh air into the joint?" he cried. "She's quadrivial! She's worse! She's damn'

16

near hypothetical!"

He left the door open behind him and came inside, glancing swiftly around. They waited for his message, for this was Andy Allen, range-boss of Los Alamos. The great ranch of King Connell was now managed by Lit Taylor, the King's son-in-law and a power in the Territory since he had wiped out Frenchy Leonard's killers and rustlers. Andy was Lit's right hand.

Lit was laid up with a fractured thigh, else in tonight's council he would have out-ranked Jim Moore, both as representative of the Territory's largest outfit and as the retired deputy sheriff who had been responsible for bringing the Law west of the Rowdy River.

"Lit's a-layin' out at the ranch jerkin' at the hitchrope. He's just downright surreptitious, because he couldn't come in tonight," grinned Andy Allen, who loved long, strange words solely for their own sake. "So he says to me that I better grab my foot in my hand an' lope into town to tell you-all he's backin' Curt Thompson quadrilateral an' complete."

"Taylor's record entitles him to consideration," Tom Card said smoothly, nodding. "But, it seems to me that this condition we face demands concerted thought — the best thought of all of us. So, the opinion of one man should be considered only as one man's view — even if he *is* Lit Taylor of Los Alamos. Now, as I remarked in the beginning —"

"Hold on a minute, Card!" interrupted Jim Moore. "Curt, you mind stepping outside for a spell? You see, we have got to settle on something tonight and maybe the talk'll be freer if we can be to ourselves, like. Just as soon as we settle on what we're going to do, I'll send you word."

"It's all yours," Curt nodded calmly. He moved toward the door, but paused on the threshold to look back at them with that small, humorless smile. "But don't you forget what I said. You can have me, or you can have Sam Bain — but you sure as hell can't have us both! Either you-all give me a chance to corral this trackless bunch lone-handed, or I hand you back your little tin star — right now!"

He drifted away from the court house, rolling a cigarette. He flicked a match upon a thumbnail and cupped his hands about the tiny flame. He drew in smoke and looked up and down the street.

"It's pretty," he thought, lifting his eyes to the sky where the great yellow stars were like scattered topazes upon black velvet.

"Mightily pretty . . . And that bunch back there can send me riding again. I wonder — would the stars be as lovely — Colorado-way — as they are here?"

Grimness went out of his smile with the thought. He looked toward the lights of the Palace, then moved softly downstreet until he stood in the shadows beneath the wooden awning of Halliday's store. Here he could look across at the long front of Tom Card's place, where saloon and gambling-room and dance-hall alike were crowded tonight.

It was a favorite haunt of Curt's at night — Halliday's store. For from it he stared directly across the street into the wide, unshaded window of Tom Card's office; stared directly at Shirley Randolph's dark little head and clear-cut profile, while the girl worked upon Tom Card's account books. And it was virtually the only opportunity Curt had to watch her to his heart's content.

Chapter II

Half a year, now, the girl had been in Gurney, keeping books in Tom Card's office, riding out into the hills on a horse bought during her first month in the county seat. And Gurney really knew no more about her than on that day when the stage had brought her from Ancho and the railroad.

Very vividly, Curt remembered that day. For he had ridden over into the Diablos after a crazy Mexican murderer and had cut into the Ancho-Gurney road on the way home with his prisoner. He had stopped the stage, shackled the Mexican beside the driver, and, with their horses tied behind, had shared the stage's interior with Shirley — the only passenger.

"I hope I'm not bothering you," he had said to her. And —

"Not in the least!" she had answered in a tone as far away as if she sat upon some height at least as remote as the blue peaks of the Soldados ahead.

But a little later, while covertly he stared — much as he was staring now — at the clear, pale cameo of her face, the wide, fixed dark eyes, she had turned to ask him a question — ask if he knew a cattleman named Villiers. Curt had known nobody of the name and she had withdrawn with a word of thanks.

"And I rode with her all the way," he recalled, now, "clear up to Mrs. Sheehan's hotel. And thought, like a damn' fool, that in a week — if she stayed here hunting her Villiers man — I would get to know her!

Ah, well! I was younger then. . . ."

He watched, now, while she began to clear the table that was her desk. Slightly, he nodded. She was ready to go home to Mrs. Sheehan's — and he would trail her unseen as he had so often done — or ready to buck the tiger in the Palace's gaming-room, as she sometimes did.

She had gone to work for Tom Card the day after arrival, and against the Palace's tawdry background she was always glaringly out of place. No man ever spoke to her except to answer her. None ever made advances — partly because Tom Card shielded her, but more because of her own aloofness.

When Curt decided that tonight Shirley was gambling, and crossed the street to the Palace, he saw her standing in the midst of the men before Newe at the faro table. She made her bets while Curt watched. She won, lost, won again, and none of her neighbors even stared openly.

"Lovely! Lovely!" Curt breathed, watching the slim straightness of her, the quiet assurance of sleek, black head. *Lovely!*

Daily, he saw her in Mrs. Sheehan's dining-room. His seat was next to hers. But he was no nearer acquaintance, friendliness, than he had been when he helped her from

21

the stage that first day. His only consolation was that neither Tom Card nor Sam Bain had penetrated her reserve more than he. And both the big, handsome gambler, the equally eye-taking Lazy B owner, were as obviously fascinated as Curt.

A rasping voice behind him broke in upon his brooding. He turned, to face the speaker without pleasure. Zyler was one of the regulars in the Palace. Somehow, he lived, had money to spend, without doing any work that Curt knew of. He was most typical of the Palace loafers.

"Well," Zyler inquired, "whut'd they do to you? You still chief deputy, or — just a deputy?"

The fact that he could not answer the question was enough to infuriate Curt, apart from his dislike for the questioner. But he was sheriff — if only for this final half-hour. The star he wore under goatskin *charro* jacket was a shield for such as Zyler. A sheriff could not hit them. So, he looked sleepily at the grinning one, and when he spoke, it was drawlingly.

"Your question's wrong, Zyler. You must ask if I'm Acting Sheriff Thompson or — just Mr. Thompson, an outstanding private citizen. Or — don't ask questions at all. That's still better."

22

Zyler burst into raucous laughter. The temptation to step in and smash a fist to the open mouth was very strong, but Curt controlled himself.

"*Sh!*" he said softly. "You bother people. And you're not the sort to go bothering folks with carelessness. I'd think about that, Zyler . . . It may be skin on your nose."

At the faro table Shirley Randolph turned. Dark eyes came to Curt's face, shifted to Zyler's, then to Curt's again. Curt saw. Somehow, it had power to infuriate him — sight of her there, a part of Tom Card's set-up in the Palace, as this smirking shoulder-striker, Zyler, was a part of it. She *was* a part of it. Even the aloofness with which she stood among the cowboys and townsmen did not alter the fact that she was a part of it all.

He stepped closer still to Zyler. And the laugh died in Zyler's mouth. He was taller than Curt. He had to let his chin drop, bend his head forward, to look down into Curt's smokily dark blue eyes.

"Zyler!" Curt said in an undertone — too low for anyone else to hear. "Take this warning — or *don't* take it! Don't ever open your mouth to me, again! *Ever!* Don't ever even look at me, again! Least of all, laugh when I'm around. For you'll strain me, Zyler . . .

I'm not a strong character. I don't have a lot of will power. Right now, Zyler, I'm on the edge of taking that gun of yours away from you and just beating you to death with it. I —"

Zyler's small, dark eyes dilated. He stared fixedly at Curt, who stood so close that their shirts brushed.

"I get spells!" Curt whispered. "I'm subject to 'em. Spells when the sight of certain men — like you, Zyler! — sets me wild. And I have to tear things to pieces. Like — like this!"

His left hand slid up and caught Zyler's gun arm above the elbow. He had fingers like steel hooks — Curt. Now, they clamped on Zyler's arm and the taller man's face twisted agonizedly. "Walk to the door with me, Zyler," Curt breathed. "I'm not going to hurt you — now! Come on!"

He turned Zyler and, without slacking his grip, moved at Zyler's side to the door. They went out upon the sidewalk. Tighter, Curt's hand clamped Zyler's arm. He leaned a little toward Zyler.

"You lousy bum!" he said savagely. "I ought to've slapped your face in there, before 'em all, and made you pull that bushwhacker's gun of yours — or run! Do you think *you* can slap leather with me?"

24

"No!" Zyler whispered. "I — I ain't huntin' trouble, Thompson. I — I — just ask' you a civil question. I —".

Out here in the semi-darkness his swagger was gone. Curt could hear his labored breathing. He could feel the arm he gripped shaking.

"Keep out of my road, then! I've been a peaceful man, since I came to Gurney. *Since I came to Gurney*, Zyler! But —"

"I don't want trouble!" Zyler gasped.

"Then don't put yourself in its way. You've watched Tom Card and Sam Bain and you've developed notions. You've aped their ways until you think you're something. That's going to get you killed! Maybe *they'll* last out the war, but you won't! Don't let those two talk you into a wooden overcoat."

He twisted and with the slight-seeming movement, Zyler spun across the sidewalk, staggered on its edge and fell sprawling in the street.

"Was that — necessary?" Shirley Randolph asked from the doorway at Curt's left.

Curt moved quickly away from the Palace wall and toward Zyler, now getting up.

"Get out of that door!" he snapped at the girl. "Zyler! You touch that hogleg and you'll drop it in hell!"

Zyler immediately elevated his hands and

hurried toward the bar-room door down the walk. Curt turned. Shirley was outside, now. She turned to the right — the direction of Mrs. Sheehan's hotel. Curt stepped after her. She heard the rap of his heels on the planks and turned.

"If it's no trouble," he said conversationally, "I'd rather walk beside you than trail fifty feet behind — the way I've always done before."

"What?" she cried. "Trail behind me? What do you mean?"

"You are an innocent!" he grinned, and fell into step with her. "Do you think that I've let you walk these streets at night by yourself? Night after night I've dogged along behind you and seen you into the hotel."

"I certainly didn't know it! And I don't think I like it, now that you tell me! Why should *you* — I mean — you said 'let' me walk the streets at night. Since when have you had anything to do with my affairs; any right to *let* me do this, or forbid me? It seems to me, Mr. Curt Thompson, that you take a good deal upon yourself!"

"It's a family habit. Not so strong in me as in some of the others. Why, in our family album there's a tintype of Great-Uncle Ebenezer Zachariah. There was a man for you! *He* stayed a widower until he was sixty-five, then took on himself a widow with eleven children. Now, I'm an impulsive soul — as you noticed back there when I was having my — *discussion* with Zyler. But I've always been able to control myself, in the neighborhood of widows with more than ten children."

She laughed faintly. It was a strained sound — as if (Curt thought) she had not laughed for a good while. Instantly, she was serious again. He looked at her grave face, in the light of a store's window.

"I asked you, then, if it were necessary to knock Zyler into the street. It seems to me that you — rather go out of your way to court enmity. At least, you have the reputation of a quarrelsome man; a man with a good many enemies."

Curt laughed carelessly, watching her.

"I'm an abandoned soul. But I'll bet I'm a brand that could be snatched from the burning. It's just that — oh, you know the song:

"First took to drinking,
Then to card-playing,
Got shot in the breast
And I'm dying today . . .

"A cowboy like me, associating with the

wrong kind of people, he gets off to a bad start. Now, if you'd sort of take an interest in me and set aside a half-hour every day to show me how to lead a better life —"

"I'm serious!" she said, with irritation. "You're entirely satisfied with yourself. That — sticks out all over you. You wouldn't be anybody in the world but Curt Thompson. And you think Curt Thompson is just about right, as he swaggers along the sidewalk. Even those of us who — well, who think that he's a rather nice person —"

"My God!" Curt breathed piously and stopped her short with hand upon her arm. He turned her a little, so that the reflected light they were leaving revealed her face. "Do my ears deceive me? You — you really think this swaggering Curt Thompson is even *rather* a nice person?"

"I said — rather! Let's go on."

"I don't give a whoop, now, whether that bunch of yappers down at the office leaves my star, or puts in the Stuffed Chaps! It's been a lovely, lovely day! *You* think I'm nice —"

"Of course" — there was the faintest shade of malice in her tone, now — "I'm not the only one who thinks you may do. Nor am I the one who holds that view most decidedly . . ."

"What are you talking about?" he asked her, in real bewilderment. "I've got friends here, of course, the same as enemies. What you take for quarrelsomeness is just laziness: I want to bring out into the open the people who've got the old knife ready to dig my back. It saves trouble to know on what side the fence people are. Zyler, for instance. Sam Bain. Tom Card. That whole slew. They're only dangerous to the man who lets 'em get behind him."

"Tom Card and Sam Bain are both friends of mine. We won't discuss them. Certainly, I won't listen to your talk about them. What I was saying —"

"What I was thinking is — *I* knew a boy once who had a pet skunk. But, go ahead! Every baby has to sit down on at least one red-hot stove, to learn about getting burned. You were saying —"

"Mrs. Young, at the racket store, is convinced that Mr. Thompson is Texas's greatest product, to date."

"Oh — Marie!" Curt laughed. "She's a darling. If I'd ever had a sister, I would have wanted her to be just like Marie. But we're talking about you. Would it be asking too much to ask that you do a little reforming in my direction? I'll bet it would make a different man of me — not right away, of course! But in a reasonable length of time. Say, five-ten years . . . And how I'd love it! Will you, Miss Shirley?"

They were at the steps of Mrs. Sheehan's hotel, now. Shirley turned and stepped up, so that she could look down at him. She laughed.

"Don't be silly. I do think you're a nice person — no rather about it. But that's all. I'm not taking in any boys to reform. Seriously, though, it would be pleasant to see you — seeing straighter, I suppose I wanted to say . . ."

"Such as — and how?" Curt demanded, when she hesitated.

"Why, not letting some irritated snap-judgment give you the wrong impression about good men!"

Curt reached out deftly and captured her hand. He took off his hat and stood looking up at her.

"I thank you," he said softly. "I know what you mean. But only time will tell whether *your* judgment is right, or mine. And it needn't keep us dry-gulching each other, need it — the fact that we don't see some people alike? I'll try to remember that I'm hasty-tempered, when some — stranger next drifts in and I have to size him. I really will. Meanwhile —"

"Meanwhile — what?" she demanded after an instant, and tried to pull her hand away.

"Meanwhile, I could wish that you were a school-teacher."

"Why?" she asked unwarily, in a surprised tone.

"Because, in all the best books, the school-teacher marries the cowboy! And I approve of that!"

"*Which* cowboy, though?" she said quickly, and pulled with more of urgency against his unyielding hand. "Good-night, Mr. Thompson!"

There was light enough coming from the hall to silhouette the slender, shapely figure; to let him see clearly enough the pale oval of her face and the dark eyes steady upon him. He drew a long, slow breath. The impulse — but it was more than impulse; it was desire — to draw her close and hold her, bend and find her mouth, was strong. But he knew that this was not the moment to move; this girl was different from those he had known in his happy-go-lucky wanderings. So he forced himself to speak lightly:

"Which cowboy . . . Yes, that's a point I'd have to consider, all right. Because I would want to know which cowboy to shoot, in case things didn't work out the way I wanted. But, in a serious matter like that, Miss Shirley, you — you'd be careful, wouldn't you? Promise me you'll be careful and not go jumping into matrimony without a lot of good advice!"

She laughed — and it was a lighter, an easier, sound, this time. Still she pulled against his hand. "I can promise that, I think!" she told him. "Now —"

He bent a little and lifted her hand, to kiss the palm. She made the slightest gasping sound and stiffened. He released her hand and straightened.

"Good-night," he said softly. "It's been the *loveliest* day!"

Going back toward the court house, Curt thought of the girl, rather than of the arguments in the sheriff's office. He had gone a long step forward, tonight. With another girl, it would have meant little, but Shirley Randolph was not like — Marie Young, for instance.

So to have walked beside her from the Palace to the hotel; to have got from her admission that she had thought about him sufficiently to have the impulse to quarrel with him; to have been able to tell her, even lightly, that he wanted to marry her — that was much ground gained.

32

"But," he asked himself, "what gave her that notion about Marie? Just because we hurrah each other, people get the notion that there's something to it, I reckon."

Then his thoughts slid away from both women. For, no matter what he might say to Shirley, about not caring whether the county's prominents put Sam Bain in as acting sheriff, or left him in Smoky Cole's place, he *did* care. He cared very much. He wanted to be sheriff of Gurney. It was his life and he wanted to succeed in it.

Marie Young was still in the tiny racket store when he came up to the door. She and Pancho, the Mexican boy-of-odd-jobs, were putting covers on the counters. Curt leaned in the doorway and watched unobserved for a moment.

"Just a little more to the right," he said critically. "I do hate to see things slaunchwise and anti-godlin. There! That's it. But it's certainly ducky that I could come by."

"I notice that you waited until the work was done, though," Marie told him scornfully. "You cowboys! If one of you had to work as men in the East work, he'd just pass out. The other day two cowboys were standing outside there and one asked the other: 'What are you doing now, Steve?' and Steve said: 'Nothing, John.' And John said —

almost excitedly: *'Where?'* Steve said: 'Over yonder, about thirty miles.' *Work!* Imagine a cowboy trying that!"

"You mustn't talk about people that way," Curt reproved her gravely. " 'Specially the people of your adopted country. Cowboys haven't the *time* to put in at common labor. They have got thinking to do. That takes up a lot of time."

"Thinking! A lot of thinking you do!" she jeered. She was small and pretty, very blonde. It was hard to credit her with twenty-three years and widowhood. She was very like a schoolgirl, Curt thought, as he looked affectionately at her.

"By Gemini!" he confessed ruefully, "I have done a good deal of it tonight! Thinking, I mean."

She told Pancho to bar the back door and came up the store to stand beside Curt. There was trouble in her wide, blue eyes.

"You don't expect them to put Bain in over your head? Surely —"

"I know they won't do that!" he assured her grimly. "But they're as apt as not to put him in. Card's electioneering down there, now."

"They won't be idiots enough to let you go!" she said angrily. "You've done the work of the office ever since Lit Taylor quit.

Everybody knows you have."

"There are some who don't like the way I've done it. But — it's no never mind! They'll suit themselves. But if they do put Bain in —"

He snapped his fingers eloquently and she watched him frowningly. He grinned down at her.

"Going to close up? I'm wandering around until they make up their minds down at the office."

"It's ironing," she said. "Old Marie can wash, but I can't afford to let her iron. Want to come in for a while?"

"Thanks! I wish I could. But there's the beat to walk. When our precious marshal gets out of bed, I'll be lighter on my feet. See you tomorrow. 'Night!"

"Good-night," she said slowly. "And, good luck, Curt. You — deserve it."

"You're a honey!" he told her warmly. "But, I've told you that before."

"Not exactly. But — I'm glad you think so."

She stood close to him, watching him. Then she drew a long breath and moved toward the door into her housekeeping rooms.

"Tired?" Curt asked sympathetically.

She nodded without turning and went on.

He stepped out when Pancho came to lock the street door and drifted aimlessly toward the Palace, passed it, crossed the street.

The latest outlaw organization was in his mind as he walked. In the sheriff's office, he had not told quite all that he knew of this mysterious gang which left no tracks behind. For, the week before, when he had looked over the scene of the stage holdup, he had found — as he had found upon the ground in the other robberies — horse tracks leading toward broken country. But, following cautiously, he had come upon a place where one of the riders had dismounted to tighten a cinch. Just a couple of footprints and yet —

"It's certainly a new play for the Territory," Curt thought. "*A woman,* riding with a gang like that . . ."

He had been quietly investigating during the past week. Then Tom Card's efforts to make Sam Bain acting sheriff had brought about this meeting of tonight. What woman in the Territory was of the type to fit in with what Curt was beginning to term "The Trackless Bunch"? He had mulled over the puzzle; trying to picture every woman he had ever seen, on every ranch or mountain-farm; trying to pose her in overalls and boots, masked with a bandanna, throwing a gun down upon a stage driver and messenger. So far, the effort had been without success.

Slowly, now, he moved on along the sandy street, turned at Mrs. Sheehan's and went softly along the rear walls of the buildings which fronted the single main street of Gurney. He was merely following his regular beat, doing what he termed "riding herd" on the county seat of night — a duty assumed since the marshal's illness.

Well past the sheriff's office, he turned left again and so returned to the main street. Suddenly, muffled footfalls sounded behind him. He turned alertly as a dark figure came running toward him.

"Thompson? Thompson?" a voice hailed him. "Well, I got you —"

Curt moved like a cat into the shadows of a wall. His hands twinkled up, dived beneath the jumper, crossing each other. They flashed out again with his Colts. The big hammers came back beneath his thumbs as the six-shooters flipped down to hip-level. He leaned a little forward.

The other seemed to understand these movements. He flung himself flat upon the ground and yelled earnestly:

"It's Andy Allen! Don't shoot, you blame' wolf! By George! You're certainly miscellaneous, after dark!"

Curt stood tense for an instant, then shook his head, as if he accomplished return to Gurney and a harmless environment by the gesture. He returned the Colts to their holsters and moved deliberately out to where Andy Allen was now getting up in the middle of the dusky street. He stood for an instant, looking down at the Los Alamos range-boss.

"Andy, what part of Texas do you come from?" he demanded.

"Texas?" repeated Andy, in a puzzled voice. "Howcome you think I'm a Texican? Why, I was born an' raised north of Faith. Never was out of the Territory in my life!"

"Never was in — Tarrant County, Texas?" Curt persisted. "Certain?"

"Certain! I was born up there in them great big, permeative mountings. Weighed twenty pounds an' yelled for liquor. When I was two year old I had long, yaller curls — man, I was prettier'n an epigastrium! When I was three year old —"

"You swallowed the dictionary and never have digested her yet?" Curt finished for him, grinning. "Get up out of that street, you damn' fool, and quit your lying. But — boy!" — suddenly he turned serious again — "don't you *ever* run up behind me again, like that, yelling that you've got me!"

"Makes you think them Tarrant County *gunies* have tracked you down, huh?" Andy grinned. "Well, it *was* a fool thing to do, I felt plumb therapeutic when you filled your hands the way you did!"

"Were you chasing me for something special?"

"Yeh! They been pow-wowin' hither an' yon down there in the sheriff's office. Tom Card, he said all kinds of nice things about you, Curt. Said you was a fine boy an' had a bright future before you an' was fitted for most any job — except sheriff . . ."

"Sam Bain being the bright and shining light for *that* place, of course," Curt nodded. "Well?"

"Upshot of the whole business was, you're still Big It. You got three months to land your 'Trackless Bunch,' Curt. If you don't corral 'em in that time, you're extemporaneous! They want to break the news to you, now."

Back in the sheriff's office, old Jim Moore pronounced the ultimatum of the assembly. Curt listened with brown face expressionless. He was interested chiefly in his study of Tom Card's heavy, white face and, in lesser degree, Sam Bain's barely concealed malevolence. But neither the gambler nor his protégé made any comment upon the majority's decision. They were the first to leave and Curt's eyes followed them mechanically.

Subconsciously, he was studying them, not only as his avowed opponents here, but also as rivals for the favor of Shirley Randolph. He forced himself to admit that Tom Card — big, good-looking, well-educated, wealthy — was foe enough for any man. Sam Bain was of different caliber, neither so forceful nor so brainy as Card. Too, Bain had an old, shuffling walk, the only sign of weakness in a splendid physique.

When the room was empty, except for Curt and Andy Allen, the man from Alamos stretched elaborately, settled the wide brim of his Stetson over one gray eye, and grinned at Curt.

"Yeh?" Curt inquired. "What deviltry are you hatching now? I suppose I really ought to hobble you and corral you, right now. Save running you up and down alleys, later on."

"You hurt me," Andy said sadly. "You don't know how anachronistic you make me feel, Curt. Last time it was only that Chinese cook in the U-and-Me that I took out after. Or so I'm told . . . But, tonight, I think I'll take me a li'l' bitsy *pasear* down to the

Palace. I got one of them yens to antagonize Tom Card's tiger. Want to side me, boy? Hell! It's too *internal* to be turnin' in, already."

Curt shook his head and relighted his cigarette.

"No, I've responsibilities. *I'm* no harum-scarum buckaroo with nothing but a John B. to weight down my mind. I've got to wander around and sort of circle-herd things. The Wagon Wheel's in town, full tally. And that's a bunch of hairpins apt to take Gurney apart just to see what makes her tick, if they're not watched. Well, if you're able to find your way back, after your tiger-bucking, there's a cot over there you can use. But don't you take mine — it's clean!"

They went elbow-to-elbow as far as the Palace, then Andy crossed over, jingling the silver in his pocket. Curt went prowling about saloons and street, with an alert eye for appearance of the Wagon Wheel's uncurried riders. His thoughts reverted to Andy Allen.

"Pure damn' luck that I didn't drill that happy-go-lucky idiot!" he told himself. "When he bobbed up behind me I certainly did think some of the old Jensen outfit had caught up with me . . . But, I reckon there's little use worrying about the Jensens, now, up here. They're nearly three years and a long way behind me. That's a long way behind — a long way . . . A man could start over, up here in the Territory. Get himself a little place and a bunch of cattle, to start with. Marry the right girl —"

His pleasant meditations were interrupted by the soft fall of hoofs on the sand of the street ahead. He looked up mechanically and made out the silhouette of a rider jogging into Gurney from the north. The shambling figure sagged in the saddle, slouching over the horn with head nodding as if he were half-asleep. Coming abreast of Curt, he straightened and reined in.

"Sheriff's office?" he inquired huskily. "I'm lookin' for the sheriff. I got a —"

"Why, I'm Thompson, the acting sheriff," Curt told him. "What's the excitement?"

But the man moved in the saddle with creaking of leather. Curt did not see his hand move. He did not need to see it. There was a blossoming of flame from the hand and with the Colt's roar Curt heard the soggy *thut!* of a slug going into the 'dobe wall behind him.

Mechanically, Curt jerked his own guns. Before he had them out and leveled, the man fired again — and missed for the second time. For three seconds, after that, the sidewalk was aflame with their crossing gunfire. A slug burned Curt's neck. But as he flinched, the man came sliding out of the saddle and slumped upon the sand. The horse trotted away.

Men poured out of the Palace upstreet, out of houses and other saloons. They found Curt standing grimly over the dead man.

"Don't know who he was — yet," he told them impatiently. "Carry him down to the Palace, some of you-all. I'm interested in getting a look at him."

They laid the dead man out upon the floor. Curt had never seen him before. Nor had any other there, from all that Curt could learn. He was a lank and efficient-looking customer, with pistol holster slung low on his left side for a right-hand draw, the holster-toe secured by a thong to his boot-top. He had a long, angular face, deep-lined, savage, a great hook nose and small black eyes set close upon the bridge.

"Man, you was sure lucky!" said Andy Allen, who had pushed through the crowd to Curt's side. "He got the first shot, huh? Say! What school of chain lightnin' you graduate from, anyhow, Curt? He's got three holes in him. An' all you collected was that nick!"

"One of my bullets hit his horse. It jumped and spoiled his aim," Curt explained absently, with eyes roving.

Tom Card was standing on the edge of the group about the dead man. His round blue eyes were steady upon Curt's face. Curt grinned faintly. His eyes were narrowed, almost sleepy.

"Who's this bushwhacker, Card?" he asked the gambler.

"I don't think I ever saw him before," Card shrugged.

"Never was here at the Palace?" Curt asked, with widening of his faint smile.

"Couldn't say. I don't see everyone that comes in."

Curt turned slightly and looked around him. Three bartenders behind the long bar were craning their necks to view the corpse. These Curt eyed thoughtfully.

"Mind if I ask *them* if they ever saw him?" he inquired of Card, very politely, with jerk of head toward the bar.

"Help yourself," Card said tonelessly.

So, at Curt's request, the three drink-dispensers came around and looked carefully at the dead face. But none of them — and Curt was inclined to credit their statements — admitted recalling the fellow.

Andy Allen went back to the sheriff's office with Curt. He was unusually silent until the door was shut and the wall lamp lighted. Then he looked curiously at Curt:

"How-come you as much as told Card he knowed that dry-gulcher?" he demanded. "Boy! He was collectin' tail feathers."

"Did I do that?" Curt cried. "Why, Andy! Think of that! Do you reckon Card noticed it?"

"Well, if he never, he's too lugubrious for me. *I* noticed it. So did Halliday an' some more. What was the idee? Don't try to act innocent an' nefarious with me."

"Well — come to think about it, maybe I did sort of look at Card anti-godlin," Curt said, with the same small, unpleasant smile that he had turned upon Tom Card.

He put his hand behind him and from hip pocket brought out a pint whiskey flask, almost full. He held out the bottle to Andy, then jerked it back.

"I want you to look at this, not hog it!" he warned the Alamos man.

Andy took the bottle, grinning. He turned it over and stared at the label.

"*Tom Card's Palace Special* . . . Well?"

"I found it in that bushwhacker's jumper pocket, that's all. Funny . . . He came at me from the edge of town. He was a man riding into Gurney from Portoway. And yet — he

45

was packing a bottle of Palace tarantula-juice; almost a full bottle. And he somehow didn't look to me like a saving man who'd be light on his liquor . . ."

"Oh!" Andy said, staring at the label again. "Like that!"

"Of course," Curt shrugged, "it's possible that Card told me the truth; that he had never seen that drygulcher before. Somebody might have given this bottle to the fellow; somebody in the Palace might have sold it to him without Card knowing. But — here's Tom Card, pulling the political strings to get me out of the sheriff's chair and get Sam Bain in — for some good reason of his own that I'd enjoy knowing."

He reached for the bottle, uncorked it and sniffed, then put it to his mouth and drank. He handed it back to Andy, who lifted it in his turn. Curt crossed to his cot and sat down, to fumble for tobacco and papers and build a cigarette. He put the edge of right bootsole against the heel of his left boot and pushed, then sat with that boot in his hand, eyes narrowed, very thoughtful.

"Tom Card wants a sheriff he can handle," he said slowly. "He thinks the business is arranged. But he stubs his toe, here, tonight. The majority decides to bear up without Sam Bain and keep me in. So — less than an hour after I win, and he loses, a bush-whacker rides into Gurney, maybe from right around the back of the Palace. He speaks to me and I tell him who I am. Then he whangs away at me. Maybe there's not a bit of connection, but — if one of those slugs had gone two inches to right or left of where it *did* go, tell me — who would be sheriff right now?"

"By George! You mean you think Card had this *gunie* up his sleeve all the time, for an extra ace in case he got objurgated here, like he did! Well — I swear it sounds polemic to me. *I* wouldn't put it past Tom Card. That's one — slick — gambolier!"

"Card never did like me," Curt said as he pulled off his other boot. "Let's have another drink of that, Chief Hollow Gut! He never did like Smoky, either. He wants to run Gurney. He's made a play or two in that direction, before this. But every time he bumped into Smoky, he snubbed himself against a tough old stob. But with Smoky out of the picture for a while, he thought he saw his opportunity. He certainly wants to pin his own candidate onto the sherff's badge."

"Didn't Card an' Bain come to the Territory together?" Andy asked frowningly. "If not together, right along about the same time, anyhow? I recollect, now, how Sam, he bought the Lazy B from Old Man Ledbetter, about the time Card bought the Palace an' started out to make her the biggest joint in the whole Territory. Of course he did! They're like — *that!*"

He held up two fingers close together.

" 'Course! I would've put two an' two together before this, if I hadn't been battier'n a damn' esophagus!"

Curt looked at the lowered level in the bottle and held it out. He shrugged out of the fringed, embroidered goatskin jacket and Andy, drinking, stared at the John Wesley Hardin holsters, sewed slanting on a skeleton vest, that held Curt's Colts. He stared, too, at Curt's brooding face.

"It was bad enough when King Connell ran the Territory," Curt said slowly. "Then Frenchy Leonard and his gang rode high, wide and handsome and nobody could touch 'em. They committed murder right in Gurney streets and laughed it off. But, I tell you, if Tom Card gets control of the county offices, Frenchy's day is going to look like a religious Sunday!"

Andy tossed the empty bottle into a corner and nodded owlishly:

"Card's just usin' this Trackless Bunch business for a blind, huh? Because you ain't landed 'em, he can say you ain't the man for the sheriff's job an' Sam Bain ought to be put in."

"That's about the tale. But — right here and now, Young-Cowboy-Sitting-On-A-Rock-With-A-Big-Word-Hanging-Out-Of-His-Mouth, I start the wheels rolling. And I seem to look around the office and notice a hole that ought to be filled. A hole that'll take a good, heavy deputy to fill. What say, Andy? Reckon Lit Taylor can struggle along, sort of, out at Los Alamos, without you? It'll be hard for him to chouse the dogies along, with nothing but a loopful of little bitty words. But I'd like to have you, if you'd like to come, cavorting around the scenery pretty close to me. Just till we heel-and-head this Trackless Bunch."

"It's askin' a lot of Lit," Andy reflected weightily. "It'll be a strain on him, no doubt! Nary man left who's out of *A-b is Ab* in the primer. But, if she's hard on Los Alamos, she's fine for the sheriff's office. We can ride out an' ask Lit. Maybe he'll see it our way an' let me euphemise around with you a spell."

CHAPTER III

Shirley turned in her chair when Curt spoke
to her. Andy Allen, who had trailed Curt
into the dining-room at Mrs. Sheehan's,
nodded awkwardly as Curt said to the girl:

"You know the Word Wrangler of Los Alamos, Miss Shirley? Mr. Dictionary Allen."

"Ah!" Andy said vaguely, but with feeling.
"This hairpin, Miss Shirley, he's one of the
trials we got to put up with, like cactus, or
taxes, or water in your whiskey."

"I've heard about him," Shirley nodded.
"I suppose I should offer congratulations?"

Curt nodded energetically. He looked
steadily at her until — very suddenly — she
looked away and was flaming red.

"I think so!" he told her, when he had the
chair at her right. He kept his voice low. "*I*
certainly think so."

"And now you're sheriff again —"

"I don't mean that I ought to be congratu-
lated about that!" he said, in surprised tone.
"I" — he hesitated artistically — "I reckon
I was thinking of something else. But, if you
want to congratulate me because they didn't
chop my legs off, I'll take that, and kindly
— from you."

"What else has happened to you?" she
demanded. But she looked at her plate.

Curt grinned. He accepted a plate from the Mexican girl who waited on the table, then leaned toward Shirley a little.

"It's a sort of secret. But I'm going to lead a different life. I'm going to be worked on — maybe reformed."

"Idiot!" she said viciously. But he saw the effort she made to keep from laughing. "I was serious."

"I'm afraid that's your trouble — the only thing I see that's wrong with you. You're too serious. You ought to do a frivoling thing a day. It's like an apple — a frivol a day, you know, keeps the doctor away."

"And what would you suggest?" she prompted him. Now, she faced him and seriousness had vanished. He thought that she looked five years younger, or — as if a weight had been put aside for the moment. "What sort of frivolity occurs to you?"

"Riding with me!" he answered promptly. "That black horse you bought from Halliday is getting fat and lazy. Will you ride with me?"

"Perhaps. But not today. We'll talk about it later. But I didn't think you'd have a lot of time for — frivolities. The — what is it you call them? — The Trackless Bunch is enough to occupy your time, isn't it?"

Curt did not want to talk about the Trackless Bunch. He found the other avenue of discussion much more interesting, for one thing. For another, he was a wary young man and experience had taught him that the less an officer discussed his problems in public, the less chance there was of his ideas becoming known in advance. So he grunted, now.

"I'll call around, tomorrow," he said. "To ask you to set the day for the first ride."

"Better say — if able!" Andy Allen put in, darkly.

Shirley was beginning to push back her chair. Curt got up and helped her. She looked at Andy and smiled. Tolerantly, Curt thought.

"Do you think this Trackless Bunch will shoot him?"

"Not unless they get a chance," Andy assured her. "But if they was to have that chance, they'd grab it too empirical to be funny, that's all!"

Still she smiled and Andy, watching her, seemed to grow irritated.

"What's funny about it?" he demanded bluntly. "With that old wolf, Smoky Cole, off the range, what's goin' to trip 'em a-tall, except Curt Thompson? They get shut of Curt an' they got the world by the tail with a downhill drag. For who'd be weaseled in to take his place? Sam Bain!"

"Well, let's don't worry about losing Mr. Thompson," Shirley soothed him — as if Andy were no more than ten or so. "So far, they haven't actually shot anyone, or opened a campaign to remove all the sheriffs of the Territory. So —"

"Huh?" Andy grunted, staring at her. "They haven't started — You have got pretty eyes, Miss Shirley. But not what I would call very good eyes! If you hadn't heard, still, it looks to me like you could see —"

"Shut up, nitwit!" Curt commanded angrily. For he saw that she had not been told of the shooting.

But she turned slowly to him, dark eyes narrowed, to look closely at him. And with sight of the red weal upon his brown neck her face paled.

"Somebody — shot at you?"

He nodded, keeping his face a mask. He lifted a shoulder uncomfortably and let it sag again.

"Some ambitious bushwhacker. But that's all we know. He may have been the Big Boss of this outlaw gang. Or he may have been John Wilkes Booth. *Quién sabe?*"

"Oh, I see. You didn't catch him. I heard some shooting after I had gone to bed. But

53

I thought it was just the Wagon Wheel boys, enjoying themselves. And you were shot at."

Curt nodded again. Now, he wished that she would go. He had got up able to think about that grim, dead figure without much emotion. He could pass over the mental picture of the man with the reflection that the business had been none of his choosing. Now — the fellow came between him and the girl. He did not want to tell her that he had killed the would-be assassin.

She nodded jerkily, face very white. She looked at Andy Allen, who was watching her grimly, with a shade of contempt on brown young face.

"I'm sorry I talked like an idiot," she said. "I — don't seem to get used to the Territory. I know that men shoot at each; that they kill each other. And still, I don't seem to understand. I hope you'll not meet any more of that — that kind, Mr. Thompson."

"Thanks!" he nodded dryly.

He watched her go across the room and when she had passed through the door he swore softly. Should he have told her that he had returned the bushwhacker's fire and killed him? Was it better to let her hear that from someone else? What would she think of him — who had talked to her lightly, as if no dead man lay in the back room of the

Palace, tied inextricably to an invisible notch on his gun handle? Would she step back from him the next time he saw her, calling him cold-blooded?

"Hell!" he said viciously, and sat down again, to pick up his fork and begin to eat mechanically.

Andy Allen stared at him sidelong, and nodded as if he had found something looked for. But he made no comment. Nor did Curt speak again until he had gulped his coffee and got up.

"Let's go see about the inquest," he said curtly. "I want to get started for Los Alamos. It wouldn't be fair to take you away from Lit unless he's willing. But I do hope that he feels public-spirited . . ."

The inquest was merest formality. Nobody could identify the dead man, and Curt's brief statement was almost the only testimony. Curt brushed aside the curious who wanted to buy him drinks in exchange for talk about the gun-fight.

He and Andy got their horses out of the corral. Curt drew a long breath when he sat his long-legged buckskin and looked at Andy.

"Some folks are inquisitive," the Los Alamos man commented, with jerk of the head toward the men downstreet, watching. "I'll bet they're wonderin' where we're headin' to, Curt."

"It's likely. That carbine of yours loaded? If not, better feed some shells into it when we get out of town. Then let it ride light in the scabbard. *Maybe* that'll turn out to be just one of my notions."

He could not hold gloom for long. As they rode down the Diablos' slopes and over the mesquite flats toward the great ranch of King Connell, not only Gurney faded, but worry, as well. After all, he told himself, nobody could hold that killing against him, or call it anything but the natural, the instinctive, self-defense it had been.

He fell to talking with Andy about fighting, and the work of an officer in a near-lawless land. Andy listened, put in a word occasionally, but his gray eyes were narrowed, a little puzzled.

"Like that business of last night," Curt said with careful carelessness. "I reckon a policeman back East might have handled the thing in a different way. But — chances are *he'd* have been dead at the end, not the dry-gulcher. Because he would not have had the habit I have formed, of being suspicious of men I don't know — suspicious and ready to get into action, without even knowing I am."

Andy nodded gravely.

"Thinking about it, then, I can't see but that trying to *arrest* that fellow would have just got me killed."

"Right!" Andy said earnestly. "Parenthetically an' ambidextrously correct. An' I can't see, for the life of me, how *she* could think otherwise for a minute."

"What?" Curt grunted, reddening furiously. "*She?* why, what are you talking about?"

"Miss Shirley!" Andy cried amazedly. "*You* were. Why, you poor nitwit, you're about as hard to see through as a busted window. You been worryin' ever since breakfast about what she'd think of that killin'. Don't try to hoorah me!"

"No such thing!"

"No-o? Well — she's worth worryin' about, *amigo.* I like 'em a li'l' beefier, an' with red cheeks, but even so ——"

"Hell with you!" Curt said dignifiedly. "You're like every other rattle-head puncher I ever saw. Maybe you'll change for the better when you're older."

They made a lazy nooning, sprawled by a curve of Alamos Creek, eating bacon and biscuit and beans while the horses grazed. They were smoking afterward when Curt, lying flat upon his back staring up at the sky, rolled like a wolf and got a gun out. He trained it upon a clump of brush thirty feet up the creek's bank. "Come out of that!" he called savagely. "Come on out — with a good grip on each ear!"

The brush rustled. Zyler stepped out, hands carefully lifted so that they brushed his prominent ears. He tried to look surprised, and hurt.

"Reckon you figured it was somebody else huh?" he said nervously. "Like — like that fella last night."

Curt stared at him for ten seconds without speaking. Then he looked at Andy with helpless little shrug.

"This fellow's getting to be one of my Office Pets. I swear, I don't know what to do about him, Andy . . . I keep stepping on him, but he won't fly up and let me have a shot at him. He runs along the ground trailing a wing, you know; acts like a mother quail. And how can I shoot him?"

"It's hell!" Andy nodded gravely, rolling over to prop his head upon one hand and regard Zyler thoughtfully. "It's one of the trained Fidos from the Palace, ain't it? The wind is sort of to me, an' I'm hard to fool on smells."

"Something like that. Today, for instance,

Tom Card said to Zyler that the sheriff was riding out and he'd like to know where to. So Zyler got his billygoat and came riding after us, Andy. And it came natural to him to slide into that brush like a snake. But he made more noise than he figured. And so —"

"Always hurrahin'," Zyler grinned weakly. "Me, I'm goin' to Porto. Fella there has got a horse I may buy. But I cut you' trail an' — well, I didn't want to run up onto anybody unless I was certain who it was!"

"You're going to Porto?" Curt said slowly, frowning at Zyler. "Why" — he looked at Andy — "we — that is — we're headed for Los Alamos."

"I thought maybe you-all was hittin' for Porto, too," Zyler ventured. He had his hands down, now.

"Us?" Curt cried quickly. "Oh, no! We're for Alamos. Ain't we, Andy?"

"Well, I thought we could ride along together, that's all. An' if you've decided not to whang away at me, just because I slipped up on you like I done, I'll be goin'."

Curt watched him leave. He shook his head irritably.

"You can't *push* him into trouble! You can't insult him. He just won't understand that you're talking about him. But — maybe

59

one of these days I'll make him believe I am going to pull and puncture him, and he has *got* to try to beat me to the draw."

"Now, what'll he do?" Andy inquired, getting up.

"Either try to beat us to Porto and see what we're up to, or — and that's more likely — hightail it back to Gurney to tell Card we're snooping Porto-way. That's the hell of being a liar, Andy — you want to remember that. A liar is the easiest person in the world to lie to. All you have to do is feed him the truth in big doses. You saw it work, then. Let's hightail it, boy. I would like to make Los Alamos before it's too dark. Get back to town tomorrow."

They rode through the afternoon without event. The moon rose, a vast yellow disc that barely cleared the jagged hills. The arroyos and wallows were flooded with shadows that seemed as thick as blue-black water and the moonlight filmed the wide stretches of bushgrown plain and made them yellow as pale gold. They fell silent, jogging on until, from a hogback, the home ranch of Los Alamos appeared below them.

"An outfit!" Curt grunted absently, staring at the alfalfa fields and irrigation ditches, the home pasture and corrals and neat rows of 'dobe *vaquero* and *peon* quarters.

60

They rode down toward the yellow squares that were the lighted windows of the *casa principal,* the great house of this cattle barony. Men came out to the corral and Curt, swinging off his buckskin to give the reins to a *vaquero,* told Andy Allen that Los Alamos was different under Lit Taylor's management, more cordial to the Law.

"I remember one time I rode out here with Smoky. Just a couple of years ago, but during Frenchy's time as Big Auger of the Territory. That time I was afraid the Alamos hands would poison our horses — after they'd shot us in the back!"

When their horses had been unsaddled and fed, Curt and Andy went up the neat walk to the house. Sudie-May Taylor — who had been Sudie-May Connell — met them.

"Did you have to bring Andy home, Curt?" she inquired. "Lit was worried about him, after Andy left. He remembered that Chinese cook that Andy treed, last trip to town."

Curt grinned at the slender, yellow-haired girl.

"Andy's pure as the snow, this trip. How's Lit?"

"A terror! Every night he swears that he'll be riding next day. He's in the front room, now. The King sent us a box of books from

New York, before he sailed for Queenstown. Lit and the baby are reading *Grimms' Fairy Tales* together. They're as new to him as to her."

In the long beamed room that King Connell had modeled after an Irish squire's hall, Lit Taylor's lean six feet were stretched in a massive Spanish chair. On the wide arm his small yellow-haired daughter perched with the book, her feet comfortably in his stomach.

"Dat," she was saying, "is castle. De princess's ranch."

"Hi, Curt!" Lit grinned. "How's the Sheriff of Gurney, boy? Or —"

"It's still that," Curt nodded. "Thanks to you and some more well-wishers. They gave me three months to turn the country into a Sunday school and get her quiet enough to let you hear an old cow swish her tail. How's the leg?"

"Maybe I'll ride a little, tomorrow. Sit down. Had supper?"

"No, we're riding the chuckline. But there's no hurry. I came out to talk over this damn' business with you, Lit, and — to borrow Andy, here, for the duration of the war."

"Ah, no! Not Andy! Why, he's the prop of our declining years and all that. Besides, he's got every critter on the place so educated, now, that they don't understand the rest of us. And there's everything in the world to do, Curt — you know that. It's going to be right on the edge of the beef-roundup, before I'm able to straddle Nigger Toe again and do any real riding."

Sudie-May came in. The baby climbed down and looked gravely from face to face. With the big picture book dragging, she went over to Curt and caught his shell belt. He swung her up and settled the *Grimm* comfortably for her.

"Gun!" she said and pushed the book away. "Want gun!"

"So that's the kind of children you raise, Lit!" Curt said helplessly. "Here! Take a couple of shells instead. I know it's asking a lot, Lit. But I do need a deputy. I need a special brand of deputy!"

"Can't you deputize one of the Howards?" Lit suggested. "I rode with them enough, in Frenchy's day, to know 'em from the back. They're fighters and they're stayers. Young Abe would like it."

"If you absolutely can't do without Andy, I'll have to get Abe or somebody like him," Curt shrugged gloomily. "But you know well enough that sometimes it's as important to know better than to fight, as it is, other times, to know you've got to get down into the old last ditch and count the shells and figure on using the last one of 'em. Abe is a fighting fool. No argument about that. He'll fight at the drop of a hat and go out and find the hat to drop, if he happened to be bareheaded. But not always wise in his fighting. And that reminds me — I had to kill a bushwhacking hairpin, last night!"

He told the story briefly, beginning with the conference. The baby's fingers relaxed. The cartridge dropped and she shifted on Curt's shoulder, moved her head and went to sleep. Sudie-May got up and put out her hands. Curt shook his head.

"Don't bother. I like 'em. Some day, I'm going to have fourteen of 'em."

"Wait till you've tried one awhile!" Lit grinned. Then his dark eyes narrowed. "This damn' leg!" he said viciously. "I ought to be riding with you, Curt. We've lost stuff, the same as some others. And we owned part of Rawlin's bank, up at Faith. We'll be assessed two-three thousands for that robbery. And we're in the Gurney bank. If it should be hit — and there's no reason to expect this bunch to let it alone — we'll have more assessments. I ought to be helping you!"

"No," Curt said, and gestured toward the small head on his arm. "No, you're a married man and a pillar of society. It's all right for a wild-eyed saddle tramp, like me, to put his scalp on the foresight of his Colt and dare somebody to jiggle it off. But you've got no business hunting trouble. And there's going to be trouble, Lit. I feel it in my bones!"

"Who's behind it?" Lit grunted. "Have you given a lot of time to trying to figure that?"

Curt shrugged. Sight of Sudie-May, perched now on Lit's chair with hand in his dark hair, set his mind to wandering. He could not help picturing Shirley Randolph in that intimate, possessive pose; not picturing her as if she *must* one day sit so, but visualizing her as he would like to see her.

"What?" he said rather vaguely. "Oh, no! I've tried to put names to the tracks we've found. But I haven't had a bit of luck, so far."

"Smiling Badey?" Lit inquired, and Sudie-May nodded.

"I had that notion. But it came to me pretty straight that Badey and his bunch pulled out of the Territory, right after Frenchy's rub-out. They're supposed to be clear down in Chihuahua. But, whoever it is, it's rough people! And when you add to that the fact that Tom Card's trying to get his thumb on the county offices —— Well! The man who rides with me is going to see life. Trouble's coming through the smoke!"

"An' that's why Curt naturally wants me!" Andy grinned. "Come on, Lit! Give's a chance. Let Sod Xavier wrestle with the work. It's only for a month or so, likely."

"You have to!" Sudie-May told Lit suddenly, and decisively. "Much as we'll miss Andy's conversation, we have to do that much for the sheriff's office. Let him take two or three days to turn over to Sod, then go with Curt."

"I reckon that's the truth," Lit nodded. "All right."

Sudie-May was last to see Curt. She stood in the doorway as he swung into the saddle and adjusted his Winchester. Curt rode up and sat with hands folded on the big horn.

"I forgot to ask — how is Mrs. Young?" she inquired. Her tone was so inhumanly innocent that Curt stared suspiciously.

"Why — Marie's fine," he told her. "I saw her just before we pulled out. I didn't tell her we were heading this way — some people were around. Any messages?"

"I'll be sending Manuel in with the buckboard tomorrow. Tell her there'll be a list coming to her. A lot of things for the baby

— for her clothes."

Curt grinned and shook his head.

"Funny! You making baby clothes! And you were about the wildest proposition I ever saw, when I came into the Territory."

"People change," she said — and laughed.

"Do they? Sometimes I wonder . . ."

"Curt!" she said suddenly. "You're not thinking of that Randolph girl!"

Then, when he merely stared at her, she whistled liquidly and long.

"I can see why," she nodded at last. "She is beautiful. And — as the King always preached, breeding will show, in a horse or a person. It shows in her. It's just that —"

"Well?" Curt demanded. "It's just what?"

"Oh — nothing. I'm a fool, Curt. She's so mysterious. We don't know all about her and she keeps Tom Card's books. So — the tongues wag, and I'll be as big a busybody as some others if I'm not careful. I wish you luck, Curt. I'm for you. And I think you'll have luck. For you're the kind to make it."

"Why — thanks! That's about the first consoling word I've had. Of course, I have got a few little details to settle, before I think much about my personal affairs — this Trackless Bunch, and Sam Bain, and Tom Card. But I *do* thank you for your good wishes. Tell you! If ever you get to be a widow and I'm a widower — let me know, will you?"

"I'll do that! Give Mrs. Young my message and — take care of yourself, Curt. I'm glad Lit *has* that broken leg!"

As he rode toward the county seat, Curt's alertness was mechanical for a while. Somehow, Sudie-May's calm acceptance of the fact that he was in love with Shirley seemed to make the girl stand nearer to him. He thought of her, as she had been in the shabby dining-room, staring white-faced at the bullet-burn on his neck.

"Breeding," he said aloud. "The King's right! It does show in horse or man. She has got all the signs. You can tell it in her talk, in the way she stands and walks. And she keeps books for Tom Card. I wonder what the story is . . ."

Presently, being very much a man of action, he found himself studying the puzzle of the new wave of depredations, trying to cut through the curtain of mystery which dropped after each blow of his "trackless" outlaws.

And he scowled at the lonely land ahead. Since the stage robbery which had been the Trackless Bunch's first job, inaction had been his lot — inaction except for fruitless riding. He had ridden to and around the scene of every robbery except that of the bank in Faith. But study of the ground and inquiries in the neighborhood, quiet watch for men spending too much money — none of these routine methods of detection had produced anything.

"Except that cute little footprint," he told himself. "And it's pretty hard to build up a woman that a jury can see, from that print on the trail to The Points."

He had to try something else — but what? None of his inquiries brought him information of any gang headquartering in the Territory.

"It could be a wild bunch from just anywhere," he shrugged. "There's plenty of hard cases all around. Some of their women are up to riding out with the men on a holdup, or a job of rustling."

He took a short-cut he knew slightly, in mid-afternoon. It was a stock trail that led down a cañon grown up with junipers and small pines. A tiny spring-fed creek wound through the grassy bottom of the cañon. He gave the buckskin his head and jogged along smoking.

But at the first faint click of a shod hoof, rapping a stone ahead of him, he pulled in and drew the carbine from the scabbard. He listened, heard but one horse and thought of Zyler. He rode the buckskin over behind a boulder, making him walk slowly, all but noiselessly. He waited, then, carbine across his arm. The other rider came on at a walk. Curt looked around the inner side of the great rock, saw a black horse's head, then the chunky black's rider. He tickled the buckskin with a rowel and rode out into the trail.

"This *is* a pleasure!" he said smilingly, as Shirley jerked in her mount and turned, first white, then red.

"Why, I — You startled me! I didn't think anyone ever came here and you — You were gone to Porto, I heard."

"Porto? Who said that?"

"Some man at the Palace. I was playing faro and a man spoke behind me. Does it — matter?"

"No-o. It doesn't matter. I was just curious. For I went to Los Alamos. This one of your favorite places? I've been through here once before. I caught a gay young horsethief about a mile down the cañon, last year."

"*Caught* him?"

Curt nodded, studying her. She was different, today. There was constraint in her manner. It was as plain as the effort she was making to be natural.

"I never shot a man I didn't *have* to!" he

70

blurted, almost without thought. "That man the other night — *he* was sent to collect my scalp. He just made sure he had his man and opened up."

"How did it happen that he missed you? A man would be chosen for assassination because of his efficiency, wouldn't he? I mean —"

Curt stared at her. The blood came up to make his bronzed face dull red. His mouth tightened until grayish spots shoved at the corner.

"*I* know what you mean!" he finished for her, savagely. "That if he'd been a bush-whacker, he'd have *got* me. I suppose that's the tale they're telling around the Palace! Well — I have never posed as a gunslinger, particularly. But the man who cracks down on me had better keep his mind on his business. He had better collect my tail feathers, first shot, or he's going to be in the middle of excitement. Well! That hairpin may have been efficient enough. But he *didn't* score a hit his first shot. And, after that, his horse was rearing."

She stared at him for an appreciable interval. Under his hard, steady eyes, blood came up to flush her cheeks. Dark eyes softened.

"I'm sorry," she said. "I — That *is* what's

being intimated, not only at the Palace, but by certain men around Gurney. I've heard it stated — and denied — in Mrs. Sheehan's dining-room. As I heard it — when I heard it — it did sound plausible. I shouldn't have repeated it, though . . . I see that, now."

Curt did not soften. He sat the buckskin primly:

"Tell me something, if you feel like it" — his tone was contemptuous drawl — "is that sentiment held by Tom Card?"

Then, when she made no answer, he nodded.

"I see it is," he said. "I would have been surprised if he hadn't told that story."

"Perhaps it seems plausible to him — as it seemed to me!" she flared. "You don't like Tom Card, I know, but it does seem to me that you might concede him the right to hold an opinion."

"Why, I'm not denying him the right to do anything he wants to do!" Curt said quickly. And now he was smiling, if not pleasantly. "Well? Do you go on beyond here?"

She shook her head, silently, watching him.

"No, this is my limit. And I have to be getting back, now."

"Then, if you don't mind, I'll side you."

They pushed on down the little cañon, stirrup to stirrup.

"How is Mrs. Taylor and that precious baby?" Shirley asked him, when they had gone a hundred yards without speaking.

"Fine! Just fine! Sudie-May has changed from the wildest little tomboy this Territory ever saw into the prettiest little housewife I ever saw. She tells me" — he stopped for a moment — looked thoughtfully at Shirley's inquiring face — "that people change. Even — girls."

Shirley laughed.

"I suppose that's possible. If people change, why not girls?"

"She's an admirer of yours," Curt drawled. He was still watching her. Watching her and thinking of what Sudie-May had said, about her beauty and her obvious breeding.

"I didn't know that. I have spoken to her once or twice — that's all."

"Well, that's about all you've done, heretofore, with anybody in Gurney or around. So — like the rest of us — she had to form her opinion just from seeing you go from the Palace to the hotel and back again."

She seemed to wait for amplification of this, but Curt did not continue. Instead, he held up his hand.

"Wait a minute," he said. "That cinch of yours is loose. First thing you know, the saddle's going to slip."

He got down and held out his hands to her. She turned in the stock saddle, put leg over and let him swing her to the ground. While he tightened the latigo, she walked over toward the cañon wall.

"What is this pretty little cactus?" she called to him.

"That's a baby barrel cactus. What the Mexicans call a *biznaga*."

Then his wandering eyes found that spot where the girl had stepped in soft earth between two rocks and he stiffened. Impressed there was the print of her tiny boot-sole. He looked quickly at her. He could not help it. For his thought flashed back — rather as if a button had been pressed in his brain — to the scene of the last robbery of The Points stage. And it was as if he stood again there upon the trail to The Points, staring down at the small bootprint. Angrily he told himself now that *any* woman's foot, booted, would make about that sort of print. The fact that he had been hunting for a woman whose foot would fit that bootprint made him unduly suspicious, foolishly suspicious, now.

Shirley turned to him. He kept his face

74

well under control. He put out his hand to take her arm and they walked together back to the horses. He helped her into the saddle and, when she had found the stirrup, he looked up into her face.

"Nonsense!" he told himself. "Pure damn' nonsense! The *idea* of a girl like that, riding with a bunch of stick-up artists!"

And yet — he could not help recalling how she stood among the hard cases in the Palace gaming-room, making her bets at the faro layout, to win or lose with no more emotion visible than a man would show. She had nerve. She had the determination that would take her through whatever she planned.

She looked down at him, and met his steady stare. For an instant there was softness in the dark eyes, the red mouth. Then — as always — she seemed to get hold of herself, to consciously steel herself against emotion.

"Let's go on," she said. "I have to get to work, Curt."

"So do I," he nodded. "What with this mysterious stick-up gang" — he could see no change in her expression with mention of the Trackless Bunch — "and my plentiful supply of ill-wishers in town — I'm properly a busy man."

He mounted and they rode on silently, the girl ahead, following the narrow trail. Curt was content to lag behind for the moment, to watch the straight slimness of her in the saddle, to puzzle the many contradictions he found in her every time they met.

They went on to the end of the cañon, to where the trail led out over a bench that had a high, but sloping, left wall, and overhung a precipice on the right. The going was slow, for the bench trail was narrow and floored with loose rocks. Curt was pushing up toward the girl when, somewhere in the scrubby pines up the slope, there sounded the flat, metallic *whang!* of a rifle.

The echoes rang up the cañon behind Curt with the crash of great sheets of glass broken. The slug — and the second slug — made tinny noises among boulders on the bench edge, to Curt's right.

The buckskin jumped. Shirley turned in the saddle. Curt snatched instinctively at the stock of his carbine, gave over the attempt, and instead jerked a shell from a loop of his belt.

"Get going! Get out of this!" he yelled at Shirley. "Give him the quirt!"

And he snapped the .45 cartridge at the black. It struck the animal's haunch and he jumped forward. Curt stooped over the saddle-horn and rammed the rowels into his buckskin's sides. He heard a dull, thudding sound and felt the saddle vibrate under him. There was a lead-colored scar on his saddle-fork to tell where that slug had glanced off. Then the horses were gallopng on that perilously narrow trail, with the steep slope and the rifleman — or riflemen — on the left and a hundred feet of space under the riders' right elbows.

Curt let the buckskin find his own footing; there was nothing else to do. Himself, he watched that bunch of brush from which blossomed the mushrooms of smoke that heralded bullets. A couple of hundred yards ahead the trail turned off the bench into tall pines. There was shelter there from the bushwhacker — if he could reach it.

The girl's black disappeared into the pines. The slugs were kicking up gravel all but under the buckskin's flying hoofs, or striking like droning wasps against the loose rocks. Time and again Curt was stung by flying bits of rock. Then, with the timber not ten yards ahead, a bullet struck the buckskin. The horse squealed. His hindquarters buckled for an instant and he slipped on the edge of the bench. He struggled frantically, his hoofs clawing at rock and dirt on the brink.

There was no room to dismount. Nor time, either! Under his elbow Curt saw, far below, the jagged rocks at the cliff's foot. Then he flung up his hand and caught the gnarled limb of a tree on his left. He gripped it with both hands. It was ten to one, he thought, that the branch would break, but he held it desperately and, too, gripped the buckskin's sides between his knees while savagely he raked the animal's flanks with big Mexican rowels.

Then the buckskin caught a hoof, some-how, and got back on the trail. Curt let go his hold on the branch. A moment later, still chased by the buzzing slugs, buckskin and rider were sheltered in the great pines and Curt was gently pulling from over the girl's face her shaking hands.

"You — you weren't hit?" she gasped. "It seemed impossible that one of those bullets shouldn't hit you! I saw them striking the gravel under your horse."

"He creased my horse's leg — nearly sent us over the cliff," Curt said grimly. "But — just like that other fellow, in town — he didn't get me. It was close enough, though."

He looked back at the bench trail. His arm was still around Shirley and, since she made no move to free herself, he was content to hold her against him.

"I don't know of a thing I'd enjoy more than slipping around on that *gunie* and presenting him with my shell belts, a shell at a time," he said between his teeth. "Even a good look at him would please me. I like to know who I owe for a session like that — and then pay off the debt . . ."

She looked up at him fascinatedly.

"You — you've paid such debts?" she said — and it was as much statement as question.

"Certainly!" he nodded, without thinking. Then he frowned at her. "I've not lived in nice places, a good bit of the time," he added.

She sighed and straightened, leaning away from him. He smiled at her.

"Well — we now take up again whatever it was we had in mind. Riding, wasn't it? Well, Shirley —"

She gave him an answering smile. And they rode close together, the buckskin limping slightly, until from a height of the Diablos, they looked down upon the huddle of 'dobe houses that was Gurney. Curt stared, and when he spoke, it was more or less mere thinking aloud:

"That's twice that Sam Bain's missed the sheriff's star by inches," he drawled. "I wish

I knew if this is another little item to chalk up to Tom Card's account . . ."

"Tom Card?" Shirley said quickly, turning upon him. "*Why* do you say that, Curt? Because someone shoots at you, does it *have* to be Tom Card? Especially, when you haven't the slightest evidence pointing to him. I know you're wrong. Tom Card's not that kind. *He* wouldn't lie in wait for anyone, to shoot him from ambush without giving him a chance!"

"No-o?" Curt drawled politely. "I wish I had your innocent trusts — no, I don't, either! — *I* want to keep on the right side of the grass roots. But, if I could believe that, it would certainly ease my frazzled mind a lot. You see, Card wants me out of the sheriff's office. And, even if you *can't* see it, Card or Sam Bain, either one, would get a man they wanted in the easiest way."

"I don't believe it! You're prejudiced because they were against you at the meeting the other night. But, because Tom Card honestly believes that Sam Bain would make a better sheriff than — anyone else, is no reason that he would *assassinate* the other candidate."

At which Curt began to whistle with incredulous guile and the girl jerked her horse about angrily and spurred down the slope. Not another word was spoken until they reached Gurney.

Chapter IV

Going toward Mrs. Sheehan's hotel for breakfast, Curt stopped at Halliday's general merchandise store to buy Durham. Halliday, short, thickset, red and cheerful of face, turned twinkling, blue eyes upon his customer from where he arranged newly arrived merchandise upon a back shelf.

"Hi, Curt!" he grinned. "How's the actin' sheriff? We kind of showed Card a few, I reckon, on that deal. You still got some friends around here, boy. An' if you manage to drop your loop over this-here Trackless Bunch of yours, the Tom Cards an' Sam Bains, they'll have to swap their brass band for a jew's-harp an' play low-down."

"I'll corral 'em!" Curt promised grimly. "I've got not a bit of evidence right now, Halliday, but it's there somewhere. If a man just looks long enough, and hard enough, he's bound to pick up the end of any string, eventually."

"Right you are!" Halliday assured him. "An' any time you get things fixed so you can use a little help, just holloa! I'll get down the old Sharps an' show some of these *gunies* how we used to get buffalo-hides. Man, I was with Billy Dixon an' the rest at 'Dobe Walls. Old Betsy, up there, she has barked in her time at the Comanches an' Kiowas. She's not too rusty to heave a slug at these thievin' stage robbers an' rustlers."

"Where did Card and Sam Bain come from, Halliday?" Curt inquired abruptly, twirling his Durham by the sackstrings.

"Now you tell me, an' I'll tell you!" shrugged the storekeeper. "Just drifted in an' — you know as much as anybody else, I reckon."

He grinned suddenly:

"Speaking of Tom Card — a hairpin named 'Picnic' Walker took the Palace down the line last night, in a poker game. Card, he sat in an' so did some of the Gurney folk. But she finally boiled down to a battle between Picnic Walker an' Card. There was eight-nine thousand in the pot when Picnic, he smole a smile, an' he laid down a straight flush to beat Card's four kings. An' the joke of the business is — about seven thousand of Picnic's money had just come out of the faro game right there in the Palace! More than that! The little lady — Miss Shirley — she walked out last night an' she bucked the faro game an' *she* won about a thousand! Oh, it was a sickish night for Tom

Card, I tell you!"

Entered now Sam Bain, at his queer, halting gait. He looked straight through Curt Thompson and moved over to a counter, nodding to Halliday.

"Mornin', Bain," Halliday grunted, expressionlessly.

"Want a knife," said Sam Bain. "Busted the blade off mine yesterday."

He looked over the display that Halliday laid upon the counter and finally picked up a heavy pearl-handled jack-knife and opened it.

"Regular baby bowie," he grunted, inspecting the wickedly pointed four-inch blade. "Reckon I'll take it, Halliday. Keep her handy in my pocket an' notch the ears of the first Smart Aleck that crosses me."

It seemed to Curt that Bain's dark eyes flickered sideways toward where he lounged silently against a post. He laughed softly — but quite audibly.

"Funny how dark-skinned folks always turn to the knife," he drawled amusedly. "Mexicans and niggers and such-like. . . ."

Sam Bain turned furiously upon him. Curt's violet-blue eyes were calmly, steadily upon Bain. And he had folded his arms, so both hands were hidden beneath his goat-skin jumper. A detail which Gurney had come to appreciate, in Curt Thompson.

"Meanin'?" he growled, but without hostile move.

"Just anything you *want* it to mean. I'm the most obliging fellow in the Territory, Bain. Any time you don't like something I say, just let me know and I certainly will be pleased to back it up to the limit."

"I reckon!" Bain said unpleasantly, turning back to Halliday.

"You ought to," Curt nodded. "For it's so."

"Four dollars," said the storekeeper. "She's a fancy item an' she brings a fancy price. I hope she don't bring you no bad luck, Bain . . ."

Bain paid him without reply, and turned to the door.

"One of these days," Curt drawled, "I'm going to take that hairpin apart and scatter the pieces. But that's the hell of being sheriff! I've got to wait till I'm pushed, before I start the ball rolling."

"Reckon he'd shoot?" inquired Halliday, staring through the doorway at Sam Bain's big, retreating figure.

"I reckon him the worst kind!" Curt assured him earnestly. "Because he won't let himself be shoved into a fight until he's *sure* he's got the best of the breaks. And he'd knife you, or he'd shoot you from behind, first chance he got. He's a killer, Halliday, make no mistake about that! I — have seen his kind before . . . I — have tangled ropes with a couple. Well, see you some more. Going to breakfast, now."

"*Adiós!*" nodded the storekeeper, keeping his disappointed curiosity out of face and voice. He watched Curt through the door, his twinkling blue eyes speculative.

"Come mighty near to tellin' somethin', then," he muttered. "Just caught himself in time . . . Yes, sir! That boy has seen trouble in his time an' he's seen her through the smoke. From Texas . . . Hmm! I have seen lots of Texas hairpins in my time. Some good, some bad — mostly they was somethin' extra at the fightin', good *or* bad . . ."

He shook his head, shrugged, and went back to the shelves.

Curt slipped into his chair at the table in Mrs. Sheehan's and received from the Mexican waitress steak and eggs and coffee. Shirley Randolph was not in the dining-room, but there were others of the freelance townfolk to fill most of the long table. Curt ate slowly, hoping to out-wait his neighbors and to see the girl.

Gradually, the dining-room emptied, until finally Curt was left alone. He sat smoking over his third cup of coffee straining his ears for sound of Shirley's coming. But when footsteps rapped in the little hallway at the foot of the stairs, it was only the enormous Mrs. Sheehan. She put her head inside the dining-room door, but Curt was at the table's far end and thus hidden from her by the L of the dining-room wall. She grunted to herself. Curt's eyebrows lifted at the satisfied sound of it. The old woman acted as if pleased to find her breakfasters gone.

He heard her cross the hall to the front door, then to him carried clearly the voice of "Bobo Johnny," shotgun messenger of the stage. Curt got up quietly and moved to the front window of the dining-room, from which he had a partial view of the messenger. He saw that Bobo Johnny had a paper-wrapped package in his hand. Evidently, he had just received it from Mrs. Sheehan.

"To Mrs. Patrick Rafferty at Ancho," the messenger nodded. "I'll put it in her hands, Mis' Sheehan. Papers about the O'Donnell lawsuit, as usual?"

"Well, if ever that blame' suit gets to goin', we'll maybe be rollin' along in our carriages. It's fine of you, Johnny, to take the trouble to come clear up here for my packages."

"Nothin' at all," the messenger assured

her. "Any time I can do somethin' for you, Mis' Sheehan, just say the word!"

Curt went back to his chair. So Mrs. Sheehan was involved in a lawsuit! And, evidently, she had no wish to publish the fact. He turned his head quickly. Light footsteps sounded on the old stairway. He straightened expectantly. But Shirley did not come into the dining-room. Instead, he heard her stop in the hallway. "Did you get it off, all right, Mrs. Sheehan?" the girl asked her landlady.

"Just gone, dearie. Bobo Johnny'll give it to my sister, as usual. Don't you be worryin' now. It'll get there in plenty of time to do the trick. 'Papers about the O'Donnell lawsuit — as usual?' says Bobo Johnny. Ah, me! 'Tis a wonderful liar you are, Teresa Sheehan!"

"I don't know what I'd do without you!" the girl said — so earnestly that again Curt's eyebrows went climbing.

Then he heard the girl's footsteps approaching the dining-room door. Hastily, he pulled a newly received reward notice from his shirt pocket and pretended engrossment in it. He looked up vaguely as Shirley came down the table toward him, then got quickly to his feet and seated her.

"Good-morning," she said evenly. "It's

rather late for you, isn't it?"

He studied her for a moment before he replied. Then he shook his head and smiled twistedly:

"I suppose if I said that it's not late, not early, but to my mind just right —"

"I wouldn't understand that!" she told him quickly — and coldly. "You've not usually been here so late. That's what I meant. I'm later than usual —"

She stopped and Curt watched her. She was talking without thinking of what she said. He understood that. Whether he came usually earlier than this, or later, was of no importance. It did not justify all this discussion. She was worried — he knew it well enough — about what he might have overheard of Mrs. Sheehan's exchange with Bobo Johnny, and of her own remarks to Mrs. Sheehan. "I have been studying this dodger," he said poking a finger at the reward notice.

"You seemed to be absorbed," she nodded, and he thought that she looked a little less strained. "What is it?"

"It's what my old school-teacher might have called an *arresting* bit of reading. It will be an arresting document if I get a chance at the subject. It runs to the effect that El Paso County has missed one Slim

Upson from its midst and would like to have him back. Not because the aforesaid Slim is an outstanding citizen and a pillar of the Pass City, but because they're anxious to use him up in a first-class hanging. He's wanted for cattle rustling, horse stealing, stage and bank robbery — and murder. There's a reward on his head of three thousand dollars, offered by the State, the family of the murdered man, and certain public-spirited citizens."

He read mumblingly, and grunted.

"About six feet tall, dark hair and eyes, and weighs about a hundred-seventy. That's the trouble with a printed description. Most of these notices carry descriptions that'll fit half the men you meet. No marks and scars, here, to make life easy for a sheriff."

The Mexican waitress brought her breakfast. Curt stirred his lukewarm coffee and pretended to study the dodger. Actually, he studied the clear loveliness of the girl at his side. Who was she — really? What was she doing in a cow-country county seat, playing at book-keeping? He had met a good many men in his wanderings from Texas to the northern ranges who 'went by' or 'called themselves' various names. But mysterious women — particularly women of obvious breeding like this one — were not in his experience.

He watched the soft, yet firm curve of her jaw, where it met slender, round throat. He drew a long, slow breath. She looked at him questioningly. He smiled again at her, his one-sided smile. He asked her what she was thinking about.

"I was thinking," she said, "of all the men moving on the earth, calling themselves by names that are not their own, followed by — by awful papers like that one . . . They can never know a peaceful moment. When they lie down at night, they know that on the morrow someone may look at them and recall that — that Slim Upson is wanted in El Paso, and that he is so tall, weighs so much; that he will bring three thousand dollars, delivered alive or dead . . ."

He nodded frowningly, watching her narrowly.

"What do you feel, when you see one of those hunted men? Is he just — just something valuable found by chance? Do you think of him, at all? I mean, as a person! Or do you just say to yourself: There is something in man's clothing that means three thousand dollars to me! and — arrest him?"

"You don't like me, do you?" he countered abruptly. "You have changed, since the night — it seems ages ago — that I walked here with you from the Palace and you told me that I was a — rather nice person. You have decided that you were wrong; for I have definitely said that I think Tom Card is a smooth, deep, murderous proposition. So I must be wrong!"

She shook her head and stared at her coffee. He waited, but when he saw that she did not intend to answer, he shrugged and went on broodingly:

"I haven't changed. Not a bit. What am I? What is there about me that you'd expect to change? In years, I'm not very old. But those years have been pretty crammed. I was doing a man's work on a horse, before I was twelve. Going to school between times — a poor school. I learned more from my mother than from any teacher. Then — well, I left home. I was sixteen. By the time I was twenty I had seen the cow-country from Milk River back to Texas. The same reason sent me away again. Not quite three years ago. I rode into Gurney one day and hit up Smoky Cole for a job on his one-cow ranch on Organ Creek. He had hired a man for that. But he pinned a badge onto me. And now — I'm Sheriff of Gurney . . ."

Absently, he got out tobacco and papers and made a slim cigarette. He flicked a match-head on his thumbnail and set the tiny flame to the paper's end.

"What I'm driving at it — if I'm not formed, I never will be. The first time you ever saw me, in the stage that day I was herding the crazy Mexican, I was there for you to size and decide about. I was one of three things — something to ignore, something to dislike, or — and this is what I've hoped, Shirley — a man you could like. But you've acted as if I was one thing and then the other — a nice person, then a sort of enemy. I don't know why you feel that way about me. There's nothing much I wouldn't do, if you asked me."

Still she stared at the spoon in her fingers. He blew twin horns of smoke up at the oil lamp above the table.

"I haven't changed a bit. I'm the same man I was when you came to town. Except, of course, for what you've done to me . . . Shirley — do we have to stand off from each other? Do you have to push me away, then let me come a little closer, just to be pushed away again?"

She nodded and her lips formed a single word. *"Yes!"*

"I'm not poking into your affairs. I've thought a lot about you; wondered why you were here; what there was here to keep you. But I'm not asking questions. I'm just trying to tell you how I feel — and how I'll go on feeling, no matter what you say to me."

Hesitantly, as if it were against her will, she lifted bowed dark head a little and looked at him sidelong. There was warm color in her face, now, and the dark eyes were soft as he had never seen them. He moved quickly, hand coming up with the cowboy's swift, deft sureness. She was leaning against him, his hand was under her chin, tilting her face upward. He kissed her and, for an instant, she was motionless.

"Darlin'," he said huskily. *'Darlin'!"*

Then she jerked, twisting away from his mouth, pushing against his shoulder. She said "No!" in a stifled, shaken voice. He began to frown. She said:

"Let me go! Let me go!"

He straightened, arm coming from about her. He was still frowning. She was very red. She stared at the plate before her. The dress rose and fell upon her breast and he saw that her hand was shaking.

"That — that wasn't fair," she whispered. "I didn't know you'd do that. And you will never do that again. Never!"

"You mean" — Curt hunted for the words he wanted, speaking very slowly — "that it didn't mean anything to you! That you didn't expect me to kiss you? That — that you didn't *want* me to kiss you?"

"Exactly!" she said in a hard, steady voice. Now, she looked at him. And softness, warmth, had gone from her face. "Let's don't ever go through that again. Don't mistake a casual friendliness for — for anything more."

"Casual — friendliness . . . I'm not much of a word wrangler. That's Andy Allen's department. But I remember reading the word 'casual' in a book, one time. It means — oh, something you can take or leave alone — am I right? So a casual friend would be a friend that you like all right when he's around, but you don't give a hoot if he never comes around."

He got up and recovered his high-crowned black hat from an empty chair. He stood looking at her, violet-blue eyes smoky in bronzed face. Oddly, he felt very little emotion. He shook his head at last.

"Before I go out — would you mind telling me if, when a casual friend — just any casual friend, you understand — takes you by surprise and kisses you, do you always — being off-guard — kiss that casual friend with a lot of heat and generally like a girl who gets a big thrill out of it? But, no! That wouldn't be a fair question to ask you. I see that, now."

He crossed leisurely to the dining-room door. In the hall he put on his hat. Mrs. Sheehan was coming down the stair and her square red face was forbidding. Curt looked absently at her. Normally he, like the rest of Gurney's male population, walked very softly around the large and belligerent lady. But now he met her grim stare casually.

"An' what are you doin' at breakfast at this time of the mornin'?" she demanded. "My hours —"

She stopped, to stare at him. Curt hardly noticed. He went on down the hall toward the street door. There, he turned. Mrs. Sheehan had come to the foot of the stair and was watching him. "What?" he said vaguely.

"I said: My hours are until eight o'clock —"

"Oh!" Curt nodded. "Oh, yes. Well, as hours go, I reckon they're all right."

And he went on out, to stand on the sidewalk and look up and down the street. Then he moved toward the court house, but when opposite the white front of the Palace he stopped, and his hard mouth-corners lifted in faint, unpleasant smile. He had stepped down into the street when Marie Young, behind him, called his name.

Curt turned slowly, unwillingly, to face

her. She was smiling and mechanically he returned the smile.

"Hello," he said as cheerfully — and as lightly — as he could.

"And how is the gay young Lothario?" she inquired maliciously. "Oh, don't look embarrassed! I wasn't the only one who saw you escorting the lovely Miss Randolph into town. Some of the boys tell me that it must be *wonderful* to be a sheriff. They say that all a sheriff has to do is to ride around on a big buckskin horse and meet lovely ladies out on the range — and — discuss cases with them, I suppose?"

Curt looked sourly at her. She took a step backward and put her hands up.

"You wouldn't shoot a woman, I hope!"

"I would spank one, pretty completely!" he assured her. "Marie, I swear I don't know what to make of you."

She smiled at him, but the blue eyes were serious.

"Sometimes, I — think you *don't,*" she nodded. "But you will admit escorting Miss Randolph back to town, now, won't you?"

"I'll admit that — and more!"

He stopped, collecting his thoughts. The girl stood with a suggestion of stiffness watching him.

"Yes?" she prompted him, when he did

not continue quickly. "You'll admit — what?"

"That Miss Randolph is one lady who's beyond my powers of understanding. And that, if I enjoyed escorting her back to town, it was no fault of hers."

"Oh!" Marie Young said softly. "Oh! Then you *didn't* enjoy the ride?"

He shook his head.

"This is not to be spread around. Nobody knows anything about it so far as I know, except Miss Randolph — and, of course, myself and the gentlemen concerned. As I came across the Devil's Bench trailing her, somebody certainly scorched my ears. There wasn't a chance to shoot back. It was all I could do to keep my horse on his feet in those rocks, on the edge of that cliff. All in all, it was a complete rout of the Sheriff of Gurney. Well — when I suggested that probably the bushwhacker was one of Mr. Card's trained poodles, I got my ears scorched again. But that time it was done by Miss Randolph! She doesn't let anyone talk about Tom Card when she's around."

"They certainly intend to get you, Curt!" Marie whispered. She was very pale and she had stepped up close to him again.

"Of course, it might not have been Card's doing," Curt shrugged. "He's not the only

97

enemy I've made in my time behind a Gurney star. And there's our Trackless Bunch to think about, too."

"And you — being the reckless cowboy you are — take all kinds of foolish chances! Curt, you *have* to be more careful. If — I mean — You owe it to your friends not to take so many chances!"

"Why, I don't go hunting dangerous spots," Curt said surprisedly — and laughed. "But — Maybe I'm old-fashioned, but I always have believed that when you take a job as officer you have to go where an officer is needed."

"And — this morning — is an officer needed in the Palace? Or did you just feel like going over to poke up the animals a little bit, to see if they will really bite?"

"You little devil!" Curt said amazedly. "Can you read tea leaves, too? I *was* heading for the Palace for a little drink, and a little amusement, but how you knew —"

"Well, you escort me to the store, since you're so good at escorting ladies. Perhaps I can persuade you not to bother the animals this morning."

She took his arm and they walked together along the sidewalk toward her door. Reaching it they stopped. Curt grinned affectionately at her.

"Listen, girl! I've got work to do. I can't be sitting around here entertaining you taxpayers."

"Work! What work are *you* going to do, now?"

Curt grinned.

"I'm going to try some high-up detective methods, over in the office. This business of just hopping onto a horse, and riding out all over the scenery on a chance that you'll run into the people you want — I understand that's old style. Hard on the horse, too. I'm going over and sit down at my table with a pencil and a paper. And I'm going to figure out this Trackless Bunch business. If the New System works, it'll save a lot of time."

She looked up suspiciously at his solemn face. Curt nodded. He would not have admitted it, willingly, but her cheerful friendliness and, too, the fact that next only to Shirley, Marie Young was the prettiest girl in the country, had somehow lifted him from the despondence with which he had come up the street from Mrs. Sheehan's.

"Yes? And just what *is* this system by which you're going to catch the Trackless Bunch?"

"Well, it's like this. We know that this is not a little gang. There must be several men in it. Say, a half-dozen, anyway. Well, here's what I do: I take my pencil and my paper and I make a half-dozen circles on the paper. In line, of course! Then I try to fill in those circles with the faces of the men in the bunch. If I can just do it —"

"Curt, one of these days, somebody who doesn't appreciate your particular brand of perverted humor is going to take out his great, big pistol. And he's going to shoot you dead!" Marie told him exasperatedly. "Come on in, now. Tell me about Sudie-May and little Sue. And how's Lit's leg, these days?"

She put her hand up and caught his sleeve. He pulled back with exaggerated stubbornness.

"I tell you I can't loaf, now. I've got too much on my mind and you'd talk and talk, about this and that. You'd run all the important thoughts out of my mind. A man can't mess around with women in office hours. They're for spare time! Le' me go!"

So he was standing very close to her and her hand was on his sleeve and he was smiling down most cheerfully at her, when Shirley Randolph said: "Excuse me!" behind him.

If Marie Young noticed the other girl, she gave no sign.

"I've told you, probably a thousand times, that you're the most aggravating boy in the Territory —"

Curt turned slowly, so that Marie faced Shirley.

"Come in, Miss Randolph," Marie said casually. "That silk got here last night. All right, Curt, you're excused for the time being. If you're a good boy all day, you may have supper here, tonight. I think there'll be apple pie."

"Thanks," Curt said tonelessly.

He had not looked at Shirley. He did not look at her, now. He moved away from the door as the two went on into the store. On the sidewalk's edge he stared blindly toward the court house. "Hell! After what she told me in the dining-room, I could walk down the street in the middle of a Sultan's harem, and it wouldn't signify, to her. Still —"

He turned and walked grimly up the street, crossed over and pushed on the swing doors of the Palace barroom. There was only a sprinkling of customers in the big room. Neither Tom Card nor Sam Bain was in sight when he stopped at the long bar and jerked a thumb toward the Cedar Valley bottles on the backbar. But when he had poured his drink and stood staring moodily at the glass, he heard deliberate footsteps behind him, coming from the gaming-room off which Card had his office.

"I didn't know that you were an early drinker," Tom Card said evenly, from his shoulder.

Curt turned easily, hooking an elbow on the bar. He looked the gambler thoughtfully up and down.

"I reckon not," he drawled. He continued to stare at Card.

"Shirley tells me that you were shot at again."

Card came on, to lean against the bar and face Curt.

"Why" — Curt drank and put the glass down, picked up the bottle and watched the steady amber stream as he poured — "it had most of the ear-marks of a bush-whacking. I've seen a few of the things and I've got to the point where I can almost grade 'em. That was a good Number Two. Not a Number One — they ought to have collected my tail feathers. But a first-class second-class job — good place, good time. Just poor shooting."

He drank again and refilled the glass. Catching sight of himself in the bar-mirror, he noticed that the liquor had brought a reddening of bronzed skin. Very quickly his eyes would be glassy, the pupils dilated. He nodded at Card.

"Have you picked up any clues on this — what do you call it? Trackless Bunch?" Card asked. His heavy face mirrored only polite, not too keen, curiosity.

"You ever know an officer" — Curt listened to his thickening tone with satisfaction — "that ever got anywhere by going around and talking to all and sundry about clues he'd picked up?"

He lifted his glass and drank while he grinned at Card. The gambler shrugged. His blue eyes were very steady, very watchful.

"Have another?" he asked after a moment.

Curt hesitated artistically, then shrugged.

"Well — maybe it'll help, at that. When I'm studying something, Cedar Valley does seem to brighten me up . . ."

He drank again. Perceptibly, now, he slumped on the bar. And his pupils were dilated.

"I'll tell you something — confidential," he said. "This business sort of had me down for a while. But I've been wearing a star around Gurney, it's a good while, now, Card. And in that time, naturally, I have made some friends and figured out places to get information. And I'm not up a tree any more. I'm beginning to collect stories. I'll collect more, now that I've found one

103

man that'll talk about this Trackless Bunch."

He nodded solemnly at the gambler, who in his turn nodded with interested expression.

"Yes, sir! That's the way these things go; you can't see a thing ahead, then you turn up one little bisty — I mean *bitsy* — old clue and — hell! It begins to *rain* clues."

He moved his empty glass around in tiny circles, watching the wet streaks it made.

"You wait! I'm stepping on the bottom stand — standing on the bottom step — but I'm ready to walk places, Card. Yes, sir! Going stairs-up! Inside a few days, I'll know who the big fellows are. Know who hired that bushwhacker, the other night; who had the fellows shooting at me, yesterday."

He poured whiskey at his glass, spilling liquor all around it. Card watched without speaking. Curt lifted the brimming glass and nodded grimly at him. He splashed himself when he waved the hand that held the glass.

"You wait!" he said ominously. "Corral 'em all."

"That's certainly good hearing," Card said. "Well — I had better be getting to work, Thompson. See you!"

Curt put down his glass and turned. He fished in overalls pocket and brought out a

104

handful of silver. He spilled it on the bar, but watched Card in the mirror. Deliberately, the big figure crossed the bar-room, vanished through the archway into the gaming-room.

The bartender waved aside his money. Curt stared stupidly at him. The man of drinks grinned.

"The boss gi' me the sign: Sheriff's drinks are on the house, today."

"Well, that's kind of Card," Curt nodded. "Maybe I'll do something to him — I mean for him — some time."

He went slowly, almost steadily, toward the swing doors and out. He crossed the street to the court house and, when he was in his chair behind the table, he got out a sack of tobacco and papers and with steady fingers made a cigarette. As he lighted it, he leaned back and grinned at the ceiling.

Noon came while he sat smoking, staring out through the door thinking. Occasionally, someone passing looked in and spoke and he nodded. Then he heard footsteps — more than one man's. They came up to the door and stopped. He sagged a little in his chair, with eyes almost closed.

"Yeh?" he said drowsily. "What's it?"

He had never before seen the two men standing in the doorway. One was an inch or so over six feet, lean, hatchet-faced, with ears that stood out from his head so that he had an interested, almost a startled, expression. The other was six inches shorter, with sloping, muscular shoulders, and a stupid round face stubbled with reddish-gray beard. Both were booted, shabby.

"You the sheriff?" the tall man demanded harshly. Then, when Curt nodded, he came inside.

"He's the fella we got to talk to, then, Al," he said to the short man. "Lift them drunk feet of yours —"

Al nodded vaguely and trailed after him. The tall man came over, to lean on the table. He blew out breath noisily while savage little eyes studied Curt's negligent figure.

"Maybe we got some information," he said at last. "*I* do'no. Al got it. But that was about the last time he was sober enough to know what he was doin'."

Al laughed. It was a bubbly giggle.

"Wasn't sober, then! Just wasn't pickled!"

"He was up at Porto, Al was. Sleepin' with old Cortina's pigs in the corral. He heard a couple fellas talkin'. An' next mornin' —"

He reached inside his coat. Curt watched narrowly from under drooping lids. He had not relaxed his pose of semi-drunken indolence. But the tall man only produced a worn and dirty paper that looked like an old letter.

"Look at this," he said, and leaned beside Curt to put the paper on the table. "Looks to me like —"

Al had lumbered up beside him. Now he threw himself forward and a thick arm whipped around Curt's throat. The tall man straightened, his hatchet face twisted in triumphant grin. He reached left-handed under his coat, jerked out a Colt and struck at Curt's head.

Curt swayed, kicking the chair from under him to bang the tall man lightly. He snatched at the righthand gun under his jacket, stiffening his neck against the pressure of Al's throttling arm. He got out the pistol and let the hammer fall. But Al jerked him and the bullet missed the tall man. Curt whirled suddenly and Al was between him and the other. Curt poked his gun behind him and felt the muzzle dig into Al. He fired and Al screamed and let him go.

A pistol roared from across the room. Something picked at Curt's shirt. Automatically, he continued to turn and fire at the tall man, who was backing through the rear door. He saw a long splinter fly off the door's edge. Then the man was outside and

Al had fallen upon him again, from behind. The thick arms pinioned Curt's above the elbows.

Curt let his knees bend and hurled himself forward. Al slid over his head and rolled away. He was fumbling under his coat when Curt stepped over and rapped him across the head with long Colt barrel. Then he slumped.

Curt ran to the street door. Except far down the street nobody was in sight. He ran back, to jerk open the rear door. Fifty yards away he saw the tall man riding fast, looking over his shoulder. Toward the corral, perhaps thirty yards behind the office door, two saddled horses came trotting. One was his own buckskin!

He ran that way, caught the buckskin's trailing reins and went into the saddle without touching stirrups. He spurred savagely after the tall man, whose lead had increased to nearly a hundred yards. But presently he began to see that the buckskin — still slightly lame from the bullet burn on his leg — could not overtake that splendidly mounted fugitive. He turned back and trotted toward the office. At least, he thought grimly, he had got one of those bushwhackers.

"And he'll talk — I wouldn't to a *bit*

surprised if he talked!" he told himself grimly. "I'm past feeling kindly toward my enemies. I'll find a way to make him talk. It's a chain: he may not know a thing beyond the name of the man who hired 'em. But that man will know more —"

Halliday appeared in the back door of the office. Other men were behind him. His stentorian voice carried plainly across fifty yards, to Curt.

"Collect anybody?"

Curt shook his head and rode on up to the door.

"Just half of 'em," he said. "That fellow in there — Al, the other one called him. Maybe he'll be plenty to give me the information I want —"

"What?" Halliday grunted, staring. "Fellow in here? Why, Curt —"

"He didn't get away?" Curt cried. "He didn't come to —"

Then he saw Al, sprawled where he had fallen. He looked at him and now he saw blood spreading upon the rough planks of the floor. He stared.

"Why —" he began vaguely. Then he brushed through the half-dozen men with Halliday and crossed the room. There was a smoke-blackened hole in Al's shirt.

"Didn't — didn't *you* do it?" Halliday

asked him, frowning.

"Hell, no! There was no need! He grabbed me from behind —"

Rapidly, grimly, he told his story. Halliday shook bewildered head.

"That's queer! That's damn' queer! I was the first man in — so far as I know. I heard shots — then, after a little bit, another shot. I come a-runnin'. *He* was just like that. Nobody was around."

Curt looked at the door leading into the empty jail. Shorty Wiggin, the jailer, appeared now in the street door. Beside him was Sam Bain.

"What's it?" Shorty grunted.

Curt told him. Then they searched the building and found it empty.

"It's easy enough to figure," Curt told Halliday furiously, when they stood alone. "Al was a spent shot. He might talk. He would have talked before I got done with him. Somebody was watching that precious couple of murderers, to see how they made out. That somebody popped in here as I left. He — or they — shut Al's mouth."

"Any — notions?" Halliday asked softly.

Curt's face tightened.

"I told Tom Card — just to devil him — that I was getting a line on the Trackless Bunch — *por Dios!* Would that have scared him? Mention of the Bunch? But I told him, too — I wanted to see his face — that I was going to know who sicked that bushwhacker onto me. I sort of expected a visit, after that. I got it! But —"

He shrugged.

"So far as I can see, he's still in the clear — officially. Unofficially, of course, I'm naming a slug for Mr. Card!"

CHAPTER V

Andy Allen stared at Curt across the pine table in the sheriff's office.

"Then, except for your bushwhackers, nothin's happened? You never come on a thing, the whole time I was gone, huh?" he inquired.

"You've been gone — how long?" Curt grinned. "But the answer is — no! I've done a lot more chasing around. It got me just as much as all my other riding. Nothing at all! And no sign of any tall bushwhacker. No identification of the dead one. No trail to his killer."

He had never mentioned that small boot-print found on the trail after the robbery of The Points stage. In the beginning, he had kept that discovery to himself because he wanted no warning to get to the outlaws.

Since his glimpse of Shirley's bootprint on the short-cut from Alamos, he had had even less impulse to mention his theory.

"Look here!" Andy said frowningly. "We been talkin' in a circle for an hour. Ain't it just about time that bunch broke loose somewheres else? If only we could guess where they're goin' to pull the next job, then we could get in there ahead of 'em —"

Curt shook his head.

"I thought of that. But it looks to me like too big a contract. Too many things they could do, Andy; too many places they could go. My notion is that if nothing else develops, Andy, we're due to raise some saddle corns. For it's my belief that this Trackless Bunch of ours is pretty damn well organized. The way Frenchy's used to be. There must be one man — maybe two — at the head, to do the scheming, and tell the understrappers where to hit the lick and how to scatter. Nearly always, dealing with a gang like this, you find scouts and spies thrown around, to pick up talk about good, profitable jobs. Maybe we can find one of the spies and make him talk. We'll try that. If we don't have luck, we'll try something else. Catching criminals is a business of trying a lot of roads until you hit on the one your man walked down. So —"

Knuckles rapped the door. Curt lifted a hand to the front of his goatskin jacket. He looked at the door, then at Andy. Andy shrugged and let his hand drop into his lap near pistol butt.

"Come in!" Curt called.

A small, dusty man slipped in quickly over the threshold and hooked the door shut behind him with a heel. He leaned against it, as if weary, breathing hard, looking nervously from Curt to Andy Allen.

"The sheriff!" he said. "Who's the Sheriff of Gurney?"

"I am," Curt grunted. "What's the trouble?"

"If — if I let something slip out to you, will you see that it's kept quiet?"

"Well, that depends a whole lot on what you have got to tell me," Curt shrugged.

"It's about this — this bunch that's been giving you people so much trouble. But, unless I'm dead certain nobody's going to hook me up with the talking, I'm not going to talk. *I'm* not going to get killed, because I talked too much at the wrong time."

Curt stared tensely at him. Left hand on the table was tight clenched.

"The Trackless Bunch," he whispered. "You mean — the Trackless Bunch?"

"The what? I don't know about any *track-*

less bunch. But this gang that's been sticking up stages and raising hell generally — I think maybe I *do* know something about them. Question is — is it safe to tell?"

"I reckon you can count on us to protect you," Curt assured him. He leaned forward, with eyes narrowed. "Now, what's the word?"

"I've been working for a nester up on Williams Creek. He's a big, sulky fellow — new to the Territory, I think. Well, in the last month quite a few men have ridden up to his cabin after dark. He goes out to talk to 'em. I got sort of suspicious and I tried to overhear the talk a couple of times. No luck. But I was up on the hill behind the cabin, a couple of days ago, and I saw smoke over by an old cabin. I sneaked up as close as I dared. There were eight or nine men camped there. Then a cowboy came by that afternoon and told me about this outlaw gang and how the Sheriff of Gurney was looking for 'em. So I slipped off and rode here. I'm willing to bet that it's your gang, over at the old cabin."

Curt studied the news-bringer. He was in middle twenties, apparently, though his thin face was masked by a heavy brown stubble. A white scar gleamed in the beard on his right cheek. He looked to be the drifter-kind, of whom Curt had seen many.

"Who's this nester?" he demanded.

"He calls himself Ben Vickers. I think he's from Oklahoma. If you can get a good posse, I'll lead you to where you can see the cabin. After that — well, I'm not a fighting man and you can excuse me from the battle."

"Boy!" breathed Andy Allen ecstatically. "She looks penurious! Looks like we're goin' to get our ridin', Curt! An' that suits *me* right in the middle of where I live."

"I'll get Halliday — and Powers the blacksmith and — oh, four-five others of the old-timers," Curt decided. "You stay here till I get back, Andy. Get this fellow — What do you call yourself, stranger?"

"Quinn'll do," shrugged the news-bringer.

"Well, get Quinn something to eat, if he wants it. Then get our horses ready in the corral. Throw some extra shells in the saddlebags, too, Andy. For if this is really our Trackless Bunch, there's going to be plenty of powder burned when we hit 'em!"

Shortly before midnight, the posse rode quietly out of Gurney. Curt had gathered five of the best men in the county seat — or the whole Territory — for such work as lay ahead. There was old Halliday, with his

Sharps fifty across his arm; the huge, slow-moving, slow-thinking, and utterly fearless Powers, Gurney's blacksmith; "Comanche" Smith, a gaunt, leather-faced freight-contractor who had spent his whole life along one frontier or another; Merle Sheehan of the hotel — ex-cavalryman, hardly smaller than the blacksmith and a rifle-shot of note even in the Territory. The fifth man was Ike Francis, a squat, grizzled cattlebuyer who was an old Texas cowboy.

In the van of the posse, Curt rode beside the man Quinn. None of the party needed a guide to Williams Creek, but Quinn had turned in beside Curt as they rode softly away from the corral in the rear of the jail.

"Reckon this nester smelled anything, when you hightailed it off the ranch?" Curt asked, after an hour's steady riding.

Quinn grunted vaguely:

"No, I don't think so. You see, I never did like the place, or the work. One time — two weeks ago — that was, I said something about quitting and Vickers raised hell. Told me I'd agreed to work for him six months. I hadn't, really, but he told me that if I tried to quit before the six months was up, he'd break my neck. He looked as if he meant it, too! So, he'll probably think that I just saw a chance to light a shuck and took it."

"Good enough!" said Curt. "I'd hate to have that bunch sneak off on us."

They rode on as swiftly as the rough trail and the darkness permitted. At dawn they were on the bank of Williams Creek. Quinn reined in and held up his hand.

"Vickers's cabin is about four miles from here," he said nervously. "Up the creek and west. The old stone cabin is closer — about a mile up the creek and not more than a hundred yards from the water. This cattle trail along the bank leads straight to it. And there's cover right up to the little clearing the cabin stands in."

Old Comanche Smith squinted upward at the sky. On the eastern horizon the grayness was touched, now, by the faintest, most delicate, flush of rose. Comanche spat thoughtfully into the creek and cocked an eye at a mocking-bird that, roused by the slight sounds they made, had fluttered out of the dew-wet bushes and perched upon a slender branch above their heads.

"Pretty mornin' — to cash in," he grunted. "Mile to go. We can get there as they roll out for breakfast."

They rode on. Presently, a horse nickered in the woods to the left. Quinn had been riding with eyes going from side to side, face very tight beneath the heavy brown stubble of his beard. He pulled in and listened, then turned his horse out of the trail and into the bushes.

"Wait a minute!" he whispered to Curt as he went. They reined in, hands on weapons. Then his voice came reassuringly. "It's one of Vickers's. I'll run him back a way, so he won't get scared and go dashing ahead. If he did, they'd maybe be alarmed. Go ahead. I'll catch up"

So they rode on again, more cautiously. Comanche Smith spurred up beside Curt. His gaunt jaws worked rhythmically upon his tobacco.

"Better let me scout up the trail, son," he suggested. "It won't take long an' then we'll be damn certain about what's ahead."

He vanished around a crook in the stock trail. The others took advantage of the halt to bring bacon and bread from *alforjas* or coat pockets and eat breakfast in the saddle. Minutes passed, until half an hour had gone. Still there was no sound from Comanche. Curt began to fidget; Halliday and Sheehan, beside him, looked grim.

"Could they have got him?" Curt wondered aloud. "We'd have heard a shot, but they might just have stuck him up . . ."

"Along the border, the Mex' hide by the waterholes" — this was Sheehan, speaking

118

out of his cavalry experience — "an' they drop a loop over y' head . . ."

"Let's go on!" said Andy Allen. "Say! Where's that absorbent hairpin that was guidin' us? He was here, then he wasn't —"

"Cold feet, maybe," shrugged Curt. "No time to bother about him now. Let's ramble! I don't like the smell of this."

Rapidly, but cautiously none the less, they pushed up the trail at a trot. Nearing what they judged to be the mile limit set by Quinn, they slowed a bit and each man threw his long gun across his arm. But no sign, no sound, of either the Trackless Bunch or Comanche Smith was anywhere in the green quiet. Nothing but the splash and murmur of the water in the stony bed of Williams Creek.

A mile was covered, but they found no sign of a trail, or of a stone cabin. They drew rein when another quarter-mile had shown nothing but the narrow cattle trail leading up the creek-bank. They looked in some puzzlement at one another.

"Wish we had that Quinn!" they said grimly, all together.

Now came the soft thudding of a horse's hoofs. They pushed back into the bushes and lifted their rifles. But old Comanche

heard the rustling. He called to them reassuringly, yet with irritation in his voice,
and rode up to them. He stopped his horse
and scowled at Curt.

"There's somethin' blame' funny about
this business!" he grunted. "I scouted this
whole damn trail. No rock cabin an' I never
found hide *or* hair of the Vickers place —
no sign of any nesterin' so far's that goes!
Where's that fella Quinn you had for guide?
I want to talk to him some!"

"Hasn't showed up yet," frowned Curt.
"Reckon he could have been putting up a
deal on us? And what for? Let's hightail it
back and see if we can find him. Maybe he
just got tangled up on his landmarks. He
looks sort of like a pilgrim — rides like one."

"He couldn't have got much mixed up,"
grunted Comanche. "Williams Creek starts
right up yonder, in a bunch of springs. But
let's go hunt him."

When they came back to the place where
Quinn had gone into the bushes after the
horse, they separated and scoured the
woods. No sign of the fellow. But old
Comanche returned to the trail leading the
jaded animal which Quinn had ridden. It
bore neither saddle nor bridle, now. Comanche was grinning sardonically.

"Maybe he was a pilgrim," he said to

Curt. "But he was up to somethin' an he certainly played us for a flock of little woolly baa-lambs! I found the place where he had that other horse staked out. He shifted his hull from his pony and rattled his hocks to the east. He certainly lit out in a mile-high cloud of dust, too — an' be damned if that's Spanish! No use us tryin' to catch him."

"Now, what's it all about?" Curt wondered. He looked around frowningly, beating his hand softly, absently, against his overalls.

"Maybe the fella comin' can tell us," suggested Halliday, jerking his head downtrail, Gurney-ward.

They listened and after a moment all could hear the drumming of hoofs. A lean cowboy came fogging it around an elbow of the trail. His brown face was very serious. He slid his horse to a stop before them.

"Bank was robbed last night, Sheriff!" he cried. "Ed Showalters, the cashier, was downed. The gang blowed the safe open with blastin' powder, grabbed the money an' hightailed it before folks could catch their breath. They run off most of the horses in town. So, it was two hours before we could get after 'em."

"So *that's* what it was all about!" Curt

snarled. "And I, like a damn sheep, fell right into it!"

"There was some others with you, son!" Halliday consoled him, and the others grinned shamefacedly. "You wasn't a bit more took in by that *gunie* than the rest of us."

"Well, let's hit the trail for Gurney. They'll be yelling for my scalp in dead earnest, now!"

"They will, of course," Comanche nodded. He laughed grimly. "They'll cloud up an' rain all over you. But — hell! We'll be the same as an umbrella over your devoted head, Curt! Us in this posse, we *got* to stand up for you, to save our own faces. We got to say that you was dead right — an' I still think you was — to come out here. Because we came along with you an' *we* never looked slaunchwise at Friend Quinn."

They left the cowboy to trail them on his tired horse and headed for Gurney at a hard trot. Curt was furious. If only he had been clever enough to see through Quinn! But the man had been clever, a consummate actor. Curt thought of his promise to *protect* Quinn from vengeance of the Trackless Bunch. He laughed sardonically.

"If ever I get my hands on you, Mr. Quinn," he thought, "or get you inside

Winchester range, your next acting will be right around Gates Ajar!"

He turned grimly sideways to Andy, who had spoken.

"I said — what does he look like?" Andy said jerkily. "Quinn? I got a sort of picture of his outside generally. But what would he look like, with his face mowed and his hat on the other side? *I* can't figure it, Curt. Not even metaphysical!"

"*Por Dios!* You're right! He — sort of fades away when I try to see him. Well — even so, we ought to be able to tell him, if ever we run into him. Easy!"

"How's that?" Andy asked bewilderedly.

"Why, the minute he sees any of this bunch, and thinks about how we followed him *just* as far as he wanted us to come, he'll let out a roar. We can tell him by his laughing."

Gurney was like a ghost town, when the grim-faced posse rode in at noon. Curt guessed that every able-bodied man who could find a horse had ridden out on the trail of Ed Showalters's murderers. Ed had been a popular man, a moving spirit in Gurney dances and amateur theatricals. He had friends up and down the Territory.

Curt led the posse up the main street and they swung down before the square, one-story brick building that housed the Stockman's Bank. As they crossed the sidewalk toward the open door, Harrel the president appeared in it, his big figure all but blocking the opening. He was haggard, square red face set like stone. He looked them over, sun-squinted gray eyes narrow, very bright. When he stared at Curt, his thin mouth twitched. But he said nothing. "Let's have the story," Curt said tonelessly. "We left town about a quarter to twelve. So —"

"Must have been somethin' after one," Harrel said slowly. "An' they had it planned about perfect. Puttin' everything together, from what I found out today, they was countin' on us bein' fresh out of sheriffs an' all . . . So, five-six of 'em rode in. They knew Ed Showalters's room. They got him out of bed, quiet, an' brought him down here. Judgin' by them blastin' the safe open an' killin' Ed, I reckon they got Ed's key off him an' went in the back door. Likely, Ed wouldn't open up, no matter what they tried on him. Ed was stubborn as a mule. Anyway, they tied him up, then they shot him. An' they flopped the big safe over an' blowed the door to pieces. The noise waked everybody, but the horses in the livery corrals had been let out and run off."

Curt moved toward the door and Harrel

124

stepped back to let them all inside. The single room of the little bank looked much as if a cyclone had swept it. Behind the wooden rail that divided the interior, tables and chairs and a bookkeeper's desk were overturned and smashed. The big, old-fashioned safe lay with doorless front up-turned. Fragments of quilts caught Curt's eyes. He poked a charred rag with his toe. "Anybody recognize the quilt?" he asked Harrel, and the banker growled.

"Mrs. Sheehan. They come from one of her empty rooms, she says. A room that hadn't been rented for a week. She knows the pattern. She made the quilt. No trail there. She didn't have any strangers in her hotel."

"How much did they get?"

"About thirteen thousan' — all the bills an' gold in the bank. Left six-seven hundred in silver. I don't give a damn about the money. It'll put a sizable dent in us, but we can stand it. We'll assess the stockholders. What I'm beefin' about is the way they done Ed Showalters — tyin' him up an' mur-derin' him."

"Now, why would they do a thing like that?" Curt frowned. "You'd understand their tying him up *or* shooting him, but why both is more than I see . . ."

"You might *ask* 'em why they done it — when you catch 'em," Harrel grunted scornfully. "If you ever do catch 'em."

"I'll catch 'em, all right!" Curt assured him grimly. "Ed Showalters was a friend of mine, too. I'll hang the deadwood on this Trackless Bunch and hang a few of the murderers on a handy cottonwood limb."

"Talk's cheap," Harrel snarled. "If we paid you to talk you'd be right valuable."

"You're doing a good deal of talking yourself!" Curt reminded him coldly. "And the most of your talk, Harrel, is just plain blatting — like a sheep's. I've been listening to you and Tom Card and some others of your kind a clean bellyful! You sit up and, the minute something happens, you expect the sheriff to wiggle a witch-hazel switch or do some sort of hocus-pocus, then tell exactly who's the guilty man. According to you, a sheriff is a sort of mind reader, seventh son of a seventh son. If you were in my place, you wouldn't know a bit more than I do, about who is in this Trackless Bunch, or where they hang out."

"I ain't goin' to take that kind of talk from any Smart Aleck kid!" the banker snarled. "By God! I was hustlin' steers up the trail when you wasn't dry behind the ears. I —"

"You're wrong! You're going to take it! You'll take it off me!" Curt assured him furiously. "You're an old-timer and all that. You've got the name of being level-headed, mostly. But right now you're blatting like a sheep and I'm tired of listening to it. You and Tom Card aren't running the sheriff's office. Not yet!"

"Right!" Tom Card said evenly. He was in the door behind Curt, who turned to face him. Card stood with heavy, handsome face impassive. Shirley Randolph was at his elbow. "We're not running the sheriff's office. We don't *want* to run it! It's not our work. What we're asking is that *you* run it — as a sheriff's office should be run. We want to see this Trackless Bunch of yours caught."

Sight of the girl, so intimately beside the big gambler, infuriated Curt as almost nothing else could have done just then. But the effect of his anger was to produce a surface calmness of face, a slowing, a thickening, of his drawl.

"Card," he said very softly, "when I want your advice, I'll ask for it. Until then, and so long as I'm Sheriff of Gurney, you keep your conversation to yourself while I'm around. I'm responsible for results, not methods. You keep to yourself your ideas

127

about what I'm doing, or not doing. No tin-horn gambler is going to give me orders. Least of all is any tinhorn going to rawhide me. Not while I'm as healthy as I am, today!"

For an instant there was a tiny quivering of the gambler's heavy face. Curt, coldly, deadly furious, watched him narrowly. His arms were folded, his hands stiffened, for lightning cross-arm draw. But only for an instant did Card waver on the edge of sudden action. He was too much the gambler to discount odds such as those hinted at by the younger man's concealed hands, slightly drooping shoulders, suggestion of catlike poise.

"And in the meanwhile," he said in a thoughtful tone, "this Trackless Bunch of yours must just go on its way. We mustn't say anything, mustn't even prefer to have them caught. Dear me! It's a great deal you ask of us."

"The bunch will be caught," Curt drawled, keeping his face expressionless. "It won't be so long in the doing, either."

"How long?" Card inquired, unpleasantly.

"Within a month. I'll take — just a third of the time allowed me the other night."

"All right!" Card nodded grimly. "I'll call that bluff. A month from today, the gang's to be in jail, or accounted for. Or Gurney will understand that you're just the mouthy kid I've said you are. One other thing — either way, one month from today I'll personally call you to account!"

For the first time, Curt let himself change expression. He smiled faintly, blue eyes metallic.

"That's different. The time limit holds just for the official business. For you, Card, there's no limit. Right now, before I get to work, will suit me perfectly. You can get your Principal Poodle, Mr. Sam Bain, and Zyler and the other Fidos, and we'll see if you can cut the mustard today."

"We'll be glad to!" Andy Allen nodded eagerly. "I always do feel detrimental on Tuesdays."

But Halliday, who had been muttering to Sheehan and Powers and Comanche Smith, moved abruptly. He stepped to Curt's side and put a hand lightly on his shoulder. But not in such fashion as to hamper any movement of Curt's arm, in case of a sudden move from Card. For he was an experienced gentleman, Mr. Halliday.

"I'm going to horn into this," he said grimly, staring at Harrel, and at Card. "Most of what Curt's said is plain fact. A certain clique of you have been after Curt's job. You've nagged an' you've belly-ached. You've been rawhidin' him plenty an' — like he says — just blattin' like old sheep. That goes for you, Harrel, well as for Card here! But there's some several of us in Gurney, in the county at large, solid behind Curt. We figure he's doin' right well an' if he's given half a chance, he'll bring in this gang of thieves. An' we aim to see that he gets a chance, too! Maybe some of you are kind of disrememberin' that it's the county elects a sheriff. The whole county. It ain't the bankers, or the storekeepers, or the gamblers, or yet the saloonkeepers. The county elected Smoky Cole sheriff an' Smoky, he put Curt in an' he backed him to the limit."

He waited, but there was no reply. He turned a little:

"Now, about this little argument, Curt. You got a good-sized job on your hands an' you owe it to everybody to handle that before you start tanglin' with your personal enemies. If you have just *got* to paint for war, I reckon nobody can stop you. But we wish you wouldn't. Business before pleasure is the best motto."

Tom Card's round blue eyes were ominously steady on Halliday. Curt saw a pulse throbbing like a tiny hammer in the gambler's throat. But Halliday was not one to be impressed by lowering stares. He looked at Card carelessly, just as he looked at Harrel. Card's eyes shifted to Curt.

"A month from today," he said with flat finality.

Curt nodded. He was watching Shirley. The girl's face was very pale. She seemed to see nothing, hear nothing, of what was going on.

"All right, Andy," Curt said briefly. "This will probably be a famous day in Gurney's history — the Day of the Bank Robbery and the Big Wind. But we can't stop to mark it down, now. Let's get out in that trail."

Passing Shirley, he looked steadily at her and she met his probing eyes with a long, unreadable stare, then turned, putting arm lightly on Tom Card's arm. It was Andy Allen, not Curt, who swore viciously when he saw the gesture.

They mounted before the bank, waved briefly to Halliday and the others, got sandwiches and rode out of town. The trampled trail was easy to follow. In mid-afternoon they met the Gurneyites coming back.

Three Wagon Wheel punchers in the van drew their horses to a halt and turned comfortably sideways in their saddles.

"Out-Injuned us, Sheriff!" one confessed and the others nodded. "We followed 'em easy enough till they hit that big patch of rocks, the other side the Tinajas. After that, it was pay your money an' take your choice. We separated an' spread all over that section, but there's fifty rock-floored cañons leadin' every which way from hell to breakfast. An' it ain't likely it was cows or horses we was trailin'. Them six fellas likely split up an' went nine different ways."

They waited silently while Curt stared blindly at the ground. Other riders coming up, pulled in around them. At last Curt shrugged lean shoulders.

"We'll see what we can do from the other end," he decided. "Anyway, we've met one man out of the bunch."

And as they jogged back toward Gurney, he told the Wagon Wheel boys about the wild-goose chase upon which "Quinn" had led them and of Quinn's disappearance. They listened with much interest and, at the conclusion, smacked their hands delightedly upon chaps-legs.

"He's a slick one, now, ain't he?" cried the tall cowboy who had told of the trailing. "Yes, sir! he's certainly among them present four ways from the jack! Quinn, he calls himself, huh? Well, I reckon we'll kind of keep a lookout for Friend Quinn. He's one of them hairpins that's so slick you can't feel safe about where they are, till they're hangin' up in plain sight."

Back in the sheriff's office, Curt spun a chair about and spraddled it, with arms folded upon the back and chin up on arms. He regarded Andy wearily and that young man grinned back at him cheerfully.

"We're sort of hubbing hell!" Curt grinned.

"Why, things *are* sort of hypothetical," Andy agreed. "But, hell, Curt! We'll rope an' brand 'em, yet. Keep your tail over the dashboard an' your head up, my old man used to tell me, an' you're bound to run into somethin' — if it's nothin' but the corral fence!"

"That was a fool bluff I made to Card," Curt said gloomily. "But he galls me till I don't know whether I'm horseback or swimming."

"I reckon she — I mean *he* — did," Andy nodded, innocently.

Entered Halliday, now, while Curt was glaring at his deputy.

"Got somethin' to show you, son," grinned the storekeeper. "Don't know as she means much an' don't know as she don't. But my Mex' boy, Manuel, he was projeckin' around the back of the bank right after the gang hightailed it. An' near-by the place where they'd left the horses, Manuel picked up this paper . . ."

He held out the tattered newspaper, his thick forefinger indicating the date line. It was the Ancho weekly, smudged on one side, passably clean on the other.

"Ancho — Friday of last week," said Curt, very thoughtfully. "You reckon the gang dropped this, Halliday?"

"No doubt about it. My guess is that they brought the powder in a sack, with this paper for a linin', maybe. An' they dumped the powder into somethin' handier to handle than the sack an' out come the paper."

"I didn't notice any strangers around town, before we pulled out last night," Curt said thoughtfully. "Don't know much about Ancho, though I've been there a time or two."

"I was in the Palace an' the Star, last night — you found me in the Star, remember? I never seen any strange faces, either, as I recollect. Nobody from Ancho, so far's I know. But this-here paper's too recent to've been brought into Gurney by folks in this neighborhood, in the ordinary run of things. No-o, Curt, I reckon some of our Trackless Bunch is holin' up in Ancho.

Maybe it's Ancho folks altogether."

"I've got to do something, if I'm to back that bluff I made to Card," Curt shrugged. "If that gang's holing up over in Ancho, that's something to know. And a sight more than we knew before. So — I reckon I'll ramble over there and have a look at some of the leading citizens. They do say that some pretty hard cases are drifting in."

"When do we start?" Andy inquired happily, hitching his gun forward.

Curt grinned pleasantly at him.

"We've got to split up. You've got to stay here and ride herd on Tom Card and his merry Fidos. If Sam Bain should ride in and start something, you can bend a gun over his head — or drill him — just whichever you feel like. But don't you damage Tom Card any! I've already got my brand on that hairpin."

"And it'd mebbe hurt *her* feelings, too," nodded Andy, with solemn maliciousness. "See the way she cuddled up to him, today, Halliday? She —"

He went over backward with a howl of simulated terror as Curt moved toward him. He landed upon the floor with grotesque waving of long legs.

"Man, you never see such a *gunie,* to take his love affairs incipient!" he grinned at Halliday, when he had righted his chair. "Now, me, I could handle a whole harem easier'n Curt — All right! All right! I ain't sayin' a word! If you want to be retroactive in your misery, you certainly can for all of me!"

"I'm going to get some sleep," said Curt, and he grinned in spite of himself. "I'll hightail it Ancho-way before daylight."

CHAPTER VI

Only a few, and those Gurney's earliest early birds, were out, when Curt herded the drowsy and complaining Andy Allen to the street. They stumbled along in darkness toward the bar of yellow light that lay across the sidewalk before the U-and-Me restaurant.

"But why do *I* have to crawl out, the night before, because you're headed for Ancho?" Andy wanted to know. "My stars, Curt! It's not sanitary! I don't mind ridin' herd on you young fellas, but nobody's goin' to jump out an' say *Boo!* at you, this early."

"This is part of your official educating," Curt told him grinning. "Sheriffs, Andy, they often have to stay up all night, and things like that. I've got plans for training you: We'll find a good, deep hole somewhere, after I come back. And you can sit up all night for a week, watching it. Just for practice. Now, don't you come into the U-and-Me until that Celestial has got my breakfast ready. He is not fond of you, my son. And I'm not going to miss my coffee, just because Quong Lee's shy of you."

"Oh, he'll never get egotistical about me in the daytime," Andy shrugged. "He knows I'm a night traveler."

"Just the same, you'll stay outside until I've got my order in! And if Quong wants to curry your forelock, after you drive up, don't yell at me for help. That sort of thing is absolutely a personal matter between you and Quong. If he takes a look at you, and decides that the right way to say good-morning is by taking an iron spider and making it fit you like a tight hat — that's just an Oriental peculiarity, to my mind. So —"

He went into the long, narrow room that had no tables, only a counter with high stools. At the far end wizened Quong Lee was busy at the range. Two of Sam Bain's Lazy B riders and a hostler from the freight corral were his only customers. The little Chinese grinned at Curt.

"Hi, She'ff!" he greeted him. "Catchum cloffee?"

Curt nodded as he came past the other

137

men and took one of the stools. Quong put before him a big "iron ware" mug of coffee and waited. Curt looked down and said:

"Black as hate and hot as hell and sweet as love and strong enough to float an iron wedge!"

Quong grinned with repetition of the ancient cow-camp formula. He turned back to the range and Curt said:

"Steak and eggs, Quong."

The door creaked again and Quong turned. He bristled — for all the world like a shriveled cat facing a dog. He put out his hand toward the half-brick on the range's edge and spat mixed Cantonese and mutilated English at Andy Allen, who had stopped halfway down the counter with hands uplifted.

"Him come along you, She'ff?" Quong demanded of Curt.

Very gravely, Curt turned on his stool and studied Andy. Then he shook his head and looked at Quong.

"I never saw him before."

"Why — why, you lowdown illegitimate!" Andy cried. "He's an umbilical liar, Quong. Me, I'm a deputy sheriff. That lyin' scoun'el hired me, hisself! Look at my badge!"

"Looks like Montgomery, Ward, to me," Curt shrugged, after a moment of staring.

"They sell 'em to young cowboys for eighty-seven cents, three for two and a half. If you want to feed him, Quong, I reckon it's all right. But I'd charge him extra. Show him some two-dollar ham and eggs."

"No damn good!" Quong snarled. "All time chaseum China boy — *yell!* No likeum! Too hell much noise! I feedum. But — no mo' monkeyshine, you Andy!"

"Better make him pay first," Curt suggested. "County's not paying his feed bill! You remember that, Andy, before you start ordering."

"What?" Andy cried indignantly. "County don't pay?"

"Only when you're away from home," Curt told him inexorably. "Rest of the time it's out of your own sock. Maybe that will make a difference in your appetite!"

"Oh!" Andy said serenely. "Like that! A'right, Quong. Gi' me about a gallon of coffee an' some hashed-brown spuds, an' spread four-five fried eggs on top about a yard of steak. An' — is that fried pies I see over there? It is! Gi' me two-three of the apple, unless you ain't got apple, an' have to give me some other kind. You see, Curt, I'm away from home, now. Speakin' hermetically, just between you an' me, all the home I got is the LA wagon. And' *that* won't

139

be out till the beef-roundup."

The pop-eyed Lazy B cowboy on Andy's left had been staring with a scornful curl of the lip at his neighbor. Perhaps the foolery between Curt and Andy deceived this newest hand of Bain's. Now, he made a sniffing sound that perfectly conveyed disgust — and brought Curt's attention to him. Curt observed that the cowboy had eyes like a bad horse — with much white showing. But he was not much interested until the Lazy B man said unpleasantly:

"By God! I traveled a good deal in my time. I seen a hell-slew of shurfs an' so on. But if this Gurney shurf's office don't take the cake, I never seen nothin'."

His companion jogged him hastily. The other cowboy was a bald-headed fat man, who had worked for three or four years in the country. He was very well acquainted with both Curt Thompson and the efficient, if young, range boss of Los Alamos. But the pop-eyed man drew impatiently away from the warning elbow, continuing to stare belligerently at Andy's blank face. He shook his head at last.

"Yes sir! I seen shurfs hither an' yon. An' if this-here Gurney shurf's office could just *eat* itself out of its troubles, it'd be Hallelujah Time, right now!"

Andy sawed away at his steak with a dull knife. He seemed not to hear. Nor Curt.

"I reckon different parts of the country, they got different notions," Pop-Eyes drawled. "Some places, a shurf has got to be this or that. Other places, it's somethin' else. But I can see, now, what they want in Gurney. No wonder Sam Bain ain't wanted for shurf, here. He ain't a good enough eater an' so he lost all the Chink cook vote!"

Andy chewed solemnly and swallowed. He looked at Curt:

"What you said last night — that still go?" he asked drawlingly. "I can have anybody but Card?"

Curt frowned at him.

"Now, Andy! I was just saying that because I thought I would be out of town. You wouldn't ever hold me to that!"

"I certainly would!" Andy cried indignantly.

"I wish I hadn't promised you," Curt mumbled irritably, around a full mouth. "I'm always making fool-promises and living to wish I hadn't."

"But you did promise! You admit that. An' there's no fair backin' out now. A man's promise ought to be just as effervescent as his bond!"

"All right! *All* right! It's all yours."

141

Andy grinned and turned upon the Lazy B man. He looked him thoughtfully up and down and at the last he nodded.

"Did you ever get half-killed?" he asked mildly. "Don't tell me! It won't make a bit of difference. Because inside eight minutes, you're goin' to be able to answer that question *yes*. An' up to your dyin' day, you're goin' to thank your analytical stars that I'm a good-humored man around meal-times!"

The pop-eyed man gaped at him. Suddenly, he swore and let his hand fall toward his belt. Andy went toward him in a surging motion that let him wrap his arms around the pop-eyed one. He twisted and the other's hand fell away from a pistol's butt. The stool crashed over, and Andy pushed Pop-Eyes a little way from him and looped a right fist to the thick, unpleasant mouth.

Pop-Eyes staggered toward the wall. Again, his hand clawed at his Colt. Andy ran in and knocked the reaching hand away. He jerked the Colt from its holster and threw it to Curt, who put up a hand and stopped it.

Then Andy hit Pop-Eyes in the belly and, when he had doubled him, drove a terrific left into his right ear. Pop-Eyes fell forward and Andy stepped upon his exposed back, to dig in high heels and rock himself before he stepped off and stooped to catch one of Pop-Eyes' ankles.

Curt had been watching the bald and fat cowboy. Now, he lifted dark brows inquiringly. The fat man put up both hands and made a pushing motion.

"Uh-uh! Uh-uh! Let him kill his own snakes! He's been runnin' off at the mouth about how puny everything is over here, ag'inst Arizony ways. Now, let him show what they'd do in Arizony, by God!"

Andy was dragging Pop-Eyes, face-down, along the splintered floor of the U-and-Me. Pop-Eyes kicked frantically, but Andy — grinning — evaded the free foot easily. He let his victim go and Pop-Eyes scrambled to his feet and rushed Andy.

Andy stepped aside and let the cowboy go past. But he followed and swung short, murderous punches to the other's face and body. Pop-Eyes crashed down and lay still.

Andy bent and searched him, taking a dagger from the sheath that Pop-Eyes wore beneath his shirt. He came back, breathing deeply but without labor, and sat down to his meal again.

"A very neat and complete job, Mr. Allen," Curt complimented him. "With a little training from the Old Expert, I believe you're going to shape up right tolerable."

"*I* thought it was right contiguous, myself," Andy nodded. "Goin'?"

Curt nodded. He said that he was through. He paid Quong and went down the restaurant, stopping for a moment to watch Pop-Eyes, who was now sitting up.

"Just between us," Curt said confidentially to the battered Lazy B man, "you'd better not make any remarks about the sheriff's office eating, after this. We know we've got awful appetites, but we're touchy about having 'em mentioned. Oh! Tell Bain, too, will you?"

He went back to the sheriff's corral and saddled his buckskin. He thought that nobody saw him ride out of Gurney, for the darkness was just now becoming grayness and lights were beginning to show in house windows.

He turned off the road after a mile and let the buckskin pick his way through the cañons and down the rocky slopes of the foothills. When daylight came, he rode the ridges cautiously, looking around from high places.

"My goodness!" he told himself, after such a look before and behind him. "I was not exactly a pilgrim, when I forked that Open A *palomina* into Gurney and hit Smoky for

144

a job. But helping Smoky and Lit and Chihuahua Joe wipe out Frenchy Leonard certainly put the finishing touches to me! And what soft shades of innocence I had left, after that, they were rubbed off me when we mopped up the little fellows that were left . . ."

During the forenoon, instinctively he watched the skyline, riding with his carbine across his arm instead of more comfortably in the scabbard. He studied the lie of the land before descending into arroyos or crossing a hogback. Inevitably, his mind went to Tom Card — and to Card's Man Friday, Sam Bain.

"Card intends to deal me plenty of bushwhacking! I wish he'd sic Bain onto me, out here in the open! I don't know of anything I'd like better than tangling with Sam, where it'd be just man to man. And probably it'd save just trouble, later on!"

Thought of Card and Bain brought thought of Shirley Randolph. He could see her with maddening clearness, slim, lovely, aristocratic — and aloof . . . But the mental picture that hurt most was that evoked by memory of her beyond the Devil's Bench, when he had gently drawn her hands from her eyes and held her so close against him that the pounding of her heart was plain against his. Softly, furiously, he cursed Tom Card.

"His kind often sweeps a woman off her feet — and to him," Curt conceded bitterly, out of the experiences of a crammed past. "Handsome and sure of himself; with plenty of money — He's a wolf, there's no arguing it. I wonder what country his back trail comes out of . . . He has seen a lot in his time and, if I could drop a loop over some of the history he's helped make, probably it'd answer plenty of questions.

With darkness, he built his cooking-fire against the wall of a tiny mountain creek, where the smoke would rise into the brush and be lost. A chill April wind had risen in late afternoon and the little blaze was pleasantly warm. But when he had cooked his bacon and boiled his coffee, he left the dead fire to ride a mile up the creek. He staked the buckskin on one side of the water and himself rolled into his blanket in bushes on the other bank.

The wind rose in the night and blew gustily, drowning out most sounds. Curt slept soundly, if lightly, without waking. He was up in the gray, still hour before the dawn, shaking his blanket. Across the creek he heard the buckskin moving as he grazed. A trout jumped in the creek. A tawny pine squirrel raced along the bank. Nothing more.

When he had crossed the stream on stones and resaddled the buckskin, he rode pretty quietly back to the place where he had cooked his supper. And when he swung down, after a long, slow stare around, he bent, whistling softly.

Near the dead fire, plain in the soft mould, were bootprints. They were large — a good deal larger than his own. And the left boot-sole was badly worn. Each impression of it showed a ragged crack across it. Beside a print, here and there, was the unmistakable slot of a rifle or carbine butt.

Curt stared grimly at everything around him. The wind had laid and now every tiny woods sound was audible. In the east the horizon, above a long, flat-topped butte, was reddish orange and the sun's brazen edge showed over the butte as he watched. Birds were all about him. Mocking-birds sang from the bushes. He was ringed about by them and this made him believe that the man of the cracked bootsole was not now in the neighborhood. The mockers would not be singing so, if a man were nearby. Curt had disturbed and silenced a half-dozen, on his way down the creek.

So he rekindled the fire and, with carbine

always conveniently near his hand, and the buckskin standing with reins trailing, close by, he boiled his coffee and ate his breakfast. Afterward, he swung into the saddle and rode on, watching the trail ahead and speculating about that rifleman who had stalked his old fire.

"I ought to have holed up close by," he thought. "It would have been pretty interesting, to step out on that gentleman!"

Then he tried to recall the exact appearance of Sam Bain's boots. But all he could remember about Bain's feet was the Lazy B man's odd, shuffling, halting walk.

It was around nine o'clock when he rounded a butte's shoulder and saw a man on a black horse, leaning from the saddle to study the ground. The man had a carbine in his hand.

Curt had only the barest glimpse of the other, finding something familiar about him. For without straightening, the man jumped his horse into a pile of great boulders.

Curt pulled back almost as quickly, into the shelter of the butte. He got off the buckskin and from the ground studied the other's position. As he watched, he saw something moving at the side of a boulder. He edged ahead slightly, and waited. When he saw the top of a hat coming slowly in view, he pushed the little Winchester forward and drove a slug at the hat. It vanished abruptly.

From the opposite side of the boulder came a bullet that rang upon a rock almost in his face, and sent splinters and dust stinging his face. He drew back hastily and rubbed his cheek.

"Out-guessed me!" he grunted admiringly. "That hairpin's no greenhorn at this. If I'm not damn careful, he's going to be *collecting* me!"

He studied the layout of their battlefield for an instant, grinned tightly and holstered his Colts. Then, rifle in hand, he crawled off to the side and got into a shallow arroyo. Here, he bent far over, he ran awkwardly but silently forward until he could cross the trail in shelter of a ridge. Then he worked back down, to come up on the other from behind.

He was edging along on his belly when from behind one of the boulders his adversary came, a slim, active six-footer, black head bare, brown face and twinkling sea-blue eyes alight with tension.

He saw Curt instantly and his carbine jumped up as Curt was lowering his own and yelling incredulously. Then he let it sag and stood staring. He threw back his head and laughed.

"Oh, *Sangre de Cristo!* She's them old friend, Curt! An' me, I'm try to wipe him out! Hah! You're fool' by them old hat trick, hey, Curt?"

"You came near to putting my eyes out," Curt grinned.

He had come to a squatting position now and was making a cigarette while he looked up at Chihuahua Joe, who — with Lit Taylor — had been his fellow deputy in Frenchy Leonard's time.

"Where have you been, Chihuahua, the last couple of years?" he asked. "Man! It's great to see you."

"Oh, w'en we're wipe out Frenchy, me, I'm get them foot w'at's itch an' so I'm scratch him by them hoppin' around. I'm go down El Paso–way, an' for Chihuahua. Then I'm come back an' work over them line around Cuchillo. Ver' nice country! We're fight them Mexican, an' them rus'ler, an' then we're ride for Cuchillo an' Galena. We're dance them girl an' drink them w'iskey an' buck them faro. Oh, me, I'm have a fine time, Curt! But, I'm want for to see this damn Territory once more. So — I'm ridin' back."

"Want a job?" Curt asked suddenly. "Want

150

your old job back — as deputy? Smoky Cole's laid up and I'm acting sheriff. Got a real job on my hands, too! Andy Allen — Lit Taylor's range-boss — is wearing a star. But it certainly would be a comfort to have you riding with me, Chihuahua!"

Swiftly, he sketched the history of the Trackless Bunch and his own precarious position. Chihuahua listened engrossedly, twisting the spike-points of his black mustache.

" *'Sta bueno!*" he grunted when Curt was done. "Me, I'm think three of us will not be many enough for these Trackless Bunch, Curt. Well? Now we're ride for Ancho, w'at?"

"Yeh. I want to kind of study the general education of Ancho folks in general; find out who's reading the weekly paper, and all that. Ancho's said to be a kind of hard-case village, Chihuahua. Maybe I oughtn't to drag you into things this way, so sudden and all . . . Shame to get you killed, a young fellow like you, with all your life before you."

Chihuahua grinned and stretched long arms upward. His right hand dropped to the pear-handled Colt and snapped it out, cocked. "Them Ancho, she's one hard-case place, Curt. Me, I'm remember from old times."

Curt nodded, getting up.

"How was it you dodged behind the rocks so gaily and so free, when I rode around the butte?" he asked curiously, as they went toward his buckskin.

"Hah! Me, I'm one damn careful man, always. An' w'en I'm ride for them O-Bar, Cuchillo-way, I'm git more careful. Around Cuchillo, w'en you're sit by them fire on the range, an' them fellas hear horses coming, you're think they're jackrabbits! They're dive from them light. An' last night, w'en I'm cook my supper an' I'm hear them horse coming, I'm slip back. An' she's damn fine I'm do it."

"Oh-ho!" Curt said softly. "It was warm . . . Yes, sir! It was warm, last night, in this neighborhood!"

"Warm? Hah! She's damn hot. Them fella, she's shoot at my fire. But me, I'm have them Weenchestair ready an' I'm sling three slugs for them fella. *Por Dios!* She's ride off very fast, Curt."

"What did you do, then? You didn't come projeckin' over to my fire on Pinto Creek, by any chance? But — no! Your feet are smaller . . ."

"Me, I'm not see any fire. I'm hole up in them rock an' sleep. W'at's at your fire?"

Curt caught up his buckskin's reins and

152

they turned back. He told Chihuahua of the bootprints around his fire. Chihuahua grinned pleasantly, rather like a cat.

"*Por Dios!* She's ver' much like them old time, hah? Like them day w'en Frenchy, she's boss this damn Territory. Me, I'm glad to be them deputy once more, Curt."

They got his black and rode toward Ancho. Curt looked ahead and grinned.

"I hope you don't get killed before you collect your first deputy-pay. Ancho is tougher, they say, than it used to be."

"She's them foot trick," Chihuahua said in a melancholy voice, "for me to ride into them tough town. But, then, me, I'm always one fi-ine, damn fool, Curt. I'm git killed — mabbe. But I'm ride with you."

Ancho, being in Ancho County, was not within Curt's jurisdiction. It was of much the same size as Gurney, but, being on the railroad, was a busier town. There were more than a dozen good-sized saloons, most of them with gambling-rooms and dance-halls in connection, as against Gurney's six or seven places of refreshment and amusement.

One thing impressed Curt, as they rode slowly up the single street toward a crudely lettered sign proclaiming a hotel. He turned

153

sideways in the saddle to grin at Chihuahua.

"Never *saw* so many hard cases in the same distance, Chihuahua! *Por Dios!* You could pick just about any of these hairpins we're meeting, as one of the Trackless Bunch."

"She's like this damn Territory, she's all pushed up near together," Chihuahua nodded. "But me, I'm see three man w'at's one time in Cuchillo. An' there will be not one of them w'at's belong to them Sunday school . . ."

When they swung down before the hotel, a Mexican boy appeared, to lead their horses to the corral in the rear. Curt stared downstreet to where the familiar Wells Fargo sign projected over the sidewalk, on the front of a squat 'dobe building.

"For a starter, I reckon I'll interview the Fargo agent," he said. "You might wander around the saloons, Chihuahua. Maybe you'll see something interesting — fellow reading a newspaper, or something like that . . ."

" '*Sta bueno!*" grinned Chihuahua. He was staring up and down the street. "*Por Dios,* Curt! I'm see one other of them Cuchillo wolves! *Pues,* if you're hear them shot, she will mean, mabbe, that I'm need you — or

I'm not need anything!"

In the Wells Fargo office Curt found a worried-looking youngster, very evidently an importation from a quieter land. Curt introduced himself as the Sheriff of Gurney and explained his call as purely social. The Fargo man nodded, staring at him.

"I wish you peace officers'd do something about — or to! — this gang of outlaws!" he cried so earnestly that Curt had to grin.

"The Trackless Bunch?" he inquired.

"Never heard 'em called that, over here. But it does seem to be a mighty good name for 'em! The sheriff, here in Ancho County, can't seem to find a track. And here *I* am, with half a roomful of valuable packages and the train two days overdue because of a wreck, and that precious gang liable to walk in and fill me with lead and walk out with the stuff!"

"They killed the bank cashier over at Gurney the other night. Tied him up and then shot him," Curt informed him cheerfully. "But we've decided that the thing's past a joke now. Either they've got to cut this rough stuff, or go at it on a sort of retail scale. If they don't, we'll have to do something about it."

"Do something about it!" The Fargo man cried furiously. "I should hope you would!

155

Look at that pile of stuff there! Look at it! It's just a standing invitation to 'em! We the same as stand in the door and yell: *Come and get it!*"

Curt glanced idly at the heap of packages on the floor in a corner, moved over and poked the pile with a boot toe. Then a name caught his eye. He stooped and picked up a small, oblong package wrapped in brown paper. The agent, behind him, watched as he read the superscription on this package.

"Mrs. Aimee R. Marsden,
New Orleans, La.
From Mrs. Patrick Rafferty,
Ancho . . ."

So *that* was the final destination of Shirley's package! Relayed by Mrs. Sheehan to her sister, Mrs. Rafferty, it was re-addressed to a woman in New Orleans! Curt stared at the little bundle. He would have given a great deal for the privilege of inspecting the package's contents. Irresolutely, he turned to the Fargo man. But the boyish, uncertain face checked him.

"How do you know that these packages are so valuable?" he drawled carelessly. "This one here, for instance. Of course, it

156

might be full of thousand-dollar bills, but —"

"That?" the agent grinned, leaning to see. "Oh, that's Mrs. Rafferty's. I guess it's as important to her as if it *did* have a wad of thousand-dollar bills in it. Papers about some lawsuit that's about to go to trial in New Orlenas. She brings a package down, every so often, and she acts as if it might melt before it gets on the train. But the contents of most of these are declared. If they aren't, I know enough about things in this neighborhood to make a rough guess at what's shipped. And there's plenty here!"

"Well, if the Trackless Bunch don't cut out their meanness we'll certainly have to do something," Curt assured him solemnly, moving toward the door. "See you some more. I hope — if the Trackless Bunch does shoot you up — it won't be permanent."

The Coney Island was the first saloon he came to. He looked over the swing doors, but saw nothing of Chihuahua. A well-dressed, handsome young man was leaning on the far end of the bar. From his bare head and a certain air about him Curt deduced that he belonged to the place. There was a vague something about this man which Curt found familiar, but what it was he could not say. He turned about, dismissing the small problem, and went hunting Chihuahua.

He found his deputy in the Silver Dollar watching a faro game about which gathered a baker's dozen of very hard-looking characters, all heavily armed, uniformly careless of clothing, and generally efficient of appearance. Chihuahua lounged over to Curt and shrugged lean shoulders. By a slight nod he indicated a desire for the open air.

"W'en I'm ride for them O-Bar, Cuchillo-way," he began, as they loafed down the street, "them Evans boy, they're run Cuchillo. One, she's city marshal an' them other, she's deputy marshal. Ver' tough customers, them Evans boy. *Por Dios!* You're ride one long time an' not find them faster gunman."

He made a cigarette and grinned at Curt.

"They're make them rule w'at's stops ever'body from shooting up Cuchillo — them w'at's for them Evans boy an' them w'at's not for the Evans boy. Both sides, she's pretty damn bad. Crooked gambling, rob them stage, kill them cattle-buyer — anything. An' them Evans boy, she's make trouble *just* for w'at robber will be on the other side. An' so, them Evans boy, she's make it so hot for them other side, pretty soon they're move out. Well! Today, I'm see here in Ancho plenty of them hard case from Cuchillo, Curt!"

"Right interesting!" Curt grunted. And interesting indeed, he found the news.

For, if Ancho County had suffered an influx of bad men from over the line, the explanation of the Trackless Bunch as successor to the Frenchy Leonard Gang was not difficult to make. It was an old story, and a common: outlaws made one locality too hot to hold them and moved on to fresh pastures. Thereafter, the law-abiding element of the new place chosen must fight to kill them off or run them out. Apparently, the Territory faced this problem.

They wandered about during the afternoon, and several times passed in and out of the Coney Island. The well-dressed, good-looking young man Chihuahua identified at first sight as one of the immigrants from Cuchillo, "Short Card" Mann. He had been a tinhorn gambler in the other camp and they learned that he was now owner of the Coney Island. Mann regarded them with what seemed to be mild curiosity, but made no move to become acquainted.

It was perhaps their fourth trip into the Coney Island when Curt, facing the bartender, observed in that white-aproned worthy an odd nervousness. He dropped a glass when serving them and otherwise showed signs of a tension for which they saw no reason.

"You ought to do something for it, fellow!" Curt advised the drink-dispenser gravely. "Look at him, Chihuahua! Haven't you seen it take hold that way before? Starts with a shaking of the hands and a stuttering and works itself up till it's a simonpure case of Epizooticus. Remember that sheepherder over on the Diamond? He caught it just like this fellow, when he was only a child with yellow curls, and died before he was ninety-one. Remember how he curled up into a figure eight knot, and passed out with horrible agony and purple spots?"

"I — I —" began the bartender.

"See!" cried Curt, nodding violently. "Look at him, Chihuahua! In the second stage already!"

But Chihuahua, though he grinned at Curt's foolery, was watching the bar-room very alertly. Now, unobtrusively, he trod upon Curt's foot. Lazily, Curt turned a little so that he half-faced the door. In it, almost filling it, was a huge and truculent figure, a bull-sized man in dusty jeans, wearing two long-barreled Colts in tied-down holsters.

"Oh, Lord!" moaned the bartender, and heedless of the snarl of Short Card Mann,

160

he sank behind the bar.

Curt glanced curiously at Mann, who faced him calmly enough, but with a pulse hammering visibly in his throat.

The big man in the doorway was lowering into the bar-room. His head was thrust forward, weaving back and forth, exactly like an angry bull. He saw Curt and Chihuahua and came swaggering in, boot-heels rapping with a hollow sound in the silence that somehow had fallen. Chihuahua slid down the bar a half-dozen feet. He watched the gladiator approach. His elbows were hooked on the bar, his blue eyes were dancing, and a little smile lifted his lip-corners beneath spike-pointed black mustache.

"Where'd you get that horse you rode into town?" the big man demanded, halting before Curt with thumbs hooked in his crossed cartridge-belts. "Answer up when I talk to you! Where'd you get that horse!"

"Horse? Horse?" repeated Curt, with puzzled frown. "What makes you think I *rode* a horse in?"

Apparently, the big man's mental processes were not of the rapid-fire variety. His shaggy brows drew together, and for an instant he stared almost bewilderedly at Curt.

"Looky here!" he roared after a moment.

161

"You answer up when I talk to you! I said — where'd you get that horse you rode in? It looks mighty like a horse I had stole from me, an if it is —"

"Sure your horse was stolen that time?" inquired Curt, in tones of deepest friendliness, helpfulness. "Maybe it just got loose and went back to its owner. Horses do that, you know, when they — well, when they haven't been paid for . . ."

Chihuahua laughed outright, and the big man, gaping at this — to him — new variety of victim, suddenly roared like a bull.

"You sayin' I stole a horse —"

His big hands twitched to the butts of his Colts. They were half-drawn and the hammers were back under his thumbs when he crashed to the floor with five bullets neatly grouped in his big chest — victim of a cross-arm draw almost too rapid for him to see.

Up toward the cottonwood rafters floated the pungent powder smoke. Curt stood tensely, with Colts leveled at his sides, grim eyes shuttling from the hulking figure on the floor to the set faces along the far wall out of range. The big man moved convulsively, a hand twitched, and there was a muffled report of a six-shooter beneath him. A bullet thudded into a wall over the heads of men standing against it. They moved without ceremony. Curt grinned sourly; one of the cocked guns held by the gunman had fired with relaxation of his rigid thumb.

"Next!" he called suddenly, so that men jumped with the thin sound. *"Next!"*

"Por Dios!" grinned Chihuahua, who was twirling his Colt on the trigger guard. "Me, I'm think nobody else will give the damn *w'ere* you're git them horse, Curt!"

Curt turned slowly to where Short Card Mann had been standing during the duel. He regarded the gambler thoughtfully, and once more Mann met his stare without emotion showing in his naturally pallid face — but with a throat-pulse hammering. "Where is your Law, Mann?" he inquired.

There was a stir behind him, among those men along the bar-room's far wall. Slowly, almost reluctantly, a lank, thin-faced individual of vaguely worried expression detached himself from the spectators. As he came forward, Curt turned from Short Card Mann to face this one.

"I'm the city marshal," announced the lank man. His small, close-set black eyes flickered down to the twin Colts Curt still held at his sides. His expression of worry seemed to deepen.

"That's fine!" Curt drawled. "Just fine, to have you right here on the job, to see this fellow come glory-hunting and go for his hardware while I was trying to find out what it was all about. All *I* want is to be sure that everybody's satisfied before I go. Of course," he added hastily, with jerk of head toward the sprawling killer, "I'll do whatever's regular about taking care of *that*."

But the marshal was looking vaguely about, seeming to seek counsel from the knots in the cottonwood rafters, from the legends lettered in soap upon the bar mirror. Curt, looking up at him after his nod at the dead gunman, found the official staring hopefully at Short Card Mann. He, too, turned to look at the gambler, but found him blank of face. The marshal shook his head painfully.

"I — well, I ain't so sure the deal's simple as that. Happens, I never saw you tangle and — well, seems to me the justice of the peace ought to sort of look into it and —"

Inadvertently, he met Curt's eyes at this point, and before their hard brightness his labored speech deserted him quite. Curt lifted his left-hand gun and beckoned with it — as if it had been a finger. "Come here a minute!" he invited the marshal.

He crowded close to the official, his right-hand gun carelessly poking the marshal in the side. The marshal's eyes seemed to rest fascinatedly upon the prodding muzzle rather than upon Curt, who was whispering softly in his ear. Then Curt stepped back with cheerfully expectant smile. He waited.

"Uh — everything's all right, folks!" cried the marshal, turning quickly to the silent watchers. If he avoided another meeting of eyes with Short Card Mann, that may have been purely an accident. "This here's the Sheriff of Gurney an' he come over on important business. It wasn't *his* fault he got into this shootin'."

Curt nodded pleasantly and, without thinking to reholster his guns, moved toward the door. The marshal fell into step beside him and Chihuahua came loafing cheerfully in the rear. They went out and down toward the hotel. Behind them in the Coney Island the deep silence which had marked their departure was broken by a single clear, disgusted voice:

"Yellow streak a yard wide!" announced the voice, and Curt laughed.

Before the hotel, Curt nodded pleasantly to the marshal. "Nice of you to come along with us this way. Thanks! But — if I were you, I *don't* think I'd go back to the Coney Island. Right away, that is."

"Uh — reckon I won't," nodded the marshal uncertainly. "Well, so long, gents."

Chapter VII

They watched him go slowly across the street and turn between two 'dobes, then went out to the corral and squatted beside the fence in a secluded spot. Chihuahua turned bright blue eyes upon Curt.

"Now, w'at's it you're say to them marshal?" he wanted to know.

"I just whispered to him that the Governor had been hearing all sorts of tales about Ancho and that *maybe* it wouldn't be a bad idea if he didn't monkey with a peace officer who *might* know a good deal about the Governor's business. I told him that certain city marshals were said to be kind of funny characters, and the Governor, he figured a peace officer like that was just as well dead, and I hoped I wouldn't ever have to shoot one, and I'd appreciate it if he'd tell those hairpins that everything was all right and then walk along with us as we went out, just to show everybody how much he thought of the Governor and us . . ."

"*Amor de Dios!*" breathed Chihuahua, staring at his friend. Then he slumped against the corral fence and gave himself over unreservedly to gasping laughter. Curt was reloading his Colts. He shoved them back into the holsters and waited for Chihuahua to straighten.

"Sheriffs don't seem so popular around Ancho," he remarked thoughtfully. "That was a pretty plain open-and-shut sort of try at rubbing me out. I wonder if Short Card Mann arranged the job, just on general principles. Or —"

"Por Dios! One minute I'm have them cold feeling by my back," grunted Chihuahua. "Them fellow Quinn, she's one real wolf, Curt. In Cuchillo —"

"Quinn!" Curt interrupted him scowling. "Quinn!"

"*Si!* Them gunman you're rub out. She's one of them fellow w'at's on them other side from the Evans boy. She's pull out of Cuchillo with Short Card Mann an' them other hardcase."

Curt slapped his hand upon leg with a force that made the dust jump from his overalls. Quinn — Short Card Mann — the messenger who had led him out to look for an imaginary rendezvous of the Trackless Bunch — *Now* he understood the vague familiarity of Short Card Mann. With three or four days' growth of beard; wearing dusty overalls and floppy hat; with a "scar" upon his cheek hacked out of the beard with a razor, Short Card Mann became "Quinn, the nester's hand."

He swore softly, delightedly:

"*Por Dios!* We have got Mr. Quinn-Mann where the hair is too short to cut?" he said, aloud. Swiftly, he sketched his thoughts for Chihuahua's benefit, and the half-breed listened with a wolfish grin.

"That night in the office, when I asked him what he called himself," Curt finished, "he gave me the first name that popped into his head. Happened, it was 'Quinn.' Chihuahua, old-timer, Mann's hooked up with the Trackless Bunch, and I reckon some of these Cuchillo hardcases *are* the Trackless Bunch!"

"*Por supuesto!* Sure!" nodded Chihuahua thoughtfully. "But me, I'm think that these Short Card, she will not be the Big Auger. In Cuchillo, she's just one damn tinhorn. Plenty sense, but — no, Mann will not rod the big bunch. We're go an' *git* them Short Card, now, huh?"

"Uh-uh! Nothing like that, right now! Mann's the first *live* hairpin that I've been able to hook up with the Trackless Bunch. So, he has got to show us the rest of the outfit before we collect him. He knows me, of course, but he can't know that I've got a thought in the world about his being 'Quinn.' So, we'll give him rope, Chihuahua — a rope with a loop in it, to hang

168

himself with."

He sat silently for a time, puzzling the whole chain of events. Came thought of the man who had opened fire upon him in the street of Gurney, the night of his retention as sheriff. He told Chihuahua of this.

"An' you're not find out who she's work for, huh?"

"Nobody would admit knowing him," shrugged Curt. "He was a long *gunie,* black-haired, black-eyed; had a big hook nose. Oh, yeh! He had two fingers off his left hand."

"Hah!" breathed Chihuahua. "Frank Farr! She's one other gun-fighter from Cuchillo! She's one good friend to them Quinn an' Short Card Mann. Me, I'm run Farr out of them saloon in Cuchillo one night. Hah! Me, I'm shoot off his heels with my Weenchestair. Ver' tough customer, them Frank Farr."

"The hell! Then — do you reckon Short Card Mann put him up to coming over to Gurney, to rub me out? I laid that to Tom Card, because Farr had a flask of Card's whiskey in his pocket and the shooting came right after Card had been licked at trying to put in his Man Friday, Bain, as sheriff."

"Quién sabe?" Shrugged Chihuahua. "Me, I'm think that if we're take them Short Card out in them hill an' find one nice, fat anthill,

169

an' we're stake him out by them anthill, with honey leading for his mouth, she's tell us all about it."

"Couldn't tell whether he was lying or not," Curt objected. "The way it looks to me, Chihuahua, it *could* be two-pronged: either Tom Card, he never knew about Farr cracking down on me and it was Short Card Mann that sent Farr over, or else — Man! This would be the answer to it all with a big A! The whole smear of little things would dovetail in one big scheme."

"W'at tail on w'at dove?" Chihuahua inquired curiously.

"Tom Card hankering to put Sam Bain in as Sheriff. Farr's shooting at me. That bushwhacker cracking down on me, as I crossed the Devil's Bench, coming back from Los Alamos. Yes! And those inquisitive gentlemen who came prowling around my fire last night. And this latest punch — this fellow Quinn who was hunting my scalp in the Coney Island. It could be, all of it, part of a Trackless Bunch set-up."

Very slowly, Chihuahua nodded. His blue eyes were bright and expectant. He waited, and Curt, turning over in his mind these several segments of his puzzle, looked at him, finally:

"Chihuahua, if some of these came from

Cuchillo — Ever hear of Tom Card? Or Sam Bain? Did they come from Cuchillo?"

"W'y — I'm not *think* so. But, of course, if they're come to Gurney so long as two year back, I'm not know him in Cuchillo. Me, I'm ride for them O-Bar just one year."

"If that guess is right! If only that guess is right . . ." Curt said to himself. "It would be lovely: Tom Card as the Trackless Bunch's big boss; Sam Bain in cahoots with him; and Short Card Mann, too . . . But I haven't got a speck of proof. It's just a guess — a blind guess."

Still, he thought, if this wild theory should prove to be fact, it would explain everything that had been puzzling him. It would clear up everything that, otherwise, remained a mystery. And the theory was verified by everything that had happened. Too, there was the troublesome matter of Shirley Randolph's bootprint, and her intimate connection with Tom Card, her quick defense of the gambler — and that mysterious package of hers, shipped around with such care to mislead . . .

He got up swiftly with face very girm. He must take a chance on that Fargo man. He *had* to have a look at the contents of that package.

"Going down to the Fargo office," he

grunted to Chihuahua. "You might sort of trail along behind. See that none of the glory-hunters drill me from behind."

But, standing in the door of the Fargo office, he faced a clean floor. All of the packages were gone. The young agent looked up; he was no longer worried of face. "Train came in. Got rid of that collection. Well, how's everything, Sheriff?"

"Damned puny!" Curt replied savagely. "Or worse."

He whirled and went back to meet Chihuahua. The breed lifted his brows inquiringly.

"I had a notion," Curt told him. "But I didn't time it right. Reckon we may's well go back to Gurney."

They got their horses and if anyone was interested in their going, Curt could see no evidence of it. He slouched in the saddle and lowered blindly at the horizon, while the horses jogged on, choosing their own gait and trail across the sandy flat studded with mesquite and greasewood and cactus, upon which Ancho was built.

Going up the long slopes of the Diablos foothills, Curt avoided the stage road that led to Gurney. It was nothing much, anyway, as a road. And if their quiet departure from Ancho was only the lull before another encounter with nameless enemies, it would be more difficult to ambush them, in the hills.

Three times that day they glimpsed distant riders off on the brushy ridges. Each time, Chihuahua's lean, brown hand slipped down to cuddle lovingly the sleek stock of his Winchester, but the riders merely reined in for a moment, seemed to look them over, then vanished like wolves into the arroyos.

"Cowboys, you reckon?" Curt inquired at last, but the sardonic one-sided smile with which he put the question was the question's answer.

"Cowboys — I'm *not* reckon!" Chihuahua returned, with a grin that seemed to mirror pleasantest anticipation. He half-drew the little carbine from its scabbard and lifted his gaze wolfishly to that far ridge behind which two riders had just slid.

"If we're have time," he meditated, "me, I'm like to go play with them fellow . . . *Por Dios!* Me, I'm help them to git sick!"

Came dusk and the range piled against the horizon ahead of them loomed shadowy and vast, like gigantic silhouettes cut from purple paper. They turned off, now, at left angles to the course they had been following. The horses stumbled along stony-floored arroyos, panted over hogbacks and descended slidingly into the next arroyo. At last Chihuahua was satisfied, and they staked buckskin and black in a tiny, grassy open space, well-hidden by brush, then went back a half-mile into a sheltered arroyo to make their little cooking-fire.

When they had eaten, they returned to the horses and rolled up in their blankets fifty yards apart, with carbines and Colts lying ready to hand. Once that night Curt was wakened by Chihuahua, who said that he had heard a distant sound. But he came back, after prowling awhile, to report that he could find nothing.

They saddled before dawn and rode alertly back to where the cooking-fire had been. And in the dusty mouth of the arroyo Chihuahua found bootprints. He called Curt and together they stood staring down at the record in the dust of four tiptoeing men. Curt bent over suddenly to indicate one set of prints with a stabbing forefinger:

"Look! Here's my old friend with the cracked bootsole again, Chihuahua! Big as life and twice as natural!"

"Ah, she's come twice for to see you, Curt, An' you're not at home. Mabbe she's different, next time, hah? Mabbe we're both home, to give him one fine welcome . . ."

They rode on very alertly, after breakfast.

The horses made very little noise, except when a shod hoof clinked, occasionally, upon some rocky slope. From the heights, Chihuahua studied the country around through his glasses. And in mid-morning he turned fiercely to Curt, after such a raking of the distances.

"Me, I'm think we're kill them wolf! *Mira!* Look!"

Curt took the glasses and lifted his bare head cautiously. Against a great boulder, not a quartermile away, two men sprawled comfortably, smoking. A horse's head showed at the big boulder's side.

"What could be sweeter?" Curt whispered, as if the men could hear them. Then he backed down the slope and mounted, to follow Chihuahua down an arroyo. "What could be sweeter!"

They went quietly along the dry watercourse for perhaps three hundred yards, then Chihuahua turned in the saddle and shook his head warningly. He pulled in and Curt followed his example. They got off the horses, let the reins trail, and moved ahead with Winchesters across their arms.

Chihuahua found a greasewood bush on the arroyo's bank. He lifted his head and looked through the shelter of the bush.

"They're not see us," he whispered.

175

"Them rock, she's between. We're climb out, here."

Curt heard a mumbling of talk on the far side of the rock. Two horses stood with heads down, ahead of them. Chihuahua began to cross the thirty yards of open that separated them from the boulder. Curt had time to appreciate the noiselessness with which the breed moved, booted feet seeming to avoid as by instinct small stones and bayonet weed. He followed as quickly, as silently, as he could. Chihuahua stopped at last, leaning on the boulder with head turned a little to the side. In profile, his face showed mildly satanic, with mustache-point, mouth-corner, eye-corner, lifted.

Curt joined him. A man was speaking lazily. Something about a woman in Ancho who was giving him "the run-around." He said:

"Long as Short Card was out of town, she was willin' to spend my *dinero.* Then he come back about the same time my roll played out an' she picked up her bed. I'm goin' to show her a few, when we get back. I —"

"But w'at if you're not *git* back?" Chihuahua inquired anxiously, side-stepping so that he and Curt appeared elbow to elbow before the two on the ground. "W'at then?"

The pair, rolling over with startled oaths, gaped up at the Winchester covering them. One was a little battered man, middle-aged, dark. The other was a cowboy of about Curt's own age, tow-haired, blue-eyed, with a daredevil face and loose, humorous mouth.

"We found your calling cards this morning," Curt said finally — and grinned. "It's certainly too bad that we missed you last night when you drove up."

"What you talkin' about?" the bat-eared man demanded viciously. "Callin' cards!"

"Por Dios," Chihuahua drawled, "if you're come just one tiny half-mile over them ridge, from our fire, then we're *not* miss you! I have them large sadness, me."

"What you talkin' about?" the bat-eared man said again. "What'd we want to see you about, anyhow?"

"Oh!" Curt nodded. "*I* see. You two didn't want us. It was the two who've gone off who wanted to see us. That makes it all clear. About those Absent Members — I'd like to see them, too. What's chances? Are they around somewhere handy? It'll be just too bad, if we miss each other again . . ."

"Look here!" the bat-eared man snarled, sitting up to waggle a hand at them. "I still don't know what the hell you think you're

177

talkin' about. But if you-all come huntin' trouble —"

"Hombre!" Chihuahua interrupted him with a small, sinister grin playing at thin mouth-corners, "in this damn Territory, nobody's have to hunt for trouble. Trouble, she's come without the hunt. An' if we're hunt for trouble, w'en we're see you like them poor pilgrim, by these rock, them trouble, she's over now!"

He patted the stock of his carbine lovingly, moved it a trifle.

"You're not wiggle them hand, *amigo,*" he suggested to the tow-head, who had been looking from face to face. "Keep them hand in sight — an' still — an' you're live much longer!"

Curt grinned. So did the young cowboy, as if the humor were not at his expense. Then Curt, sobering, studying the pair, saw the faintest stiffening of Chihuahua's indolent pose. He had heard nothing, but Chihuahua — he knew — had the ears of his Navajo mother. And he was listening strainedly, now . . .

Chihuahua's head rolled to Curt, who nodded slightly and stepped forward so that he stood in the boulder's shelter and covered both the prisoners. Chihuahua walked past them, making no sound. He vanished around the boulder while Curt, to cover his going, talked idly to the two.

"I swear I hardly know what to do with hairpins of your stripe," he said complainingly. "Some sheriffs would just organize 'emselves into judge, jury, and hangman and go on their way without even looking back. But I reckon I'm getting old and tenderhearted. Even a dirty bushwhacker that's afraid to meet anybody past twelve years old, I hate to just rub out. But you can see the jam it puts me in!"

The bat-eared man snarled and his dirty hands hooked and unhooked. The cowboy merely laughed and watched Curt. Then, from somewhere beyond the boulder, there was the flat sound of a shot. It was followed, instantly, by a splatter of shots fired so rapidly that the sound was like the rattle of a stick upon a paling fence. Curt stiffened. Automatically, his eyes went for a second toward the sound. He caught the shadow of a movement from an eye-corner and twisted his carbine the merest trifle. He shot the bat-eared man through the face and he — falling backward — slumped against the cowboy who had come to his knees with a pistol in his hand.

"Drop it!" Curt snarled, and the cowboy dropped the Colt.

"Hey — Curt!" Chihuahua called now. "Me, I'm git one!"

He came back at effortless dogtrot. He had stalked the bushwhacker while the latter — having found their horses in the arroyo — stalked the boulder. They had run upon each other.

"He's shoot them one shot. Me, I'm make him dam' sick!"

He looked down at the bat-eared man and nodded.

"Them dam' fool!" was the epitaph he gave him.

Prodded by Chihuahua's gun, the disarmed cowboy covered the bat-eared gunman with a cairn of stones. He was very quiet as they marched him over to unsaddle his and the bat-eared man's horses. Chihuahua rocked the horses away. Then he went after their own mounts. He came back, grinning.

"I'm cut that fella's saddle to doll rags," he reported.

They mounted and, with four pistols tied to their saddles, leaving behind the hopelessly smashed Winchesters, ordered the cowboy forward to where Chihuahua's quarry lay. Curt stared down at the hatchet-faced man who had come with "Al" to the sheriff's office. "Whittling 'em down!" he

180

said grimly, and told Chihuahua who the man was.

He looked at the cowboy, who faced him easily, and whistled *Sam Bass.*

"Them fella w'at's have them busted boot," Chihuahua was reminded suddenly, "she's hightail clean."

"I noticed that he was the missing one," Curt nodded, still studying the prisoner, "Fellow! We're going to leave you. You can get back to Ancho, somehow. But my advice to you is — don't go back! If you hang around with the crowd you have picked, you're liable to run into just about anything. But the most likely thing is a south-bound slug, about the time you're headed due north."

"Thanks for nothin'," the cowboy said flippantly. "But I'll tell you what I'll do — I'll tell you somethin' in exchange. This li'l' business, today, is just — about — goin' — to get you killed! Sooner or later."

"I hope it's later, then," Curt grinned. "For getting killed is just the last thing I want to have happen to me. Hightail!"

"So long — for a while!"

Chihuahua stared grimly after his swaggering figure.

"She's them dam' fool trick, Curt! W'en you're git you one bushw'acker, you're better kill him, quick!"

"I know . . . But you can't murder a man. When Bat-Ears made his jump, down there, it didn't bother me a bit to rub him out. I'll never worry about whanging away at a man who's after me. But —"

Andy Allen stood beneath the wooden awning of the Star Saloon, as Curt and Chihuahua rode up Gurney's main street. He saw them and yelled.

"Hi, Curt! Wait a minute!"

They drew rein and he came out to stand at Curt's stirrup, grinning cheerfully. He looked up curiously at Chihuahua's fine blue flannel woolen cloth, his fifty-dollar boots and equally expensive black Stetson.

When Curt introduced them, Andy's stare shifted quickly to the clean-carved mahogany-brown face and the twinkling sea-blue eyes. For Carlos José de Guerra y Morales, son of a gentleman-adventurer from Madrid and a Navajo mother, top-hand cowboy and ex-deputy sheriff of Gurney County, was known as a man of parts up and down the Territory — or wherever Territory men might wander.

"Why — why, I'm certainly pleased to meet you!" Andy cried earnestly.

"Chihuahua's going to wear a star, along

with us, Andy," Curt explained.

"Fine! That's certainly ambiguous!" Andy nodded. "But —"

He looked Chihuahua up and down, studied the pearl-handled Colt that hung in hand-stamped holster, sagging low upon a wide shell-belt of many loops, of the same exquisitely tooled workmanship. He shook his head.

"I was just thinkin'," he said, when Chihuahua's black brows climbed, "that you'd shrunk up a lot, since you left the Territory. You see, I've heard Lit Taylor talk about you a lot an' I gathered from what Lit said that you stood just a *shade* under eleven foot high."

Chihuahua laughed — for the first time that morning.

"She's one dam' fine boy, them Lit. Me, I'm think she's pick one good man for them Los Alamos rangeboss."

"Anything happen while I was gone?" Curt asked.

"Nothin' much," Andy shrugged, falling into step beside their horses as they moved on. "I been associatin' with Sam Bain a li'l bit . . . Sam's a real curious sort of hairpin in some ways. Yes, sir, right contemporaneous . . . Just this mornin', when I was projeckin' around the Palace, Sam bought me

183

several drinks. He talked high, wide an' handsome about — oh, just heaps of satirical subjects."

Curt swung down before the sheriff's office. He looked curiously at his deputy.

"Yeh?" he prompted Andy drawlingly.

"Funny!" grinned Andy reflectively. "No matter *what* we got to talkin' about, the talk'd always come back across country to Hizzoner, the Sheriff of Gurney. Yes, sir, Sam certainly was interested in Curt Thompson, an' where he come from, an' why, an' all like that."

"Some of these bright spring days" — Curt spoke softly, but with vast meaning — "Sam Bain is going to stub his toe. He is that . . . And be damned if that's Spanish! Come on in, Andy. You can list to word from the battlefields. Something tells men, Young-Man-With-A-Big-Word-Hangin'-Out-Of-His-Mouth, that the valleys are going to ring to the sound of the war whoop. Yes, sir! This peaceful land is going to be dyed a regular scarlet of red . . . We're getting next to the Trackless Bunch, Andy!"

The story of the past three days was sufficient to bring excited, hopeful oaths from Andy Allen; broken sentences lit by words of strange, mouth-filling grandeur.

"So our friend 'Quinn' is really a tinhorn,

by the name of Short Card Mann!" he cried marvelingly at the end. "Well, if *that* ain't a vituperative state of affairs! An' you perforated the real Quinn an' horn-swoggled the Ancho marshal an' captured red-handed in the pursuit of hellish designs three meretricious hairpins! Curt! Honest! I could go to your funeral this very evenin' an' preside as Chief Celebrator — an' laugh. You go hellin' off an' leave me here to mill around an' suck my thumb —"

"Nobody told you to suck your thumb!" Curt interrupted him indignantly. "Why, Andy, I'm surprised at you. Talking that way! I don't like to hear you making out that I left any such instructions. If you spent your time sucking your thumb, you certainly did it on your own responsibility. Why, *I* don't know whether the county ought to pay for the time spent in such an unauthorized occupation!"

Andy's indignation vanished suddenly. He leaned back seraphically in his squeaking chair to lock his hands behind his head and stare fixedly at the dingy plaster of the ceiling.

"Miss Randolph come back, today noon," he observed in a faraway voice. "Remarkable lovely lady, she is. Been visitin' on a ranch some'r's, I gathered. Tom Card an' Sam

Bain was certainly pleased to see her back, I can tell *you*. She wanted to know where you'd gone to, Curt, an' why you had to rush off like you did, an' when you was comin' back an' — oh, everything . . ."

"She wanted to know that!"

Curt's chair went crashing back against the wall. Unbelievingly, he stared at Andy Allen, who still regarded the ceiling raptly.

"Talk, you blame' picket-pin!" he snapped. "She wanted to know where *I* was?"

"Of course she did!" Andy assured him earnestly. "Even though she *never* said anything about it, anybody'd know she'd be interested! Anybody would be. Why, *I* wanted to know, myself, an' she's certainly just as human as I am!"

"The next time I go anywhere," Curt said grimly, very red of face, "I will sure-ly try to take you along, Andy. And if it works out that I can take you along afoot, my cup of happiness will be so damn' full it'll start the creeks to rising underneath!"

"Well, I don't see why you want to be sore at me!" Andy protested, rolling innocent gray eyes upon Curt. "I bet you she *did* want to know. Why'n't you go down to the Palace, right now, an' ask her?"

"That's an idea!" Curt said — and grinned suddenly. "Come on, Chihuahua. Palace's a

186

lot bigger than it was when you left Gurney. Lots of sights to see. Andy, I wish you'd kind of hold down the office till we get back . . . We may not be gone long. But if you get restless, why, there's always your thumb to suck, Andy."

"Nothin' doin'!" Andy declared flatly. His chair came down on four legs with a bang. He stood up. "Nothin' doin'! You're not goin' to buck that Palace crowd unless I, me, Andrew Jackson Allen, side you! When you wander into that rattler-den, young fella, I'll be instigatin' around the landscape right near-by."

He shook his head exasperatedly, standing with thumbs hooked in his belt.

"Of all the nebulous nitwits! You damn' fool! There's Tom Card. There's four-five derringer-packin' house men of his. There's Lord knows how many saloon bums that'd cut your throat at Tom Card's nod. There's maybe Sam Bain an' some of his Lazy B thieves. An' you'd walk into that! Yeh — you'd *walk* in, but they'd tote you out, a li'l' bit at a time. Make up your mind to it: If you go, I'm goin'."

"Uh-uh! You're going to stick here and dust off the furniture. I never saw such a dirty office. Two of us will be plenty."

Then Curt looked seriously at Andy.

187

"We're not painting up for war," he explained patiently. "Don't you see, Andy, that if the three of us walked into the Palace, it would look like a trouble-hunt? And they'd bring a war over and drop it down our necks. On the other hand, if Chihuahua walks in beside me, and we have our drinks at the bar, that's just a social visit and they'll take it as such."

Andy scowled uncertainly. But after a moment he shrugged resignedly. Curt banged him on the shoulder with a hard hand.

"Be seeing you," he said. "Come on, Chihuahua."

They headed toward the Palace, but on the way Curt turned Chihuahua into Marie Young's doorway. The girl looked up at sound of their footsteps, turned red, and came forward smiling.

"Well!" she said quickly. "If you haven't turned into the most mysterious young man —"

"Mysterious?" Curt repeated. "How-come?"

"You're a regular now-you-see-it, now-you-don't sheriff! Andy is just as bad, in his own peculiar way. He wouldn't tell me where you'd gone. You never did come for that apple pie either. But I understood that — meeting Miss Randolph so unexpectedly, here in the door — probably took away your appetite."

"Mrs. Young, may I present —"

"Chihuahua Joe!" Marie nodded. "It couldn't be anyone else!"

"I have them honor!" Chihuahua grinned and he bowed from the hips with a flourish, hat brushing the floor. "W'en them lovely lady know me before I'm introduc' —"

"Sudie-May Taylor told me all about you, one day. She described you and you answer exactly to her description."

"She's fine? An' them baby?"

"Both of them. Little Sue is the pet of the county. Well, Curt? Where *have* you been?"

"Ancho," Curt shrugged. "Looking around for evidence."

"And trouble? Oh, don't deny it! I could put two and two together, and explain that business of the other day. You went straight from here to the Palace and you pretended to get drunk and you did some talking. So — two men came over to kill you —"

Her voice shook a little. Curt grinned faintly.

"No-o, not exactly, I never get drunk. It's a peculiarity of mine. I have all the appearance, but my head keeps on working. If I pour it down, eventually I go out like a man hit with a club. But until I do, my brain keeps on working about as usual. I found out a little, that day — that Tom Card is certainly trying to rub out my chalk mark. But that's all I found. In Ancho —"

He shrugged, looking absently at her. He was asking himself why he could not fall in love with a girl like Marie. She was pretty, sensible, attractive enough to draw most of the cowboys of the county. And yet, when he looked at her, Shirley Randolph always came between.

"Ancho . . ." she was saying, when he gathered his thoughts. "What happened there, Curt? It's a pretty tough place, I hear."

He shrugged again, and Chihuahua, looking from one to the other of them, grinned wolfishly.

"*Pues,* if Curt, she's keep on, them Trackless Bunch will be ver' small."

"You — you had trouble?"

"Oh, another bushwhacker hunted me up and he crowded me so that I had to kill him," Curt said uncomfortably.

"Was there — more trouble because of that?" she prompted.

"No. Not because of that. In Ancho, anyway. But — oh, you might as well have the tale; I'm getting to be a regular Wild Bill Hickok without a mustache. Chihuahua and I ran into some bushwhacking gentle-men as we rode home. One thought he had me off-guard and went for a gun. I beat him to it. Chihuahua caught another slipping up on us. That's two out of the business. We turned the third one loose — with a warn-ing that he won't take."

"You — let him go?" the girl asked slowly, staring from Chihuahua's gentle, yet some-how sinister, grin, to Curt's grim face.

"She's foolish!" Chihuahua shrugged. "Me, I'm not let him go. But Curt —— She's not pretty to kill them bushw'acker, Mrs. Young. But — *por Dios!* She's not pretty w'en them bushw'acker, she's shoot you in your back! Me, I'm rather kill them other fellow than that them other fellow, she's kill me! So — some day, we're have now to kill them fellow we're let go. She's better if we're kill him w'en we're have him before."

"Chihuahua wants to see the Palace," Curt said, to change the subject. For there was something like horror in Marie's face as she stared at the smiling breed. "I told him that Card's prettied it up a lot."

"You — don't think it will cause trouble? Your going in there where they're all just *waiting* for you?"

"No," Curt said judicially. "No, I don't.

They're not going to paint for war just because I rile 'em. Card's out to get me. So, staying away from the Palace, won't soothe him, nor going there rouse him."

"And, of course, Miss Randolph's there," Marie said smilingly. But Chihuahua suddenly stared at her without turning his head. And he nodded slightly and looked at Curt, who was flushing.

"Oh — whistle something else, will you?" Curt said exasperatedly. "Honest! you have got a mind as one-tracked as a setting hen's. Come on, Chihuahua. They may shoot us, in the Palace, but they won't talk us to death about girls."

"Mrs. Young" — Chihuahua bowed and smiled at the girl — "one day, ver' soon, I'm see you again. Me, I'm them ver' great fool. But, too, I'm have them ver' fine eyes. Mabbe I'm tell you w'at I'm see?"

She looked quickly at him, and shook her head.

"I — think I'd rather you wouldn't!" she said. "But, of course, I'll see you again, soon."

Curt, going toward the Palace, made a growling noise.

"These girls!" he said angrily, when Chihuahua looked inquiringly at him. "Now — take Marie Young, for instance. She came

192

down here with a sick husband. Waited on him hand and foot. And it was just because he was her husband too. I know she wasn't wild about him. Well — he died and she kept on with that little store. Does pretty well with it, too. What I'm driving at is that she's got plenty of sense. But when it comes to a man she knows walking down the street with another girl — hell! Just like all the rest, she's got to keep rawhiding me."

"Ah, yes!" Chihuahua nodded sympathetically. "But — mabbe you're make them love to her one time —"

"What? Make love to Marie? I never did such a thing — why, she's been like a pet sister —"

"Ah!" Chihuahua said understandingly. "Now, I'm see . . . She's ver' bad, Curt, to let her be them sister. *Por supuesto!*"

They went on silently, after that, until Curt pushed one of the Palace's swing doors and stood back to let Chihuahua precede him inside. Since it was late afternoon, trade was dull in saloon and gaming-room and the dance-floor was closed. It was a great rectangle, the Palace. Saloon and gambling-hall were on the street side; forming half of the building; the dance-floor extended the building's length for the other half. Tom Card had a ten-by-ten office,

193

walled off from the bar-room and the gambling-room, in the center of the street side.

Bain and three hard-featured Lazy B riders were at the long bar's far end when Curt and Chihuahua came. They were matching silver dollars in company with four or five townsmen. They looked up and Bain regarded Curt malevolently. Curt stared at him, smiled with all the contempt he could manage, and moved over to the bar.

The door to Card's office was open and Curt had a slanting view of Shirley Randolph's clear-cut profile. Sight of the girl in that environment enraged Curt, now, as it always did. He tossed down his drink and, completely forgetting Bain and his warriors, moved over to the office door.

There was an unwritten law in the Palace that neither employee nor patron approached the girl while she worked. Curt was aware of this rule. In theory, he had always approved it heartily. But as for observing it himself —

He leaned against the door-facing and regarded her somberly. All that he knew of her — and thought of all that he did *not* know of her — crowded to his mind as he stared down at the sleek, dark head. Her mysterious past; that tiny bootprint on the scene of The Points stage robbery; her packages, so artfully relayed to New Orleans; the way she championed Card — whom everyone with eyes would have distrusted, Curt thought grimly.

As he stood looking down at her, his shadow fell across the table. She looked up frowningly, then, recognizing him, lifted dark brows inquiringly. Her expression altered faintly. It was as if — Curt told himself viciously — she had never seen him before. But he was on his guard, tonight. Marie Young might annoy him until he showed irritation, but Shirley Randolph would not! And if she could outdo *his* indifference —

"Yes?" she said coldly.

"No," he drawled, very evenly, very — absently. "For he seems not to be here. And I want to see him — *particularly.* Or almost particularly . . ."

She watched him turn toward the barroom, then back to face her. His manner was preoccupied. He looked absently through, rather than at her, as if she had been — to him — no more than a bookkeeper, an unimportant employee.

"I don't know where he is. Nor when he'll be here. If it's a message —"

"It's not a message. It's a question. I want

to ask him about a man — a short, dark, bat-eared man. If he's been here recently . . ."

"Bat-eared? Oh! I see. Why, *I* —"

"Wait a minute!" he interrupted her coldly. "I don't want *you* to tell me anything. I want to ask Tom Card. Not to hear his answer —"

She waited, staring bewilderedly. He looked into the bar-room once more, then turned his head toward her.

"Why do you want to ask him a question? If you don't care about his answer?"

Slowly, very slowly, Curt let his still face, his hard mouth, twist in the tolerant smile of a grown-up who regards a child.

"Because I want to see his face, when he tells me something or other. For I killed that bat-eared murderer *this* side of Ancho."

She was suddenly very white and her eyes were wide.

"*Killed* — him?" she said draggingly. "He attacked you?"

"He would have — given another second. And the killer who got away from the office — my friend Chihuahua Joe got him, a minute before Bat-Ears made his play. He was in the same crowd. Well — I'll ask Tom Card, when I see him."

He heard the scrape of her chair behind

196

him as he moved away, but did not turn. Even when he knew that she had got up and could look across at the bar-mirror and see her standing in the office door, he gave no sign of seeing.

Instead, he looked slightly to the side of her reflection; looked at Sam Bain, who had left his men and moved up the bar until, leaning on it, he looked straight into the office. Now, Bain looked at Curt's set face, then at Shirley, and back at Curt. He began to laugh.

Curt stopped short. He stared at the Lazy B man for an instant, then altered course. He went at deliberate step across the barroom until he stood directly before Bain.

Bain met Curt's stare for a moment. Up and down the bar men stopped talking, stared at the two, and waited. They saw Bain stiffen, saw his eyes shift from those of the younger man.

"That's a nasty laugh you've got," Curt said in the slow, thick drawl that marked, with him, the very snapping point. "I don't recall that I ever heard a laugh like it. A hyena's, of course, is similar. But pleasanter. So we'll have hyenas out of the argument. I have got no call to be insulting hyenas, anyhow."

"Say!" Bain snarled. "I ain't —"

"So, hereafter" — Curt went on as if Bain had not spoken — "you keep that laugh of yours bottled up when I'm around. I'm free to say I don't like it a bit. It makes me think of coyotes sneaking around looking for dead cows and all sorts of things like that and —"

Bain's dark face twisted. His hand was against his side, very close to Colt butt. The fingers curled, uncurled. But when Curt stopped short to stare at that hand, instantly it became still.

"Can't manage it, can you?" Curt inquired sardonically. "You can't *quite* get there. You'd give anything in the world for backbone enough to make you even a puny imitation of a man. But all you can do is wish. You get cramps in your gun-hand, now, don't you? The well-known Four-Flusher Cramps. But if you ever get a chance to sling lead at my back, or catch me asleep, you'll know exactly what to do —"

Suddenly, he stared at Bain with narrowing eyes and the the shadow of a small, unpleasant smile.

"Oh! Mind holding your foot up for a minute, Bain? Your right foot. What! You do mind? Why, I'm surprised, Bain! Or — almost surprised. A little thing like a cracked bootsole oughtn't worry you so much. Well, after all, it's not the shape your bootsole's in, that signifies. It's where that boot's been traveling, Bain . . ."

A flicker of uneasiness showed upon the Lazy B man's dark face. Bain seemed to press his shabby, runover boots harder against the floor. "I don't know what you're drivin' at," he blustered. "But it's none of your business about my boots."

"That guess is out a mile!" Curt said softly. "Your boots are quite a bit of my business — and they're going to be a lot more! You're a peculiar sort of damn skunk, Bain! I hardly know when I ever met one so peculiar. Can't insult you anyway. Can't make you act like half a man. So — I reckon we'll just have to take some other line with you . . ."

Contemptuously, he studied Bain's furious, yet uneasy face:

"You pack a gun — but you're afraid to pull it. And where's that big pearl-handled knife you bought from Halliday? The one you aimed to cut so many ears with?"

Again Bain's eyes flickered uneasily, as when Curt had referred to the broken sole of his right boot. But Curt turned away from him. Flashingly, it had occurred to him that the silence, the inactivity, of Bain's three hard-case cowboys were odd, to say the least. But when he turned that way, the puzzle became quite simple — indeed, was solved . . .

The three Lazy B men were grouped sullenly at the bar's end. They were watching Chihuahua, a good part of the time, and Chihuahua held his pearl-handled Colt up against his breast. Daintily, he touched it here and there with the corner of his silk neckerchief. But always his twinkling blue eyes were fixed yearningly upon Bain's adherents. He was smiling at them.

Not altogether were they occupied with Chihuahua, either. Just inside the door that opened into the dancehall, standing with his lean back to the wall and the sawed-off riot gun from the sheriff's office across his arm, Andy Allen kept the cavernous muzzles of the shotgun trained upon the Lazy B men.

"Barkeep!" called Curt — but the bartender was not in evidence. At Curt's second, more imperative, order, his pomaded curls and pasty face appeared *most* deliberately above the bar.

"*I* ain't takin' no chance with that cannon!" he informed Curt, with jerk of the head toward Andy Allen. "No, sir! I see her let go one time, gents, an' — *listen!* She collected half a mob an' then she reached out an' gathered in two Mex' that was comin' into town with a burro-load of mesquite roots, just to make up her full quart. No, sir! Not for *this* mixologist no flirtation with Smoky Cole's old Greener!"

"Let's have a drink all around," Curt suggested. "Take that quiet young fellow with the cannon a drink, too. All right, Andy! Drink this one and drink it deep: To Sam Bain's bootsole — for, by God! It's the only kind of *soul* he's got!"

Curt and Chihuahua set down their glasses and moved toward the front door, serene in the knowledge that, behind them, Andy still held his post with the Greener. At the door, Curt halted.

"We'll take a *pasear* down and get something to eat, Chihuahua," he remarked, very clearly. "There's an extra cot in the office that you can use. And, Chihuahua, if you happen to hear anything prowling around the place tonight, just raise up, will you, and sniff a couple of times. If it smells like a skunk, whang away — especially if it smells like a skunk with a busted bootsole . . ."

"W'y me, I'm ver' pleased to kill them skunk," Chihuahua said interestedly — and just as audibly. "I'm have them smell tonight, like you're say, Curt."

Curt grinned faintly. He knew that behind him fury fermented. Bain had been backed down by the sheriff's office, and the deed had been accomplished in full view of men who were not all adherents of Tom Card. The story would spread. It would have effects far-reaching and perhaps hard to trace to that moment. All in all, Curt was pleased.

Andy joined them at the corner of the building and they marched down the street three abreast.

"It's been," Curt remarked, in the manner of one who reviews a theatrical performance just witnessed, "what I'd call a right *soleful* afternoon . . . Bain would certainly say so!"

They were all in the sheriff's office after supper, engaged in something like a council of war, when the door was unceremoniously flung open and a huge grizzly bear of a man lunged in, his great paws brushing the butts of tied-down Colts as he walked, in what seemed a sort of unconscious readiness for battle. He stopped just inside the door and stared belligerently at Curt, who nodded at him — as did Chihuahua Joe.

"What the hell's the matter with this-here sheriff's outfit?" Wolf Montague roared without preface. "How come the bunch of you is sittin' here in the office on your

202

rumps, like a goddam bunch of goddam old maids at a goddam sewin' bee? It's gettin' so a man can't set his cigarette down without some damn' thief snatches it up. Now, I voted to keep you in as sheriff, Thompson. But I want to see some of these damn' thieves caught an' hung to the cottonwoods! I tell you —"

"Just a minute!" Curt grinned. He knew Wolf Montague very well. "You aren't ever going to tell me that you've lost something?"

"Lost somethin'! Lost somethin'!" roared Montague. "About a hundred head of big steers — that's all. Out of my north pasture. Gone like greased pigs! If this-here goddam sheriff's office was worth the black powder to blow it to hell —"

"Now, now," Curt soothed him. "Keep your shirt on, Wolf. You don't mean half of all you're saying. You're not so sore because we haven't corralled this Trackless Bunch. You know good and well that you never came to town, till you'd got your boys together and looked around everywhere for those steers. You haven't got an idea about who took 'em, or where they went. If you had, you wouldn't be here, telling *me* about it. Uh-uh! You wouldn't say a word till the smoke was lifted. So don't try to hurrah me. Sit down!"

Wolf grinned a trifle sheepishly. He sat down as invited and admitted that Curt had read his trail. He spoke cordially to Chihuahua, who was an old acquaintance.

"Well, somethin's got to be done," he said at last, leaning on the box that served him for a seat. "I do'no's *I* can say just what. If a man could just git a glimpse at 'em once, Curt, it wouldn't be so hard. What I can see I can shoot at! But they're hittin' here, then hittin' som'r's else the next time."

"When'd you miss your steers?"

"Yest'day mornin'. Might've been gone a couple days, though. I do'no'. They was up in the north pasture, like I said, fattenin' up. I'm kind of shorthanded an' I never figured, nohow, that they'd drift much. Well, yest'day, right early, I was ridin' that-away. An' I missed 'em. I picked up their trail a couple places, in the arroyos. But there'd been a right smart shower the night before an' washed out the trail in the hills.

"I come back down to the house an' I got my three boys an' we combed them ridges. But we never picked up the trail ag'in. Kept on a-huntin' for it till noon today, then I come in to see if you'd stumbled onto anything new about this-here goddam Trackless Bunch of yours."

Curt locked his hands behind his head.

Thoughtfully, he regarded the fierce-faced old cowman.

"They're a slick outfit," he grunted. "Every job they do is so well-figured that picking up the trail and trying to catch up with 'em is a poor bet . . . Seems to me, the only chance I've got of hanging the deadwood onto 'em is by finding out who's the boss, then pinning some special job on the outfit."

"Listens like sense," nodded Wolf Montague. "But can you find out who this boss-fella is?"

Curt looked at Chihuahua and grinned faintly.

"Well," he said cautiously, "I think I'm a little bit forrader than I was the other night. I have got a fine mess of suspicions. I have even got *proof* on one man. I think he's pretty high in the gang, too."

"Who's that?" Montague grunted tensely, leaning.

"No, I'm not telling — yet. The time's not right. I expect him to lead us up to the rest of the bunch. But I can't go too fast, Wolf. Meanwhile, we'll ramble out with you and have a look at this ground. When are you going back?"

"Mornin', early. Long's I'm in town, I might's well make a little money off them would-be poker sharps in the Palace. They're my meat."

Curt frowned thoughtfully at him. He hesitated, then —

"Mind doing me a favor?" he asked — diplomatically. "Don't say anything about the steers, or even about the Trackless Bunch, in the Palace. It's — well, it's a notion of mine."

"Why — all right!" Wolf nodded, staring. "But I'd as soon tell the tale to anybody, myself."

"Well, it — it might spoil something for me."

"All right," Montague shrugged. "See you early tomorrow."

When he had gone, Andy Allen looked curiously at Curt, who was staring at the door. "Well?" Andy grunted at last. "Why'd you tell Wolf to keep still about his steers?"

"I didn't *tell* him. I know him a lot too well for that! I *asked* him, you noticed. Wolf's cross-grained. You give him the idea he mustn't do something and that's the only thing he'll do. 'Wolf' Montague . . . Hell! It's 'Mule' Montague that he ought to be named."

"But why did you *ask* him not to talk?"

"To save his stubborn neck! That's why. He'll go down to the Palace and he'll start drinking. And he'll get ready to battle the whole place. He always does. Especially if he gets to losing. And if he pops off in the Palace, somebody is just as apt to try shutting his mouth as mine. And I'd hate to lose old Wolf. We're liable to need him, later."

"Es verdad!" Chihuahua nodded. "Me, I'm know Wolf them long time. She's like Curt's say, Andy."

"Think he'll keep still, because you asked him to?"

"I think so. But most of all, I hope so!"

Andy produced from its hiding-place a full quart bottle. They sat around the table, playing stud poker and drinking sparingly, for an hour. Then Andy yawned.

"Stud poker — when I never seen the like of my hole card — an' Star tarantula juice, together, they hit me where I live. Gentlemen! I feel sagacious as hell. I'm turnin' in."

Curt looked at Chihuahua, who nodded slightly.

"Let's wander awhile," Curt suggested. "We mustn't keep Andy up, Chihuahua. He hasn't learned, yet, to do his sleeping in the winter time."

They moved toward the Palace. From the dance-floor came the sound of music, for one of Tom Card's improvements had been importation of a small orchestra such as Gurney had never heard before his time. Chihuahua hummed the tune.

"*Por Dios!* Me, I'm think she's better here, now. I'm find me one blonde girl an' I'm dance . . ."

They went inside through the bar-room's swing doors. Card was in his office, Curt saw. But out in the gaming-room was Shirley Randolph before her favorite game — faro. Broodingly, Curt watched. Chihuahua observed the direction of Curt's stare and hesitated for an instant.

"She's — something new, w'at?"

"Card's bookkeeper. They say she always wins."

"*Por Dios,* then I'm love to have them receipt! Me, I'm win sometime, but always, too, I'm lose sometime. If she's know how to win all time . . ."

He leaned a little, until he could see the dealer. Slowly, he nodded, and stared at Curt thoughtfully.

"Mabbe in them game she's something I'm not understand . . . Them dealer, she's go by 'Newe' here? She's name' Newe in Cuchillo, w'en I'm ride for them O-Bar. Ver' slick dealer . . ."

"Newe," Curt nodded. "We haven't had any complaints about him, here in the

Palace. He could be using a crooked box. But it does seem that somebody would get suspicious. You want to dance? I'm going to take a look at Wolf Montague."

"*Muy bien.* An' if you're want me, Curt —"

"I'll probably shoot a couple times — and not into the ceiling, either," Curt smiled grimly.

He went into the gaming-room, and Shirley, looking up, met his blank stare. She frowned, but he let his eyes shift to Newe, who sat behind the table with black slouch hat low over shaggy brows, the inevitable match-thin brown cigarette threatening to set his mustache afire. So Newe was another Cuchillo man . . . Curt wondered if this were another link, between Cuchillo and Gurney, between Cuchillo hardcases and the Trackless Bunch in the Territory — between the outlaws and Tom Card.

Newe's small, bright eyes, shallow and hard and blue as turquoises, lifted from the layout for an instant. Meeting them, Curt grunted to himself.

"Information's not coming from him!" he thought. "Not from Newe, any more than from Tom Card. Whatever he knows — if he really knows anything at all — he'll bury so deep behind that rocky face of his that blasting would hardly get it out. But — he's using the same name here as in Cuchillo. I wonder what that means? No trouble on the back trail that he's afraid will catch up with him? Or — what?"

He let his eyes shift past Shirley without focussing, without meeting the girl's stare. The rest of the crowd bucking the faro-bank seemed to be very ordinary customers — cowboys, unimportant townsmen of Gurney, a couple of the Palace loafers. Zyler was standing at the table's end. He looked furtively at Curt, then his stare shifted quickly to the box from which Newe was taking a card.

Curt turned slowly, to look all around the room. And now he saw Wolf Montague with four men, sitting at a poker-table against the wall. Wolf's eyes were shiny — the only token of his drinking. He reached, while Curt watched him, to get a quart bottle that stood in the table's center among chips. He filled his glass. While he lifted it, he was studying his hand. He tossed the whiskey down and pushed a stack of chips into the pot.

"I'll raise that some," he said. " 'Count of the shape of my hand. I'd be plumb coward, if I never raised it."

The others shook their heads and threw

in their hands. Wolf laughed bellowingly as he reached out to drag the pot to him. A boyish-faced house man with wise, tired eyes looked at Wolf sidelong.

"Was that just hurrahing, Wolf? I mean, about you and the sheriff having something up your sleeve. But — of course it was! I knew it all the time. You can't hurrah me, Wolf."

"Hurrah you! Hurrah you! Like hell! We know plenty. We ain't spreadin' it, yet. But when we do —"

Awkwardly, Wolf began to separate the chips and stack them. He looked around the table, and asked who had the deal.

"It's Pony's deal," the smooth-faced house man said. "I still think you're hurrahing us, Wolf. This bunch is raising hell with all of us. I happen to know that the sheriff's not the only one looking for their trail. And if anything's been found — No, you can't fool me, Wolf. You're just hurrahing."

"Oh, the fool! The mouthy damn' fool!" Curt said softly, viciously, to himself. "They're just turning him inside out!" . . .

Curt moved a little toward the back wall and the glazed door that opened upon can-littered space behind the Palace. If he went over to the poker-table and tried to coax Wolf away, it would show the men there his suspicions. "And — chances are, it'd just make Wolf stubborn and he wouldn't move for hell!" he told himself. "But if I don't horn into that layout, trouble's coming. And through the smoke. So —"

He looked around. Shirley was cashing in, now. She had very few chips, this time. She turned a little and faced him. And there was no mistaking her search for him, her interest in him. She was curious about his presence in the Palace. Not only was she not looking through him, as when he had stood in the office door, she was staring straight into his eyes. She seemed about to speak to him.

That knowledge — and somehow he *knew* that he was right — made Curt's pulses jump. Then he remembered how she had talked to him in friendly fashion; how she had relaxed in the saddle at Devil's Bench in the crook of his arm; how she had met his mouth with warm, ready mouth — only to pull away from him and tell him that it meant nothing. He went on without pause to stand in the archway of the dance-hall and wait until Chihuahua came around to him, dancing with a tall blonde girl.

Chihuahua's brows raised slightly. Curt nodded as slightly. When the music stopped, Chihuahua seated his partner and spilled money on the table for drinks. Then he came to Curt.

"Wolf's blabbed," Curt said quietly, crowding the arch to let men come through. "From what I heard, they're pumping him. No chance to get him out. He'd just baulk. He's over at a poker-table. Will you take the gambling-room? I'll watch this end. No telling which way trouble'll come — from this side of the joint or the other. We'd better cover both."

"*Por supuesto!* Me, I'm have them pleasure! My girl, she's spend them money an' be happy. So —"

He went across the bar-room to the front door and vanished. Curt, turning, recoiled from Shirley who now stood directly behind him. She regarded him very gravely.

"I want to talk to you," she said. "I — looked straight at you, but you went right on by."

"What do you want to talk about?" he countered evenly.

"I'm going to the hotel. Will you — walk with me?"

"I'm sorry. But I'm busy now. I — have to meet a man. If there's something you simply have to get off your mind — it'll wait till breakfast, won't it?"

"What are you doing? I mean — how are

you busy? I heard you tell that tall man that you didn't know from which end trouble will come. What did you mean by that? Is there to be trouble here in the Palace, to-night?"

"Trouble?" Curt repeated vaguely. "Oh! Oh, you mean what I said to Chihuahua Joe. Oh, no. I meant something else, and somewhere else. But, I am busy. Getting ready for tomorrow."

She stared at him steadily, then shook her head.

"That isn't so. You are expecting trouble — here, tonight! That's why you don't want to leave. Now, will you tell me, or do you want me to find Tom Card and ask him?"

He swore under breath.

"Now, why," he asked himself, "did she have to come up just in time to hear that?"

But he faced her with indifferent expression.

"Why, if that's the notion you've got, you had better go to Tom Card."

"I will, if you won't tell me. And it's no use to say that you're not here for a purpose. For if you're not, you can walk to the hotel with me."

He saw nothing for it but to go. For in the gaming-room, he was certain, a blow would be struck at Wolf Montague because Wolf had hinted at knowledge of the Trackless Bunch. If she went to Card, the blow might be delayed, but it would be struck just the same. The difference being that it might come in a way, or from a direction, that he would not be prepared for.

He looked past her. Only the usual noises, the usual movements, were noticeable in bar-room, gaming-room, dance-hall. He hoped that Chihuahua could cover Wolf until he got the girl away from the Palace and hurried back.

"All right, then," he said drawlingly. "Let's go."

Out on the sidewalk she took his arm. The night was dark, for the sky was blanketed with shower-clouds. They went slowly, Gurney's sidewalks being no more than plank platforms before the stores, or hard-packed 'dobe earth, the gaps between building and building littered by cans and bottles.

They covered half the distance to Mrs. Sheehan's without a word. She seemed to wait for him to ask a question and he was grimly determined that he would say no unnecessary word. At last, she looked sidelong at him in the light of a store's window.

"You've made up your mind to dislike me, haven't you?"

"No," he answered promptly. "But I have

made up my mind."

They went on and when he did not am-
plify the statement, she said: "Yes?" inquiringly. "To what?"

"To let you go your way while I go mine.
That's what you said you wanted. I don't
have to be told twice."

"Don't be stubborn. Simply because I
can't feel as you — thought I should feel
—"

"Simply because you can't feel as I feel.
That's the answer. Don't try changing it.
You say you don't feel that way. *Muy bien!*
Then let it go. It's not bothering you much."

"And you?" Her voice was oddly subdued.

"I'll probably live. *No es importe.* Is that
all you had to say to me?"

"No. But you're making it hard for me to
say what I had intended saying. It's about
— Tom Card. And you."

"Well? I thought that was pretty well
settled, for the time being. I'm going to
gather in our outlaws and — Tom Card is
to come hunting me. And that's that."

"It's foolish! Utterly foolish!" she blazed
at him. "For you two — simply because you
looked at each other once and decided not
to like each other — to act like two children
— or like two bulldogs."

"Tell Card that," Curt suggested, grinning. "Tell him not to come hunting for me and I won't hunt for him — on that trail. Tell him — or have you already mentioned it to him?"

He looked quickly at her side-face, in a light they passed. He nodded.

"Uh-huh. You have mentioned it to him. And he told you in that sweet, know-it-all-way of his, not to bother your pretty head; everything's going to be all right."

"He didn't say it in that way, at all. He said — well, if you were willing to apologize —"

Curt laughed shortly, but with real amusement.

"Apologize! I apologize . . . Well, well. In some respects, Mr. Card is certainly an amusing hairpin. Is that all? Didn't he have any other suggestions? He knew well enough that I'm not apologizing. So — what else can I do?"

"Oh — you're the most maddening person! Doesn't anyone have any influence with you? Or do you have to go mulishly along, certain that you know everything — I know what I'll do! I'll ask Marie Young to speak to you. It seems that you listen to her!"

"You certainly have got a case on Card, now, haven't you?" he asked unpleasantly.

"You certainly don't give a hoot whether I get wiped out, or not. So it must be that you're trying to save Card's hide. And because you can't see through his false front, you tell me that I oughtn't to see."

"Perhaps I see more clearly — because I have more information. Certainly, when you and others say things about him that I *know* to be false —"

"You never heard me say anything about him that you *knew* to be false. You just *said* that you knew! And here's what you ought to be thinking about: How you're going to feel when —"

He stopped himself, with some little difficulty. For it infuriated him to hear her making excuses, taking up the cudgels, for Tom Card. But he had almost told her that she was going to be very uncomfortable when he ripped the mask from Tom Card. And he could not say that, no matter how much she irritated him.

"You're entitled to your opinion, of course. But I happen to know you're all wrong," he said carefully.

They stood, now, at the foot of Mrs. Sheehan's steps.

"You see," Shirley said irritably, "you won't listen to anyone. You make an opinion, then you won't admit that there is the slightest possibility of being wrong. Because you've decided that Tom Card is a person you dislike, there can be no good in him — no matter what anyone else may know! You think you know —"

"I *do* know," Curt told her grimly. "And you'll find out!"

He looked at her somberly. When she stood on the step just above him, bare dark head a little on one side, it was hard not to put his hands out quickly and draw her to him as he had done in the diningroom. It was very hard not to hold her close and kiss that provoking mouth until that studied calm of hers disappeared — vanishing in a flurry of fear of him, if he could wake in her no other emotion.

He wanted to say that he was certain of Tom Card's leadership of the outlaws; and that if Card had not been, his own jealousy would be enough to make him hate the big, sure gambler. He drew a long breath, to keep from saying it, and from saying that she was his and he would have her or nobody would.

But he held himself rigid and when he spoke, he managed a slow drawl, a tone of — almost — indifference, casualness.

"It was kind to let me walk with you. Too bad, though, that I have to play out my own hand on the strength of what I know about the rules and the men I'm bucking. Good-night."

"Good-night," she said hesitantly. Then — "Good-night," she whispered when he waited, a little puzzled.

He touched hatrim and turned away. He went straight back to the Palace, but not to the door. Instead, he slipped between the side wall and that of the building adjoining Card's place. Chihuahua, he thought, would be prowling and he might find him without drawing attention, if he went in the back.

He stopped at the corner and looked around for a moment. Then, moving carefully through the cans and bottles, he went toward the corral behind the Palace. He wanted to see through the back door of the gaming-room. This door had an upper panel of glass, but it was painted black for half its height. He turned and looked, but could not see over the painted section.

There was a faint gust of wind on his face, odorous of rain. He looked at the overcast sky and a great drop of water splashed on his face. Beyond him was a cottonwood tree and something rustled there as he looked skyward. He stared, for the noise among the small leaves seemed louder than so small a breeze would have made. And the rustling came again. He moved that way, hand at the front of his vest. And in the lower branches of the tree a dark mass showed, moving.

Curt wondered who would climb a tree at night. Some drunk might have the inclination, but would hardly have the ability. Then he turned his head jerkily. He could look from where he stood into the gaming-room, seeing part of the wall and ceiling. It came to him then that Wolf Montague sat at a table by that wall. A man in the tree might be able to see the players around that table.

He whipped the right-hand gun from its holster and lifted it. He called sharply to the dark figure above him.

"Come out of that, now! You're covered!"

Like period to his order, a pistol roared above him. The glass panel of the door rang like a muted bell and from the gaming-room came a frightened yell.

Curt moved a step to the side, pulling back the hammer of his Colt. From somewhere along the Palace's rear wall a shot came. The man in the cottonwood groaned softly and pitched to the ground two yards from Curt's feet.

"Hey, Curt! She's me!" Chihuahua called. "I'm see him fi-ine, that time. She's more dark than them leaves."

221

He came running across, making hardly more noise than a cat would have done. He bent over the motionless figure and a match flared in the darkness. He held the tiny flame down toward the blotch of white which was the face, while automatically Curt covered the fallen one. Then a drop of rain struck the match head and it sizzled out.

From the Palace men were calling. Curt heard the name "Harry" and then the added information that "Harry" was dead.

"She's dead," Chihuahua said calmly. "She's one fellow I'm see in the Palace, tonight . . . An' she's climb no more tree, hah?"

"Shooting at Wolf, probably," Curt said slowly, turning.

"W'y, I'm not have them surprise, if she's so," said Chihuahua. "An' w'en you're yell, you're make him miss."

Curt went toward the smashed door. The men there gave back and let him through. A crowd was gathered about that table at which Wolf Montague had played. Wolf's bellow rose to comfort Curt:

"Right, through the glass an' smack-dab into Harry's face!" he said. "Hey, Curt! What was the shootin' about, outside?"

"Chihuahua got the bushwhacker," Curt

told him. He came over to stand looking down at the boyish-faced house man. Harry lay upon the table as if asleep. His right hand was crookedly faced, the arm beneath his head. The wise, tired eyes were closed. There was a small bluish hole in the center of his high forehead.

"Look at that!" Curt grunted suddenly. "Aces and eights, he had — *The Dead Man's Hand!*"

He looked around and met Tom Card's blank stare. As blankly, Curt faced the gambler.

"Any — notions, Card?" he drawled.

"Notions? Why, I don't think so. Why would you ask me?"

"Why — he's one of your men. It's natural to ask you why somebody would take the trouble to climb a tree and put a slug into him. But — here's the man, now. Who is he?"

Men scuffed and stumbled through the door, carrying a stocky, shabby figure. Chihuahua brought up the van, sea-blue eyes very bright, as they roved from face to face inside.

"Some bum who's been around here for several days," Card said carelessly, with a glance at the dead man. "I don't know what he called himself. Maybe some of my bartenders do."

"Pretty good shot, for a saloon-bum," Curt meditated aloud. "Mostly, they're pretty shaky . . . Well — he killed Harry and Chihuahua killed him. I reckon we can leave the rest of it to the coroner."

Then he saw Zyler, gaping at the body.

"I thought for a minute it might be you, Zyler," he said. "But maybe I just *hoped* that, rather than thought it."

Zyler's murky little eyes widened and his loose mouth sagged. He said *"Huh?"* in a vague tone and men around him laughed. Then he looked scowlingly at Curt.

"I reckon!" he said blusteringly. "I reckon that was it."

"But maybe I'll not be wrong, next time," Curt sighed.

CHAPTER VIII

Andy Allen, sitting up with sleepy groans, stretched himself and yawned. He put his feet over the edge of his cot, and Curt, waking, groped for a boot and sent it over to crash on the office wall near Andy's head. Then he, too, sat up and flung back his quilt. Chihuahua waked without a sound and was into his boots very quickly.

"What's that?" Andy said between yawns.

"Some billydoo of yours, Curt? You an' your ambiguous love affairs!"

Curt and Chihuahua looked toward the door. Andy went across in bare feet and stooped to pick up the folded slip of brown paper that projected from the bottom of the door. He straightened and unfolded it. His lips moved, then he looked queerly at Curt, who was pulling on a boot.

"What's it?" Curt grunted, without much interest.

"Well" — Andy hesitated, then shrugged — "might's well read it, I reckon; 'Thompson look out Texas man comin' with warrant,' it says."

Chihuahua glanced at Andy, then at Curt. He began to make a cigarette. Curt held out his hand and Andy came over to give him the paper. Then he went to his cot and hunted under it for his own boots, Chihuahua yawned elaborately.

"Me, I'm hungry like them wolf!" he said. "Andy, you're snore like one young army. I'm think we're better fix your nose with the split stick."

"Ah, that's just a dream you had! I don't snore. I stayed awake one time just on purpose to see if I did. An' I never."

Curt looked at them. He understood very well that they were merely following the

225

proper etiquette in such matters. He grinned, staring down at the paper.

"Heave me my other boot, will you, Andy? 'Texas man coming with warrant' . . . The trouble with a fellow guessing is — no matter what he does, he's still just guessing."

He pulled on the boot that Andy tossed him.

"Two things are wrong with this note, anyway. In the first place, it wasn't sent by any friend. Not by a long shot! And there's no warrant out for me, in Texas, so far as I know. Now, if nothing had been said about warrants; if this note just said, *'Look out! Texas men coming!'* I probably would have got good and scared."

He laughed grimly. They watched him.

"You see, three years back, I was home — down in Tarrant County, Texas. I got to having trouble with the Jensen family. Hell! We'd *always* had trouble with the Jensens. And that's a hard-riding, quick-shooting outfit, let me tell you. I tangled with young Tom Jensen one day and I cleaned his plow — with my hands. Then he tried gunning for me. Well, I shot him up. Didn't kill him, but he was crippled for a long time."

"Well, then his two older brothers jumped into the war. I ran into 'em one night when I was with a couple of friends of mine. The

226

Jensens had three of their men with 'em. When the smoke cleared off, there was a man down on each side — dead. The Jensens were pretty well shot to pieces and I had a crippled left arm."

He stared at the wall, making a cigarette blindly.

"They sent me word they were out to get me, one way or another. My mother begged me to leave the country. And I was about ready, when they primed a fool bronc-buster they had working for 'em to try getting me. He jumped me one night in a saloon at Birdville. I didn't want to kill him. I did my best to keep from it. But he was drunk and he wanted a fight. I had to pull on him and — he died a few days later. But, so far as I know, there's no warrant out for me, on that. I left within the week. To please my mother. She's an invalid and she's buried two — my father and an older brother — with bullet-holes in 'em."

"Nothin' on the back trail, then, to worry you," Andy nodded.

"To my knowledge, no. If I'd stayed at home, the Jensens would have hung something onto me with crooked evidence, or shot me in the back. So I came up this way, and I don't reckon the Jensens know where I am. If they did, they might send a killer up to get me, but they wouldn't bother with sending warrants into the Territory. You know how much luck they'd have at that!"

He fingered the crudely written note.

"Sam Bain, or Tom Card, did this!" he said, with assurance. "Just took a chance that maybe there *were* warrants out for me and I'd split the breeze. Well, let's eat and collect Wolf Montague. Let's take a look around his north pasture."

They did not find Wolf Montague in the U-and-Me. But while they ate breakfast a cowboy told Curt that he had seen Montague going toward the court house. And when they came into the sheriffs office, Wolf was sitting there. He looked guiltily at Curt.

"By Gemini, I must've been plastered last night," he said. "Thanks, Curt."

"De nada," Curt shrugged. "What's the letter?"

"Oh, that! Why a Mex' kid come in with it, a spell back. Says it's for the Sheriff of Gurney. Then he hightailed."

It was a cheap envelope, without superscription. It might have been bought at almost any frontier store. Curt turned it over, then ripped it open. There was nothing inside. Curiously, he looked at it and saw that a single line had been printed on the inside of the envelope flap. He stared.

"Beware! Texas officers coming with warrants."

Nothing else. He scowled at it, then handed it to Andy Allen who read and looked at Curt with lifted brows.

"She's too gregarious for me!" shrugged Andy.

"Same as the other one," Curt said briefly to Chihuahua. "But not from the same party. Not *written* by the same party, anyhow."

He shrugged impatiently, jammed the envelope into a jumper pocket with the first note and moved on to where Wolf Montague was waiting outside the door.

They got their horses and rode out of town. Passing Mrs. Sheehan's, Curt's eyes wandered toward that window in which, upon a time, he had seen Shirley Randolph. But if she were there now, he could not see her. He spurred ahead to join Wolf Montague and Chihuahua, who rode in the lead.

They made Montague's line at noon and presently came upon an Arrowhead cowboy. He had been hunting trail, he said.

"No luck!" he finished laconically.

Chihuahua took the lead. For there was hardly his equal in all the Territory, as a tracker. They went slowly, now, for the range was hilly and cut by arroyos and cañons.

When night came, they had found nothing.

They cut across to one of the Montague line-camps and found at the little stone cabin a limping cowboy who greeted Chihuahua with a wolf-howl.

"Well, sir!" he said. "If this ain't like old times! Remember the time you an' Lit Taylor an' the Gurney gang hit Frenchy Leonard up at Porto?"

"*Si!*" Chihuahua nodded politely. "I'm remember ver' well. You're in them store with Frenchy an' Slim Hewes an' them other. We're shoot them hell out of you."

The cowboy tapped his crippled leg.

"Some of your doin's," he grinned cheerfully. "Well, sir! That was a warm day. I'll slap some more beef into the frypan an' we'll have plenty for everybody. I just made up a batch of biscuits."

They sprawled upon their saddle blankets, after supper. The crippled cowboy yarned about Frenchy Leonard and his day. At last Curt asked him who had rustled the Arrowhead steers. Chihuahua, very quiet, was watching the cowboy in the flickering light of the fire on the open hearth of the cabin.

"I swear, I do'no'," the cowboy shrugged. "I figured a spell it might be Smilin' Badey, but" — he looked a shade uncomfortably at his employer — "I used to ride with

Smilin', you know, Wolf. An' if it was Smilin' back in the country, I'd know it."

"How?" Montague grunted curtly. He,
too, was watching the ex-outlaw steadily.
"How would you know — special?"

"Well — not to put too fine a point on it,
because if Smilin' was back, he'd be lookin'
me up."

"Yeh?" Montague drawled. His tone was
very gentle and there was tension in the
crowded little room. "Yeh?"

The cowboy looked defiantly at him.

"Yeh! If only to git my answer when he
ask' me to come ride with him ag'in! If only
to hear me say — hell, no!"

Montague studied him intently and the
cowboy's eyes were steady. At last, Wolf
shrugged.

"I'm takin' your word for that," he said.

"You can," the cowboy nodded. "I had my
fill of that. I don't want no more bein' on
the dodge. An' I never yet sold out the man
I was workin' for."

They turned in without more talk and
were up before dawn. Chihuahua led them
away from the cabin. He grinned at Wolf.

"We're have them same notion, about
him, hah?"

Wolf looked back at the crippled rider. He
nodded grimly.

"I reckon. I knowed he was in that Porto fight, with Frenchy. But when he says he used to ride with Smilin' Badey — Well, he was right close to trouble. But either he's a sight slicker'n I give him credit for, or he's all right."

Until noon, it was the same as on the afternoon before. And finally Curt turned sideways in the saddle to shake his head and frown at Montague. "It beats me!" he confessed. "But this range of yours, the way it's cut up with arroyos and all, is just the easiest place in the world to hustle cattle over without leaving a breathmark! What say, Chihuahua?"

"Me, I'm think I'm not so bad on them trailin'," Chihuahua shrugged. "But your steer, Wolf, she's act like she's wear them dam' wings. An' when one rain come —" he snapped his fingers eloquently to indicate the entire and utter vanishing of any possible trail.

"Well," Curt said thoughtfully, "no use your taking your time to chase around after 'em, Wolf. We'll scatter out and cover the country best we can, in the direction you guessed they were heading. Maybe we'll uncover something and maybe — just maybe, Wolf — this will be the last time the Trackless Bunch will come projecking around your range . . ."

"A' right, Curt," Wolf nodded. "I ain't goin' to rawhide you no more. For I'm damned if I know what I'd do if I was in your boots. An' if Chihuahua, *he* can't cut their trail, I reckon nobody in the Territory could. Let me know if you find anything, an' when a few more Winchesters'll help, just say the word an' me an' the boys'll come splittin' the breeze."

They said "so long" to Montague and moved forward, Chihuahua leading with blue eyes studying the ground frowningly. But though they rode so for miles, combing the arroyos, they found no further sign of the rustled steers. At last, coming to the crest of the ridge, they reined in and looked at one another.

"Didn't I hear that a new fellow's keeping store in Uncle George La Grange's old place?" Curt asked Andy.

"Seems to me I did hear something about a new man movin' in," Andy nodded. "But I ain't been up around Cottonwood Tanks—away since Uncle George's Mex' woman combed him with the axe, that time."

"Might's well ramble on up there and look this new hairpin over. Can happen he's an honest fellow and if he is, he might have seen something."

So they jogged on over the hogbacks to the crossroads beyond Cottonwood Tanks, where Uncle George La Grange of the axe-wielding Mex' consort had kept a little store until the day he had pounded the woman one time too often, and she had retaliated with the axe.

"Company!" Curt grunted, when from a ridge-comb they could see the squat adobe store and make out the half-dozen saddled horses at the hitch-rail before it.

"Wonder who we're horning in on —"

"Six horses," Andy observed cheerfully. "If she's some of the Trackless Bunch we're amblin' up to, they're goin to figure out two apiece."

"Well, maybe we're acting like the damn' fools they tell about, that go hightailing it in where even angels would go around, but I certainly want to look at this bunch."

"*Por Dios!* Like Andy's figure, there will be but the two for each," Chihuahua grinned. "We're not worry, hah? Two for each, she's just fair . . ."

They rode somewhat cautiously down the slope to where the trails crossed and swung down before the store's hitch-rack. Through the open door of the place carried the sound of rough voices and low toned laughter. A stubbled-faced rider appeared in the doorway, looked them over thoughtfully, nodded briefly, then stepped back again.

They tied their horses — with fore-thoughtful slipknots that could be released with a single jerk — and went clumping across the hard ground into the store.

Five men were in the store, besides the storekeeper. And they were all strangers to Curt. He looked them over and decided that there were no pilgrims, no weak sisters, in the bunch. They were uniformly dusty and unshaven, uniformly clothed in flannel and overalls and rough jeans — and uniformly burdened with long-barreled Colts. A couple of short Winchesters stood in a corner of the room beside a sugar barrel.

They were drinking. The man who had a harmonica at his mouth, and the man who had been jigging to its music, were provided like the others with tin cups of the store-keeper's whiskey. The freckled rider who had inspected them from the door leaned now upon a pile of boxes and surveyed them blankly. It seemed to Curt that all eyes had gone to the badge on his shirt the badge on Andy's and on Chihuahua's. Then without change of expression, the six pairs of eyes had shifted.

"Howdy!" he said tonelessly. He led the way to the counter. The storekeeper nodded and the men said "Howdy" in reply. Curt gestured generally at their tin cups. "Drink?"

They looked furtively, one at the other, then, as if some grave decision had been reached, nodded in unison. They got up, or straightened, where they sat or leaned. They came over to the counter and the store-keeper — as lean and brown and still of face as any of them — produced a jug and three more cups. He filled them all and lifted his own with the others.

"To crime!" Curt said, grinning. "For what would a sheriff ever amount to, without it."

The freckled man looked at Curt thoughtfully. He had hazel eyes and red hair so dark that it was almost brown in the dim light. Slowly, he grinned.

"An' what'd a country ever amount to, without a sheriff?" he countered solemnly. "Drink her deep, fellas."

"Hah!" Chihuahua grinned. "You're play them *Skiptamaloo?*"

The man nodded and began to play. The cowboy who had been jigging set down his cup and began the ancient breakdown. Chihuahua nodded seraphically.

"Faster! Ver' much faster!" he cried at last.

He faced the dancing cowboy and broke into a tapping, whirling dance that shook the rough floor planks. As the harmonica ended on a high wail, he pulled down his black hat, hard, dropped hand to pearl Colt-butt and leaped high to crack his heels thrice together and drop like a cat.

"She's ver' fine exercise!" he grinned.

Curt was studying the men — and the storekeeper.

"How's business?" he asked him finally.

The storekeeper shrugged indifferently.

"Nothin' to write a letter home about. But I'm aimin' to stick it out a spell."

That was the sum-total of the conversation. They leaned silently against the bar and smoked and watched the two men who had picked up an ancient deck of cards. The freckled cowboy who had first come to look at them lounged out finally, disappearing through a rear door and closing it after him. Chihuahua moved a little where he stood. He stared sleepily at the front wall of the store. Then the freckled cowboy came back.

Faintly, from outside, came the muffled hoofbeats of a horse — a horse that walked away from the hitchrack. Curt heard it, but made no sign. He knew that Chihuahua was watching the door. They idled for a couple of minutes longer, then Chihuahua yawned and turned to Curt, who took the hint.

"Might's well be rambling," he said. "So long!"

"So long!" the company repeated politely, without looking up from their cards, their harmonica, their cigarette making.

There were but five horses — besides their own — now at the hitch-rack. They swung into the saddles and rode quietly on up the north trail, without looking back. They rode perhaps a half-mile before topping out of a deep arroyo and crossing a higher-than-usual ridge. Then Chihuahua set spurs to his stocky black and whirled off down the arroyo to the left.

"We're catch him quick, if she's stick to them trail!" he flung back, over his shoulder.

Hell-for-leather, they spurred over that broken country sliding at peril of their necks down the stony slopes, plunging doggedly up the far banks of the arroyos. Their horses were unusually good animals, far superior to the genral run of cow-horses. Unless the fugitive were mounted on an animal of much speed and bottom, they would over-haul him.

Finally, they were racing parallel to a trail that led vaguely back toward Gurney. Chihuahua spurred over to the trail itself, bent far over and jerked his hand aloft.

"She's come down these trail, all right!"

he yelled.

Again they rammed home the rowels and sent the horses rocketing forward. A mile passed; two. Still no sign of the vanished rider, save the hoofprints of his flying mount. Then, from a pile of rocks ahead and above them, came the vicious *whang!* of a Winchester. A bullet kicked up a dust fountain ten yards to their right.

As if it were signal for a drill-evolution, they split. Curt rode straight up the slope at a gallop, lying over his saddle-horn. Chihuahua and Andy Allen swerved to left and right and raced toward the sheltered man's flanks. They found cover among boulders and pushed their Winchesters forward to sling .44s toward the spot from which bullets were coming raggedly toward Curt — and harmlessly, as yet.

Chihuahua slipped like a huge cat from boulder to boulder. Less expertly, Andy followed his example on the right. Curt found the bullets getting too close for comfort. He dropped out of the saddle, behind the jagged reef of rock. So, from three sides, now, they combed the fellow's fortress.

Chihuahua had completely disappeared from Curt's view. His arrival upon the crest of the tumbled ridge was announced by a single shot. Then he stood up and beckoned

Curt and Andy forward. They scrambled up beside him and found him standing grimly over that lean and cheerful rider they had captured on the road from Ancho, and let go. He lay now, still sprawling in the notch from which he had been firing at them. He was bleeding from two body-wounds.

"Ain't no — great shakes with — Winchester!" he whispered. "Been six-shooter distance — would have *got* somebody!"

"What did you sneak off from the store for?" Curt asked. "Come on, fellow! You might as well talk. You're passing in your checks, anyhow. Might as well tell us everything. Your gang ran off those steers of Wolf Montague's. Where'd you hide 'em? Who's behind all this business — anyhow?"

"Wouldn't you — love to know?" the cowboy whispered. He closed his eyes.

"Me, I'm think she's tell — if we're handle him right!" Chihuahua purred. He squatted beside the lean, still figure. "I'm see one time over by them Dragoon Mountain, w'ere them Apache, she's catch one prospector. She's skin him an', w'en I'm find him, them red ants —"

The cowboy opened his eyes. He stared glassily up at Chihuahua. His lips moved stiffly and they bent toward him.

"Bring on your skinnin' knife!" he whispered, with defiant grin.

Andy Allen stooped suddenly beside the cowboy and took his wrist with professional mien. He held it for perhaps ten seconds, staring up at the afternoon sun. Then, with the cowboy's eyes dully upon him, he opened the flannel shirt and studied the wounds, placed his palm against the forehead and looked up at Curt. He grunted impatiently.

"He ain't hurt bad!" he said loudly. "I've seen lots of cases like this. Why, when I was studyin' to be a doctor, I handled dozens of cases worse than this an' never lost a one. If we take him on to Wolf Montague's where I got my instruments, I can fix him so's he'll be up an' out in a couple weeks."

Curt nodded briefly, after a moment.

"He won't move a step, unless he spills what he knows!" he said, with equal loudness. "Well, fellow! What's she going to be? A burying — or what?"

The cowboy's eyelid fluttered faintly. Curt bent. Again the lid fluttered. There was no mistaking it, this time. He was winking sardonically at Curt. Then his face twisted with pain. His eyes closed. He was silent for a while as they squatted around him. He called deliriously for water after a while and Andy went down and brought up the horses,

241

and they gave him water from a canteen.

He talked brokenly, sometimes, thrashing about wildly and re-enacting what were evidently scenes from robberies of one kind and another. Curt could not decide if these were crimes of the Trackless Bunch in the Territory, or others in which he had taken part. Suddenly he raised himself on one elbow. He was frowning as he addressed Curt in a low voice.

"He's goin' to down him, anyhow!" he said, with evidence of distaste for the information. "An' I thought that, when he tied him up, we'd just leave him."

"Down who?" Curt asked quickly. "Who's going to down who?"

"*He* is. Going to down that cashier."

Back to Curt's mind flashed the question he had asked himself when he had learned that Ed Showalters, caught by the Trackless Bunch in the Gurney bank, had been tied up, then killed without apparent reason.

"*Why* is he going to down him?" he snapped. "Can't we just leave him here? Why does he want to down him, now?"

"His handkerchief slipped down. He says that the cashier seen his face. He says the cashier called him by name! He says he's *got* to down him, now!"

Further questions brought nothing but

broken mumblings. Curt labored with him until the perspiration was pouring down his face. He tried every leading question he could conceive. He mentioned Tom Card's name and Sam Bain's — but got no response. He wondered if he could be mistaken about the connection of these two with the Trackless Bunch. Then he thought of the Ancho angle.

"Short Card! Short Card! Short Card Mann!" he said over and over. "What about Short Card Mann?"

At last the eyes opened again:

"Short Card!" the cowboy repeated faintly. "Lis'en! He says git on the job *pronto!* The big boss is still sore at you. You want to get this deal through like it was *greased.* He says he done *his* part, an' if you don't line these steers out, the big boss'll just naturally raise hell!"

His mind seemed to stick on the last phrase. Over and over he mumbled the words — "raise hell — raise hell — raise hell" — until his voice died away in a mumbling drone. Then silence. Curt looked at Andy and Chihuahua and shook his head.

"He died pretty!" Andy said admiringly. "Yes, sir. He naturally died like a wolf!"

Curt stared somberly at his feet, considering what he knew. There was no doubt now that Short Card Mann was but a lieutenant in the Trackless Bunch, a mere understrapper of the "Big Boss." The message which had been carried — or was to have been carried — by this dead man from another lieutenant — the one who had actually run off Wolf Montague's steers — proved that. But who *was* the "Big Boss"? And who was this man who had sent the message?

"Who you reckon *is* this Big Boss?" Andy asked thoughtfully.

"Sí! Quién es?" Chihuahua repeated, with dark brows lifted inquiringly.

"Tom Card!" Curt said viciously. "Tom Card — even if I haven't got a bit of proof to tie him to the gang. But I'd lay my last, orphan two-bits on the line, backing my belief that Tom Card's the Big Rod of the Trackless Bunch; that he schemes the jobs and they're carried out by men like Short Card Mann and Sam Bain!"

He got up to look grimly about him. There were loose rocks everywhere. He began to pick them up and Chihuahua and Andy, understanding, carried the cowboy over to a shelf of stone, then joined Curt in carrying rocks to build a cairn over the body. When they were done, they went back to their horses. Curt looked at Chihuahua, who waited expectantly.

"Well?" Andy Allen demanded. "What's to do, now?"

"Back to the store!" Curt drawled. "We have certainly had reason to believe that this fellow was one of the rustlers who ran off Wolf Montague's Arrowhead steers. And he was warned out of the store, or sent with a message to Mann, while we were there. Which means that if the trail between Wolf's pasture and the thieves *is* broken, we can make a pretty good guess that we picked it up again at the store."

"So," Chihuahua nodded pleasantly, "we're go back to the store an' we're help them fellow to git sick!"

"Only if they don't see the light," Curt modified that, cautiously, "We'll take 'em into Gurney if they surrender. On the way back, we'll take in the Arrowhead and see if we can match their horse-tracks with the best ones we know of on Wolf's range."

"An' if they ain't havin' any surrenderin' today?" Andy inquired. "We — take 'em in anyway, huh?"

"Pigs or pork!" Curt nodded grimly. "We take 'em in, one way *or* the other. Maybe we can't convict 'em of stealing the Arrowhead steers, but we certainly will arrest 'em!"

CHAPTER IX

On the return trip to the store, they came on the dead cowboy's horse behind the ridge from which he had made his last stand. The horse had a broken leg, which explained the man's halt to fight three of them. Andy put a bullet into the animal's head, then they passed on.

They came to where Chihuahua could study the shabby building through his glasses. With naked eyes, Curt and Andy could see that the horses were no longer at the hitch-rack and Curt swore. But Chihuahua spoke without lowering his binoculars.

"Them horse, she's behind the store in them shed, I'm think. I'm see two — mabbe three — inside."

"Fine!" Curt grunted savagely. "Now, the question is, how best to walk up on 'em. They know who we are —"

"*Mira!* Look!" Chihuahua interrupted him. "One man, she's leave them store. She's go to them shed . . ."

They watched the little figure cross the open between the store and the shed, disappear within it, and come out again leading a horse within a couple of minutes. He swung up, this faraway figure down the slope, without a backward glance. He rode toward the hills. Chihuahua turned to Curt.

"I'm git him, hah?" he said purringly.

"Trail him!" Curt decided. "See where he's headed. Andy and I'll take care of the store and the others. I think we can work up in cover of the shed and catch 'em unawares."

They watched Chihuahua mount and go fast downhill on the trail of the horseman who rode leisurely toward the foothills. Then Andy grinned at Curt and looked down at the hang of his Colt. Curt nodded and they went to their own horses.

They made a roundabout course, taking cover in arroyos and behind ridges, until from the shelter of a hill they looked straight ahead at the silent shed, the equally quiet store. They rode out into the open with Winchesters across their arms, watching strainedly the 'dobe back wall of the shed. As they rode, the store's rear door was not in their line of vision. Andy turned a little sideways in the saddle and leaned. Curt, listening also, nodded. "Somebody outside," he breathed. "Come on! Chances are he's heard the horses!"

They dug in the hooks and the horses jumped toward the shed. A man appeared at the corner, Colt in hand. He lifted it and Curt, low over the saddle-horn, heard it roar. But neither he nor Andy was struck by the slug, nor was the second shot more accurate. The man jumped back as they neared shelter. Curt almost threw himself from the saddle behind the shed and staggered. He straightened and ran to the end of the wall. He had a glimpse of the man who had shot at them. Apparently, he was about to run for the store. But when Curt fired, he whirled back to the nearer shed.

"There were five and the storekeeper," Curt computed flashingly. "Six — less the man who just rode off. One in the shed, here, leaves four in the store . . . Not so good!"

"You in the shed!" Andy called. "Come on out. We're officers. You won't be hurt, none — if you act right!"

The man in the shed made a contemptuous blatting sound for answer. Curt moved cautiously to where he could see the store. The door was shut, now, but there were two windows in the back wall and the shutters were outside. As he looked, a long arm came out to catch a shutter. He aimed very carefully, not at the arm, but at the approximate position of the invisible body to which that arm belonged. With the whiplike report of the carbine, the arm came up convulsively, then was pulled inside.

Curt sent two more shots questing into the opening. They were received with an angry yell from the interior of the store. And from the other window someone opened with a Winchester, sending so savage and accurate a hail of lead to chip off the 'dobe wall's corner that Curt slid away from it. He looked at Andy and found him grimly attacking the shed's wall with his sheath-knife.

"Good boy!" Curt complimented him. "But, first, gi' me a boost up. Maybe I can get in a shot from the roof before they look for me there."

"They'll knock you off it as hermetical as a pigeon!" Andy objected, but he came to make a stirrup of his hand.

Curt pushed off his hat and shoved the carbine to the rounded dirt roof of the shed before he stepped from Andy's clasped hands to his shoulder and so up.

He lay flat there, reaching for the carbine. And from the shed the man's voice raised bellowingly, calling to the garrison in the store that someone was on the shed's roof. Curt swore; then, Winchester in hand, he gathered himself and lunged across the roof to the front. He squatted briefly, put left hand on the roof's edge and rolled off. He struck the hard ground before the shed's door, almost at the feet of the man who was yelling.

From the store, someone opened fire. But Curt, without coming erect, had twisted his carbine about and cocked and fired almost in the same motion. The man in the door vanished. A slug lifted Curt's hair. Another snagged the blouse of his shirt under right arm. Then he had leaped inside and a Colt, flaming in the dusk there, blinded him for an instant. He sprawled, rolling. His Winchester barrel struck something and he heard an agonized groan.

He blinked frantically, saw a vague shape above him and spun about on the straw-littered ground to hook his legs around the other's legs and snatch at him. The man fell across him with force to drive the breath from Curt's body. But, almost mechanically, he groped for the pistol, caught an arm, and pushed it from him. The Colt roared and horses plunged somewhere close — uncomfortably close.

"Cut it!" Curt panted. "I got you — covered!"

"Yeh?" the man said mockingly.

He lunged against Curt's hand, rolling clear over him and off him. Curt fumbled left-handed for one of the pistols in the Hardin vest. He got it out as the man rose to his knees. He let the hammer drop and the bellow of his gun blended with the roar of the other's shot. But he felt no shock of lead and the man went backward.

He got up shakily, panting, with the Colt ready. But the man was dead, Colt in limp hand. Curt answered Andy's frantic yelling, now. They were yelling in the store, too, calling to the man in the shed. Curt reholstered his gun and recovered his Winchester. He went toward the door, to squat and study the windows.

He could see no sign of movement anywhere. He grinned mirthlessly, got the hat fallen from his victim's head and put it on the muzzle of his Winchester. Artfully, holding it low, he moved it at the door, so that it looked like a man beginning to crawl out. And from a window came a shot that sent dust scattering over him from the shed floor. But answering shot came from Andy at the corner of the shed. And a triumphant yell from Andy, also.

"Got him, Curt! Cover me!"

Curt fired two shots rapidly at the right-hand window, two more into the other. Andy plunged into the shed grinning. He looked quickly around, found the man on the floor and nodded. Then, without speaking, he faced the store.

"You cover me!" Curt said, after a moment of watching. "I'm going to get close enough to make anybody at those windows a plumb invalid!"

"All right!" Andy sighed. "I ought to know you ain't got *sense* enough to know what you ought to be scared of! Go on. Get yourself killed off."

He fired a shot at each window, and Curt, head down as if running against rain, plunged out of the door and toward the store's wall. No shot came. He flattened himself against the wall, a little puzzled. Then he worked toward the door. There was a rawhide latchstring that he could reach without exposure. He twitched it, then pushed on the door. It sagged back with squeaking of rusty hinges. He waited beside it.

"You double-damn' fool!" Andy yelled from the shed. "You — You — Don't you go in there! Not till I come, anyhow!"

And he raced toward Curt, to stop and glare reproachfully at him. Curt was listening. He heard no sound from within the dusky room. He shrugged and looked at Andy.

"I'll bet they hightailed out the front door. I'm goin in! You'd better stay here and —"

"Go to hell! You're worse'n a damn'

metabolism! I'm ahead of you!"

And he jumped inside with Curt on his heels. They crouched with ready carbines, staring about the living-quarters of the storekeeper, listening strainedly. Andy turned at last.

"That drip-drip-drip —" he said, in a hushed voice. "Over there . . ."

He moved in the direction of a window and grunted in a satisfied sort of tone. Curt had gone to the door opening upon the store itself — that door through which the freckled cowboy had gone to send the hidden man to Short Card Mann. Listening there, he turned to face Andy, silhouetted against the light from the window, standing against a cot.

"It's our friend the storekeeper!" Andy reported. "One of us snagged him in the shoulder an' he fixed that with a rag. But the hole in his face he couldn't fix . . ."

Curt looked around. There was a door from this room into the partitioned half of the rear section — that part of the back-end which had the other window. He grunted to Andy and watched him go to open that door.

"Store-room," Andy reported. "Nobody in there."

Curt jerked back the door into the store.

And a mumbling sound came to him. He listened, then cautiously peered around the facing. That freckled cowboy who had been the only one of the five rustlers to speak, on their first visit, now sprawled along the counter. He had the storekeeper's jug and a tin cup. Whiskey was splashed on the planks of the floor around him. He was moveless, except for the stiff twitching of his lips and the flicker of eyelids. Curt went toward him.

"Well!" he said. "Next time an officer yells at you —"

He stopped, for he had seen the red stain spreading under the cowboy's body. He moved a little and nodded slowly, grimly. There would be no next time for this cheerful, steady-eyed competent. The freckled one's eyes rolled to him. They were glazed with pain.

"You win!" he mumbled. "Count of — Ab. If he'd waited — let you git up — to shed — knocked you over easy —"

"Where's the rest of your bunch?" Curt asked him.

"Do'no'. Just me an' Ab — an' storekeeper — when you lit —"

And that was the last word they had from him. They searched the place, but found no evidence of the presence of more than the three of them. They came back in to find

254

the freckled man lying quietly with eyes closed, hand still gripping the tin cup's handle. Curt bent over him, felt his heart and straightened with a shrug. And from the back came Chihuahua's hail:

"Hey, Curt! She's me!"

They called him in and he entered by way of the back room. Evidently, he had seen the storekeeper. For now he looked at the freckled man and nodded. He said:

"She's one clean-up, hah? An' me, I'm find Wolf's steer! *Sí!* She's not three mile from here. Them fellow, she's take me there easy. But I'm have to shoot them rus'ler an' them two other, she's hightail fast. I'm start them steer back for Wolf's — they're have 'em in them wide arroyo an' w'en them rus'ler, she's run, them steers have nothing between 'em an' them Arrowhead. Wolf, she's find 'em in his pasture tomorrow."

"You got one," Curt said thoughtfully, "and two made a dust-cloud . . . Out of six — or seven, if we count the storekeeper and I reckon he was one of 'em — we accounted for five . . . That's hardly going to stop the bunch, but it *is* whittling. Well —"

He looked distastefully around the store, shrugged.

"I feel like burying these and setting fire to the place! But I'll have to report it, to be in the clear. I reckon we'd better hunt up a key for the door and lock the place up. Then if our noble justice of the peace won't come out to hold an inquest — and I doubt a lot if he'll take the trouble — Wolf can send a couple of men over to clean up."

"We headin' for the Arrowhead, now?" Andy asked him. He looked furtively down at the man whom he had doubtless killed and his brown face was solemn.

Curt nodded.

"Yeh. Wolf can send a man on a fresh horse to tell the judge. But I'll bet he'll hold his inquest in town and whitewash it from there. He's not going to straddle a horse if he can help it. Not with that belly of his!"

They found the key and locked the front door, having barred the back and shuttered the windows. Then they rode pretty silently toward Wolf Montague's, following the trail by which they had first come to the store. Chihuahua's eyes shifted mechanically back and forth. He watched the country around them, watched the ground over which they rode. Near dusk, when they had come again to that section in which they had lost the plain trail of the stolen Arrowheads, Curt broke a long silence with spoken thought of that dare-devil cowboy who had ridden from the store toward Ancho.

"If he'd just told us the name of the fellow who was *sending* the word he packed to Short Card," he said gloomily. "Or the name of the man who murdered Ed Showalters. For *I* believe they're one and the same. Here's the way it looks to me: Short Card Mann's a sort of go-between for the gang, in Ancho. He handles the selling of the stuff, passes on orders — all that sort of thing."

"An' the other fellow — the one that sends the messages?" Andy grunted. He seemed anxious to talk of something besides the affair at the store. "He's the Big Auger's straw-boss?"

"Just about! He leads the gang when they're on the ground. We *know* it couldn't have been Mann who killed Showalters, for Mann was with us when that happened. And it certainly wasn't Mann who rustled Wolf Montague's steers. For the word that fellow was carrying to him proves that. So —"

Chihuahua grunted suddenly and reined in. He leaned out of the saddle and put down his long arm. When he straightened he held up a pocket-knife for them to see. Curt stared, then jumped his horse to side Chihuahua. He fairly snatched the pearl-handled knife from Chihuahua's hand. He turned it over in his fingers, then threw back his head and howled triumphantly.

"Got him! Got him where the hair's short! This is Sam Bain's knife — on Wolf Montague's range — in the trail of those rustled steers! I saw Sam buy this knife from Halliday! Look at the deer's head on the handle! So — as certainly as doughnuts have holes in 'em, Sam Bain is Card's straw-boss! He's the one who leads the Trackless Bunch on its jobs. He's the one who murdered Ed Showalters, the one who let his mask slip down so that Ed recognized him and called him by name!"

"Hah!" Chihuahua said softly, grinning. His hand slid down to the butt of his Colt. "She's fi-ine! Now, we're ride in an' we're take these Sam Bain, an' go over to Ancho an' settle Short Card Mann — an' these Tom Card, too, hah?"

"Nary speck!" Curt drawled. "Nothing like that! This knife hangs the deadwood on Sam Bain with us — but only with us! We have to build up a lot better case than this. We have to show the whole Territory, remember. But — now we *know* all that we've suspected, before. We know where to watch. We are dead-certain where these jobs are figured — in Tom Card's Palace. So — it'll be wonderful if, when the gang gets more rope, we won't be able to jerk it, hard! And when we do, I think it's just naturally going to snap a half-hitch around their necks."

"Oh, nobody knows the trouble I see,
Nobody knows but Jesus!
Oh, nobody knows the trouble I see,
Glo-o-ory, Hal-le-lu-u-u-yah!"

Curt sang mournfully to himself as they jogged back to Gurney. He was in a gloomy mood again. For as he considered his problems, pictured Tom Card as boss of the Trackless Bunch — for Curt had no doubt of this identification, now — he had to ask himself: What of Shirley Randolph?

He pictured her in his mind — the slim, shapely figure, dressed always in a style that told volumes of her aristocratic past; the small, dark head that was poised so proudly on round, white neck; the clear-cut features that expressed character, will power, of far more than usual feminine strength.

Unwillingly, Curt conceded to himself that this girl would do things that the ordinary woman would lack courage to do. Her coming to Gurney, at all, was proof of that! Would she, Curt asked himself painfully, ride with a hard-case outlaw gang? He mulled this over, then shrugged to himself.

"Well, she certainly has bucked the Palace games like a man! Never asked 'em to remember that she was a girl. Just stood up and won or lost like anybody . . ."

And, if the tiny bootprint he had found on the scene of the stage robbery had not been Shirley's, whose had it been? Certainly it was unlikely that the Trackless Bunch included among its active members any of Tom Card's dance-hall girls. Curt could think of none among the berouged entertainers who would be an asset to the outlaws. Anyway, how could one explain Shirley's championing of Tom Card, her apparent dislike for the sheriff's office, her mysterious shipments to that New Orleans woman, except by believing what he would have given worlds not to believe?

"Sometimes I's up; sometimes I's do-own;
Oh, yes, Lawd!
Sometimes I's almost to de gro-o-ou-nd!
Oh, yes Lawd!"

Behind him Chihuahua and Andy Allen looked hard at one another. Suddenly, Andy grinned and kneed his horse over to side Chihuahua's. He whispered two words and Chihuahua's thin mouth quivered beneath spike-pointed black mustache; a slow smile spread upon his brown face.

Andy cast gray eyes soulfully upward and began to chant, in a high nasal tenor:

"Oh, would I were a bird!
That I might fly to thee,
An' breathe a lovin' word,
To thee so far away;
My heart would beat with joy,
To see thee once again —

"Trouble with them blame' one-sided songs," Andy stopped to remark loudly to Chihuahua, "they just tell what the hairpin's pinin' for, or the girl. Now, the chances are, the other party — he or she — ain't givin' a hoot about the love-sickness of the li'l' songbird. Don't you reckon so, Chihuahua?"

"Me, I'm think she's sound like fine sense," Chihuahua nodded solemnly.

And they fell into a long discussion of ladies and gentlemen who had been left behind by wandering lovers. They decided that it was rather cool of the wandering ones to expect the abandoned ones to wait meekly at home until the wanderers saw fit to return. They went further — with much detail — and agreed that a man in love was a peculiar sort of animal at best — as bad

as a cow that had eaten loco weed, Chihuahua thought, and Andy accepted this il-
lustration without argument.

Curt gritted his teeth and tried to think,
while the two cheerful voices behind him
went into the gloomy details of all the love
affairs they had ever seen or heard about.
An uneasy suspicion of the reason for all
this consideration of love and lovers was in
Curt's mind, but he thought of no way to
check it. Too, with the fatuity of the lover,
he could not see how anyone might have
guessed his condition. But at last he turned
sourly in the saddle:

"If you can jar loose from that sewing
circle without straining yourselves, suppose
we speed up a little bit? We want to get to
town before we have to get younger
horses . . ."

"Just what we was thinkin', me an' Chihuahua!" Andy agreed enthusiastically. "But
we see you was studyin' somethin' sad an'
metaphorical an' we figured maybe you had
an infectious reason for crawling along. We
never wanted to bust right in on — well,
whatever it *was* you was a-mullin' over, or
we'd said somethin' before this."

But Curt, with a heartfelt oath, had set
spurs to the buckskin and was racing off.
Nor did they catch up with him again until

the twin rows of buildings that fenced Gurney's main street were plain ahead. This was not altogether due to the superiority of the buckskin. Curt had the advantage in that Andy and Chihuahua rolled somewhat in the saddle as they rode and must now and then let the bridle-reins sag while they held their hands to their sides.

Curt left Chihuahua and Andy in the office while he went out to talk with Halliday about affairs in general. He found the cheerful, red-faced storekeeper empty of any particular news, but intensely interested in the evidence that had been dug up on Wolf Montague's range. For with Halliday, Curt was entirely frank.

"It'd certainly clear up everything, now wouldn't it!" cried Halliday. "Tom Card as the big boss. Bain an' this-here Short Card Mann for deputies . . . Curt, she certainly looks like we need a bale of rope ag'in! You can't handle a deal like this single-handed, son!"

"It'll probably come to where I have to deputize a bunch of you," Curt nodded thoughtfully. "But I don't want to come out in the open right now — it'd tip my hand to 'em and give 'em a chance to play their cards some other way. Wonder what they're figuring for the next job . . ."

"God knows!" shrugged the storekeeper piously. "Or the Devil! You reckon the Bunch is all hangin' out in Ancho?"

"No-o, I reckon Bain keeps some of the best on the Lazy B. I've thought a time or two that those punchers of his are sort of more than average hard-case. He keeps a half-dozen, you know. That looks queer, on a two-by-four outfit like that, when Bain and one cowboy wouldn't be strained doing the work. The rest of the Bunch would be in and around Ancho, with Short Card Mann bossing 'em, waiting for orders from Card, through Sam Bain."

"Kind of funny, to me," Halliday drawled thoughtfully, "that Sam Bain'd be ridin' point in that bunch . . . You set the town laughin' at him, Curt. Mornin' after your showdown with him, he shot that worthless Binjie Hull in the Palace. I reckon Hull, he figured Bain was proved easy enough for him to run a shady on. But Bain pulled right explosive, I gather. Hull was damn' lucky he never collected more'n two bullets through his right shoulder."

"No doubt in my mind that Bain is Card's right bower," Curt said thoughtfully. "Maybe I could have wondered if that pearl-handled knife of his might not have got into the trail of the rustled steers in some way that wasn't connected with the rustling. But, you see, Halliday, when I was hunting trouble with him, I mentioned the knife he'd bought to cut ears with. And Bain turned green! For *he* knew he'd lost that knife somewhere on the ground of something shady!"

He shook his head frowningly.

"As for his handling a hardcase outfit — my running a sandy on him wouldn't prove that he takes everything lying down. You noticed that he climbed Binjie Hull soon enough. No-o, it's a funny business, this being a tough hairpin; somebody's got the Indian sign on almost every gun-fighter. It happens that I've got it on Bain. The fact that he *might* collect my scalp, if he could make himself pull and whang away, don't signify a damn. He just can't make the grade with me. But it's possible that he's got every man under him bluffed to a fare-you-well."

He slid down from the counter and tapped the butts of his Colts, where they hung in the John Wesley Hardin holster-vest. Halliday grinned slightly.

"Bain ain't in town — if that's what you're thinkin' about —"

"He's not? Well," Curt shrugged indifferently, "it's just as well, maybe. I was going to invite him to rattle his hocks. I'm tired of all this shooting back and forth. If Bain and Binjie Hull pine to wipe out each other, that's fine. But I'm going to make 'em get out of town to do the job, where they can't maybe kill somebody worth something."

He wandered out. Automatically, he turned up street toward the Palace. But he could not see, through Tom Card's office window, the girl's figure. So he went on and found himself standing presently — and without knowing just how he came to be there — in the entry hall of Mrs. Sheehan's hotel.

"An' if it's dinner you're after" — this was a grim voice from the stairway — "I would be remindin' you that my hours for dinner is from twelve noon till one-thirty!"

Curt turned to face the vast and belligerent Mrs. Sheehan. He shrugged embarrassedly.

"No, no! I've had dinner, already!" he protested quickly. "I — I want —"

"Yes?" prompted Mrs. Sheehan. "Yes? You're wantin' —"

But Curt had lost his voice. Just in time, too, he thought. For he had been on the verge of blurting out exactly what he wanted — Shirley Randolph. He stood dumbly staring at his extended boot-toe. Mrs. Sheehan came down the stairs with the deliberation of movement enforced by her bulk. She leaned thick, red arms upon the stair-rail and regarded him entirely without favor.

"You were sayin'?"

"I — Nothing, Mrs. Sheehan. I — I guess I'll have to be going."

Steadily, the Irishwoman regarded him for a long moment, while he moved his feet awkwardly. Into her little blue eyes crept a faint gleam of amusement, although her broad, red face remained grimly blank of expression.

"You wanted Miss Shirley!" she nodded. "The gall of the likes of you cowboys! Worryin' a girl like her, as if she was no more than one of them painted hussies of Tom Card's!"

"Worrying her!" Curt cried amazedly, staring. "I only wish I could think I'd ever worried her!"

"You *have* worried her!" Mrs. Sheehan declared. "In my own dinin'-room, one mornin', at breakfast-time, it was. Did I not hear you with my own ears!"

"You were listening?" Curt cried, horror-stricken at thought of what she had overheard that morning. "Why — Why — I thought you were upstairs!"

"An' what else would I be doin' but listenin'! Will Teresa Sheehan stand by idle when the likes of you is frettin' a helpless child?"

"Then," said Curt grimly, "if you listened, you ought to know that you aren't worrying a bit more about her — while she's down there in that hole of Tom Card's — than I am! Not half as much! A girl like that, working in that holdup's gambling-house!"

Mrs. Sheehan seemed about to say something, clamped her wide mouth firmly shut, hesitated, and then her face softened.

"You needn't give yourself trouble about that," she told him. "Tom Card well knows what would happen did so much as one motion of his disturb that girl."

"I don't care about that!" Curt cried stubbornly. "It's no place for her — or for any nice girl. I can't talk to her about it. But you can, Mrs. Sheehan. And you ought to make her see it. Listen! I've got some money in the bank. Around five thousand dollars. If you could give it to her, some way, not letting her know where it came from, couldn't she go back home?"

"Well!" Mrs. Sheehan cried explosively. "If you're not a seven days' wonder! An' do you think she'd take the money? An' why should you be givin' her money, anyway?"

"I'd give her anything in the world I had. I'd even rather never see her again than see her every day in that hole of Card's, with Card and Bain grinning and hanging around her! And as for getting the money to her, you could say it was left her by some uncle or aunt or something and she'd never know the difference. Not till she was gone from Gurney, anyhow."

"You talk like a born idiot! I couldn't do it — even if I wanted to. An' I'm not helpin' you, Curt Thompson, to put that child in a hole."

"I'm not putting her in a hole! I" — he stopped and met her eyes levelly, all embarrassment gone — "I think enough of her to give her anything I own. And with no strings tied to the giving. I may be a queer person, but I wouldn't marry that girl if she *begged* me, unless I was dead certain that she wanted me as much as I want her. I wouldn't *touch* her, unless she wanted me to. That's how I feel about her."

"Ve-ry pret-ty!" Mrs. Sheehan said scornfully. "But not one word in three do I believe of all that fine speech. You're like the rest of the cowboys — you want her because she's lovely; an' maybe because she's hard to get. An' you'd take her, by fair or by foul, any way you could. Don't tell me otherwise! An' — how of Marie Young? Tell me you're not playin' for both Miss

269

Shirley an' Marie Young. Try to tell me you ain't!"

"Marie Young?" Curt cried, staring. "Playing for Marie — The trouble with *you*, Mrs. Teresa Sheehan, is that you're too meddlesome! You're like most women — though I hadn't believed that, before! You can't let a man tip his hat to a girl but you're making a match. And if you can't figure a marriage, you have to figure something elese. Marie Young is a nice girl. I like her. But I no more think about her in any other way than she thinks about me."

"Yeh?" Mrs. Sheehan drawled, but watching him narrowly.

"Yeh! For that matter, she's as bad as you are, about matchmaking of the mind. Always talking to me about Shirley; always telling me if she's seen me ride into town with her, or speak to her on the street. But she's a nice girl. She's more than that! She's a *person.* About this money —"

"It can't be done, Curt. It just can't be done!"

"Why can't it be done? You ought to be able to do it without making her suspicious. It certainly wouldn't be any harder than — getting imaginary lawsuit papers to Mrs. Marsden in New Orleans!"

"Oh! Oh, so somebody else has been

270

listenin' at doors, has he? An' that put notions in your head . . ."

Curt faced her defiantly — and cheerfully.

"You didn't bother to have a good look in
the dining-room, that morning, before you
gave Bobo Johnny the package. Or you'd
have seen me. Certainly! I heard the whole
conversation. More than that — I saw the
package in the express office at Ancho,
relayed by your sister to Mrs. Aimee Marsden in New Orleans."

"Just — accidental?"

"Just by pure accident! I was hunting
evidence about my pet gang and the agent
over there had the packages piled on the
floor. I saw yours — *hers* — in the heap.
Now, Mrs. Sheehan! You've got to listen to
me. We both want to help her. She can't
stay in the Palace. You know it as well as I
do. If she stays —"

He thought of that little bootprint on the
trail and he faced her strainedly, hands outflung.

"There's just no telling what may happen.
Let's get her out. Figure a way to take this
money and get it into her hands. It's nothing to me, anyway! What's money to a
rambling saddle tramp? Something to blow.
That's all. It's rewards. I collected 'em and
I banked 'em. Five thousand will help her

271

get away — Ah, Mrs. Sheehan! You've got to do it? You can talk all you're minded to, about Tom Card being afraid to bother her. But he's not! He's the slickest scoundrel in the Territory today. She's no match for him. Neither are you."

"He's wantin' to marry her . . ."

She was watching him narrowly, as if she analyzed him feature by feature.

"What would you say to that?"

"I'd say" — Curt's drawl was slow and thick — "that it's still all wrong! I would cheerfully go down and kill him before he could do it. And that's not just because — *I* want her. It's because I know Tom Card from way back. She'd ruin her life, marrying Card. I've seen his kind before, between Texas and Milk River. I know what they are — with brains, education, and all, running away from something back home — sitting in the middle of their schemes like a spider in a web. He's the slickest thing in the Territory, Mrs. Sheehan, as I said a minute ago. But this time the case will be tried — if it goes to trial — before Old Judge Colt. And I'll give him as near ten contrary verdicts as I have the time!"

He paused, out of breath. Mrs. Sheehan was still watching him with that attitude of intensity. She seemed suddenly to make up her mind. For her broad, hard face was wonderfully softened by a smile.

"My son, I'm believin' that you're a good boy!" she said quickly. "So much do I bank on that opinion that I'm goin' to break my promise to Miss Shirley. I'm goin' to tell you the truth about that girl.

"There was a fine old family in New Orleans, Curt; one of the finest in all Louisiana. They had been rich; they was a proud, headstrong line. An' when the father died, it was little but their fine blood an' their pride that they was left with, after his debts was paid.

"There was the mother an' two girls — Shirley bein' the oldest an' her not yet twenty. The other will be fourteen, about. An' there was a lawyer, a rich man of a family as old an' proud even as the Marsdens. An' *he* wanted to marry Shirley . . .

"But she had no love for him an' when he worried her past endurance, with talk of marryin' him an' lettin' him help her family, she pawned the bits of jewelry she had. She told nobody what she was doin'. She just started for this Territory, to find a cousin of her father's, who was said to have a ranch out here. I told you that these Marsdens were a stiff-necked breed!"

"She asked me about him — that day on

the stage!" Curt nodded. "Villiers, she called him."

"But no cousin could she find. You know how men move this way an' that, out here. An' here she was! She had no money to go farther an' back home — to marry that lawyer — she would *not* go! So she stayed here in Gurney. The darlin'! with her chin set hard like a man's.

"Tom Card was soft-spoken. He give her work in the office. An' half of the first week's wages ever she drew she held in her hand an' looked past Tom Card at the faro-bank:

" 'Is it against house-rules for me to play that game?' she says to Tom Card, an' he grins at her.

" 'Play as you like!' says he. 'An', though it's my own game you're buckin', I wish you luck!' he says.

"So out she marches an' stands beside the men, with that Marsden chin set hard. An' she loses a bit an' wins a bit, but comes off at the last with about a hundred dollars. She wanted to send it to her mother. But she wanted to keep who an' what she was a secret, here. So at last, she told me the tale I'm tellin' you. Since then, I have helped her to ship her winnin's back to New Orleans."

"Do you reckon Card known any of this?" Curt asked frowningly.

"He's a deep'n. Maybe he's guessed some. Sure, it's little of what Tom Card knows that ever shows in his face. But I think he *knows* nothin'. A part he might guess, from the mere look of Shirley. But now he thinks he's in love with her — an' I think it small wonder!

"Now, Curt, my son! I'm tellin' you all this because you've stumbled onto a part of it already. But, too, I felt like tellin' you because I believe you *do* love her — the way she deserves to be loved. You'll understand much, now, about her queer ways. An' you'll not be makin' mistakes you might have made, else. Two things I would impress upon you — if you would not lose her quite:

"Say nothin', hint nothin', of what I've told you. An' leave that five thousand in the bank, my son! Forget that you'd like to give it to her. One day, maybe —— Well, there's lots of things a young married man can do with five thousand dollars. Now, be off with you! But you remember what I've told you! 'Specially, remember what I've warned you!"

Curt went almost blindly out. He was puzzling what the harsh-faced, kind-hearted old Irishwoman had told him. But, even though

Shirley's story explained much that had puzzled him, it but increased the suspicion that had been hanging over her since his first glimpse of the bootprint in the dust of the stage road.

Desperately, she needed money to send to her family. And Curt had seen too many dollars slip from his own hands at gambling to believe that she could win steadily enough to make regular shipments of money to her mother. A proud, stiff-necked family, the Marsdens . . . Certainly, she was typical of them! A girl who could and would step out of the sheltered life she must have led, in such a town as New Orleans; who would come all alone into the savage Territory; who would bravely begin, not only to support herself, but support her family . . . Curt nodded slowly, unwillingly.

"If I were in her fix and I couldn't do anything else, *I'd* stick up a stage!" he told himself grimly. "I'd pick me out a bullion shipment or a money shipment to some bank and I'm afraid I'd borrow off the owners!"

And there came to him an odd little thrill of pride as he thought of the girl who accepted the lot commonly considered a man's, and played out her hand so nervily. For all that she seemed so hopelessly out of

276

his reach, he could not help feeling a sort of possessive pride in her.

He went absently on, until, when a shadow fell across his path, automatically he looked up.

Chapter X

Shirley had halted to stand staring incredulously at him. One slim hand was at her throat. She was very white, Curt noted. He met her stare frowningly.

"I — I thought you had gone! I — *heard* that you had gone," she said in a low voice.

Curt's puzzled frown deepened. He had never seen her so moved, so — shaken. He shrugged.

"I did go. We just got back a little while ago," he explained, with some surprise. "The way things are going nowadays, the sheriff's office is slated to eat a good many meals away from Gurney, and give a good many horseback decisions."

"I don't understand. You say you went, but — came back?"

"Why, yes. Just an ordinary little trip. The kind that's been pretty common, of late. We went out — Chihuahua and Andy with me — with Wolf Montague. He's the man who owns the Arrowhead outfit; the man who almost got killed in the Palace when that house man, Harry *Como se Llama,* was shot the other night. Montague had lost some steers to our Trackless Bunch. We followed the rustlers' trail. But —"

He stopped himself suddenly. She waited. With artful carelessness he fumbled for tobacco and papers.

"We managed to settle in our own minds, pretty well, that it was a Trackless Bunch job."

"But —" She hesitated, and Curt, watching her, found himself fascinated by the way tendrils of her dusky hair were stirred at the nape of her slim neck by the gentle spring breeze. And held, too, by the play of soft color in her clear face, coming and going.

"But you're back, now? You're going to stay?"

Something about her steady regard of him — that was almost strained — and the brittle tenseness of her tone brought Curt's wandering thoughts back. He looked curiously at her.

"Back to stay?" he repeated slowly. "Why — I suppose so. Until the next call comes. The Sheriff of Gurney is like a fire horse — apt to be called out just any time. Why?"

"Oh —" She checked herself, lifted a

shoulder and let it sag. "I — I suppose I'm just curious. That's said to be a woman's privilege."

But while he studied her and puzzled the oddities of her manner today, he knew very well that no idle curiosity had prompted those questions. She was not that kind. And suddenly — for no reason that he could name — he thought of those two warnings he had received, that Texas men were coming fast on his trail; that he had best leave Gurney. His hand went instinctively to the pocket that held the scrap of brown paper with the first warning scrawled upon it, the envelope with the second warning printed upon its flap.

Almost, his fingers went into the pocket to pull them out. But she was watching him and he caught himself, made the jerky movement a natural gesture that ended with hand dropping. He drew in cigarette smoke and let it out gently.

But he was thinking furiously about the messages — and about her. She *must* know of the warnings! If, on the trail to the Arrowhead, an ambush had been planned — and she had known of it — he might have interpreted her surprise as being caused by his return alive. But that could not be!

"She'd never be party to a dirty job of

bushwhacking such as Card and Bain hand out," he told himself. "She's not that kind. I couldn't believe that of her if she told me it herself. Anyhow, even if I could believe it — there wasn't any such bushwhacking. All the odds and ends that happened just jumped out from behind the bushes as accidents."

No . . . She could not know of anything like that. But she must know of the warnings. And certainty of her knowledge of even that much had power to infuriate him. She knew of the attempts to scare him away from Gurney; to frighten him off the trail of this gang. She knew of them and must have expected him to receive them at face value. She must have believed that he had run away.

A slow rage rose in him, at this further proof of her closeness to Tom Card, this additional token of her knowledge of all the schemes of the gambler — if not actually of the Trackless Bunch and its jobs.

In that moment he could have killed Card smilingly. But his anger was a mixed emotion. For he felt also pity for this blind, wilful girl, whose necessities had pushed her into such a situation, into such company. That pity made him very careful, now.

"Shirley —" he began slowly, awkwardly

— then stopped.

For Mrs. Sheehan had warned him against betraying knowledge of the girl's past history, her present troubles. And Curt conceded that the shrewd, kindly old Irishwoman was correct in her belief that Shirley would resent his knowledge of her problems.

"Shirley," he began again, and hunted for the words he wanted, "why do you — oh, stay in Gurney, in the Territory? Do you really like working — even keeping books — in a gambling-joint? It — You're as out of place, there —"

"I like the Territory," she said evasively, without meeting his eyes. "I like the space of it. As one of the cowboys said the other day — the world's big in this country! I like it. And — But, let's don't discuss it!"

"Let's don't discuss it!" Curt said savagely. "You come into our country, into our lives, and you do and say anything you're minded to. Then, when we speak to you, all *you* need to say is: 'Let's don't discuss it!' That's supposed to put us in our places."

He moved his shoulders angrily and glared at her.

"I say: Let's *do* discuss it! You haven't a bit of business in that dive! You haven't a bit of business in Gurney, in the Territory, if you have to stick in Tom Card's joint!

Shirley" — his voice softened — "you've pushed me around a lot. You've backed and filled and managed to tell me some pretty hard things. But, in spite of all that, you know — I *know* you know! — that I want to help you. Why, I'd do just about anything you asked, or I could think of without your asking, to help you. Anything — any time — anyhow! So, why do you have to push me away as if you're afraid you might speak decently to me? Why won't you let me help you? There's no string tied to my help. Why don't you —"

"I said — *let's* don't discuss it! I mean that. I don't need any help from you — or from anyone else! And my affairs are mine only. Why I stay here, keep books for Tom Card, is my business. I told you — I had to tell you — not to mistake casual friendliness for something else. Must I tell you that every time we meet?"

Facing her stony calm, he went suddenly very red beneath bronzed skin. He nodded. His mouth was grimly set, his eyes were smoky.

"Certainly, you won't have to again!" he assured her in thick, furious drawl.

He went past her and on down the street without looking back. The Palace loomed ahead of him. But his shifting stare found

Marie Young's door. He stopped and faced that way. Halliday, coming along the sidewalk from the Star, called to him cheerfully. Curt answered his friend with an absent grunt and stepped off the sidewalk to cross the street.

Grimly, Curt asked himself why he should play the fool any longer. Everyone was bent on throwing Marie Young into his arms — why not put out his arms? He went fast toward her door. Why be a damned fool? Marie Young was the prettiest, the most desirable, woman he had ever met — except Shirley Randolph — Shirley Marsden. And Shirley was definitely beyond him. She had played — no, he admitted, she had not led him on with any hopes. She *had* acted as if she liked to be in his arms, as if she meant surrender when she lifted her mouth to his. But — whatever motive she had owned, that was definitely past and done with. And ahead of him was Marie Young.

"She's never given me a reason in the world to believe that she thinks about me except in a sort of sister-brother way," he thought. "But — maybe I can change that. I like her a lot. She's a real person. Any man could be proud to walk down the aisle with her. *'Sta bueno!* Mr. Thompson. You'll be a damn' fool no longer!"

He stopped in the door and looked frowningly into the pleasantly dusky interior of the store. Marie Young, working at a counter in the back, faced him. His eyes refocussed to the dim light and he saw her, small, shapely, amazingly pretty.

"I'll do it!" he said grimly. "I'll do it this very day, too."

"Why — Curt!" the girl said and came toward him, smiling.

"Hello, *bonita!*" he answered. "Here I am, back again. The only place I seem to go first, when I come back to town, is the office. Then here."

"Kind sir!" she cried. "The man's paying me compliments! Why, Curt — you haven't looked at life through the bottom of a bottle? I never knew you so pleasant!"

"I'm just a pleasant person," he said carefully, resurrecting the habit of what he liked to call his "frivolous youth." "Hadn't you noticed the lots and lots of wonderful points about me, that make me stand out from the mine-run of men?"

"No-o, I can't say that I have. And what have you done with my faithful squire, Andy? He's not like his employer. *He* says pretty things and means them."

"And here I stand before you, the very soul of Truth! But that's the way it goes. A young squirt like Andy —"

"He's not a young squirt! You're not over a couple of years older and — Where did you send him?"

Curt smiled at her, but he was puzzling the difficulty found in getting where he had intended to get. Here he had come in, all ready to tell her that he wanted to marry her, and she seemed to be utterly blind to his advances.

"Nothing — special," he said carelessly. "He'll be around later on. Unless I figure him a good, long job."

"Well, then, you'll have to eat his apple pie. There's some cream for it. Houck's cow is fresh and I was first to hear about it. So I get a half-gallon, a day. That's one thing I don't like about the Territory —"

"No milk," Curt nodded absently. "It's like that all over the cow-country. Ten thousand head of cattle mean never a drop of milk. Where-at's this apple pie, and is it really good?"

"Good? I think I'll not offer you any. Andy never makes such remarks about my pies!"

"I just *asked* you! There must be something peculiar about it, else you wouldn't be so touchy over a civil question. Lead me to it and I'll give it a really expert opinion. Andy's not qualified for serious work like this. Not that I say anything against him. He's a nice boy. One of these days he's going to grow into a fine man. And his wife'll have me to thank for bringing him up properly."

"You!" she said scornfully. "A bad influence, more likely. What Andy needs is a firm feminine hand on the reins."

"I'll tell him! But meanwhile, why all the hesitation about showing me the pie? Where's Pancho? He can tend bar —"

She called the Mexican boy and led the way into her living-quarters. Curt looked appreciatively about the sitting-room. There was no other room in Gurney like it, so far as he knew. The rough-plastered 'dobe walls had been tinted buff and the floor painted. Navajo blankets, in rug-size, with colorful prints well-framed, made it a cheerful, livable room.

"Want to eat in the kitchen?"

Curt nodded and followed her into the equally unusual — in Gurney — room she had partitioned off the store's rear. He found a green willow rocker and stretched his legs comfortably. As she moved about getting a plate and cutting the big pie, he had opportunity to verify his first opinion of her. She was a girl to set any reasonable man's pulses hammering. She turned and

286

caught him staring at her. A quick flush came to her smooth cheeks, then she turned away and asked calmly:

"Did you find those Arrowhead steers?"

"Yes, for a wonder. But it was by pure accident."

"And — the rustlers?"

He watched her as she turned to face him. She was troubled, he saw. Lightness had gone from her face and the hand that held the knife shook.

"We ran onto them. Else we'd never have found the steers. It was pretty messy business. I'd rather not talk about it."

She brought the plate with a quarter-pie on it to the end of her kitchen table. He shifted the rocker and she perched herself on the table's end. It came to Curt to wonder if she knew that the position showed to advantage the lithe curves of her slim body. But she looked down at him seriously.

"What's going to be the end of it all, Curt?" she asked him. "Can you really hope to wipe out this — Trackless Bunch?"

"I think so," he nodded, when he had swallowed his first bite of pie. "We're whittling 'em down and, too, getting a line on 'em. Yes, I think we'll wipe 'em out. Then — young Andy will go back to Los Alamos; Smoky Cole will come back to the sheriff's office; and I'll get me a bunch of cows and start an outfit over beyond the Soldados. And —"

He looked thoughtfully at her and again she flushed.

"Andy's having lots of fun, isn't he?" she said quickly.

"Too much — by the way you keep harping on him! And he oughtn't to be getting notions. He's too young, for one thing. *You* could wrap him around your finger and he'd never know you were doing it. Now, I'm lots more experienced — lots wiser. *I* can beg pies from you and be around your general loveliness and keep my head. It won't be pie-making that I'll consider when I come hunting a wife. Though, of course, pie like this will be considered in your favor!"

"My goodness! Is this a proposal from the lady-shy Mr. Thompson?"

"Yes," was on the tip of his tongue. He thought that it would be amazingly easy to say it, then get up and scoop her from the table into his arms. And he had come in to make love to her. He wondered why he only smiled at her and finished the pie. She seemed to wait, still smiling faintly.

He made a cigarette and she got a match from the band of his hat, flicked the head expertly against her thumbnail and leaned to set the flame against cigarette-end. He put up a hand to catch her wrist and lifted it. He drew in a cloud of smoke and continued to hold her wrist.

"If you're done —" she began in a shaky voice, and stopped. She was furiously red, now, did not meet his eyes.

He got up and stood close beside her. His hand, or hers, began to tremble. And from the store a voice came, carrying clearly enough to them, despite distance and intervening doors.

"Mrs. Young!" Shirley called. "Busy? I've a problem —"

Curt let go Marie's wrist. She was staring at the door into the sitting-room. Curt frowned slightly. It seemed to him that he had heard her swear softly.

"Go sell her some pins," he said — and somehow was relieved. "I'll disappear through the back door."

Slowly, very slowly, she nodded.

"Yes, Miss Randolph," she answered Shirley. " 'Bye, Curt!"

Curt stalked into the office and flung his hat in a corner. Andy and Chihuahua sat comfortably in rickety, rawhide-bottomed chairs tilted against the wall. When Curt sat down and began to make a cigarette, they looked eloquently, one at the other.

"Me, I'm think them gambler, she's one funny hairpin," Chihuahua remarked pensively.

Suspiciously, Curt eyed him sidelong. Chihuahua was staring at the wall.

"One time, in El Paso, I'm gamble a little in them Criterion Saloon. I'm see lots of them gambler around. Some will be them tinhorn, but not all. I'm see one *big* gambler. She's just walk around an' watch them game. Me, I'm ask one fellow w'at's these fellow's name. She's say these gambler is s'pose' to be them silent partner in the Criterion, but w'at's his name, she's forget."

He shifted in the chair and looked thoughtfully at Curt.

"Me, I'm go back to them Criterion one other night. I'm see these gambler again. An' I'm hear his name. But I'm forgit him. Well, like I'm say, these gambler, she's them funny hairpin. Jump around all time, like them flea. One time you're see him in El Paso, nex' time, mabbe she's hang out in — Gurney . . ."

Curt straightened, frowning at Chihuahua, who gazed seraphically at the far wall.

"What do you mean?" demanded Curt.

"Me? W'at — *quién sabe? Quién sabe?* One time here in Gurney, I'm see them big gambler w'at's walk around them Criterion in El Paso. An' I'm remember, quick w'at's them name I'm hear — Tom Card!"

"El Paso, huh?" grunted Curt, with eyes flaming. "So that's where he hails from, is it? Well!"

He slumped in his chair for a while and Chihuahua and Andy watched him silently. After a time he straightened and looked at them:

"Andy," he drawled — and his tone was belied by the smoky darkness of his eyes — "how you feel, boy? Rheumatics better? Corporosity segatuate all right?"

"Um, I reckon," Andy nodded, watching him. "Of course, I never *will* be the man I was before my basilicus got infected an' gravitation set in. What's up the lil'l' old sleeve?"

"I thought maybe we could hobble your stirrups and maybe strap a slicker over your legs and you'd be able to stick in the kak from here to Ancho. I think I want to send a telegram. Yes, sir! A telegram to El Paso. For it runs in my mind that the city marshal down there might *just* possibly be able to give us some information about Tom Card. Maybe about Sam Bain, too."

"Can happen!" Andy nodded enthusiastically. His chair came down upon four legs with a thump. "An' if Card an' Bain *was* to be wanted down there for somethin' — man! Wouldn't that be theosophical?"

"Dark'll be soon," Curt said thoughtfully. "Don't start before supper. The way things are going around here, the minute one of us sticks his head out of the door it's just about compulsory for somebody to shake the loads out of a cutter in his direction."

They went to supper at Mrs. Sheehan's. Shirley was at the long table. She looked blankly at Curt, smiled politely when Chihuahua bowed and Andy nodded. Then she kept her eyes upon her plate — or showed more attention to Bobo Johnny the shotgun messenger than he was used to, or desired.

Curt ate as rapidly as possible, but neither Andy nor Chihuahua could be hurried by his example. Andy looked at Curt's grim face, then at Shirley's preoccupied expression.

"Why, Curt!" he said, in a pained voice. "You hadn't ought to gullup your meals that way. That's probably what's wrong with you, boy! You set down an' look sour at grubpile an' then you get up an' go out an' shoot people! Why'n't you do like Chihuahua an' me?"

Curt snarled at him wordlessly and continued to eat steadily. Andy shook his head and sighed dolefully.

"I'm glad I'm goin' out to Alamos tomorrow," he said mendaciously. "Maybe some of the Palace bums'll shoot me in the back while I'm on the road, but that'll be better'n havin' to work for the Sad Sheriff of Gurney. You better come along with me, Chihuahua, an' get shot an' put out of your misery."

Chihuahua laughed. His blue eyes shuttled to Curt, then to the girl's stony face. Shirley betrayed by no change of expression that she had heard Andy's thrust at Tom Card's henchmen, but a flush marked her cheekbones.

"W'y," Chihuahua said amusedly, "if two of us, we're go together, they will not trouble us, Andy. They will never stand to more than them one man."

Curt pushed back his chair and stood up. Andy sighed again, a troubled sound.

"No use talkin' to him, Chihuahua," he said gloomily. "Or settin' him a ambiguous example, even. Maybe folks in his condition just can't be reasoned with. Probably he don't like the company, too . . ."

Curt went sulkily out of the dining-room and down to Halliday's. He sat with the storekeeper for a while, grunting in reply to Halliday's talk. Andy and Chihuahua came by, a quarter-hour later. They seemed very happy. They were laughing and shouldering each other toward the sidewalk's edge. They stopped and looked into the store, looked at Curt, then at each other. Simultaneously, they burst into whoops. Halliday grinned.

"Your young deputies, they seem mightily worked up about somethin', Curt," he said.

"Ah — they been raising hell up at Sheehan's," Curt shrugged. "About ready, Andy?"

"Yeh. But you ought've stayed, Curt. Did Chihuahua have his back hair combed! Ah, me! I was sorry for him!"

"Me?" Chihuahua cried. "W'y — Andy! She's comb *your* scalp; she's not speak with me!"

"Well . . ." Andy conceded judicially, "maybe it was *both* of us that caught it, after you left. She never liked us sayin' that the Palace had bums in it, or even folks that'd take a shot at a man's back. An' she never found a thing funny about us hoorahin' you. In fact, she pointed out how different you was to us; an' she showed us how we was wrong about you: *we* thought you was sulkin' about somethin' an she says, no! You just show better manners than us; *you* don't like Tom Card an' the Palace crowd, but you don't set around a table an' pass dis —

dis — disparagin' remarks when Card ain't there!"

"Ah!" Curt said angrily. But he could not help looking steadily at Andy, any more than he could help feeling an odd jump of pulses. "She never said any such thing! It's time we got started. You won't carry any telegram. But when you get to Ancho, you'll have to use some of the gift of gab of yours on the telegraph operator. Look him over; size him up. If you think you can trust him, put your cards on the table. Get him to send your wire to the sheriff and the city marshal at El Paso, asking what's known down there about Card and Bain. And make it plain we want it all kept quiet."

Andy nodded.

"Card's known by name. But I might describe Bain, in case he used another name down there?"

"Good idea: Word your telegram about like this:

REQUEST INFORMATION EL PASO RECORD TOM CARD, GAMBLER, AND SAM BAIN, SIX FEET TALL, DARK SKIN, DARK EYES, NARROW FACE, WALKS SHUFFLING. IF WANTED EL PASO PLEASE NOTIFY ME.

Sign my name and title."

Andy nodded and repeated the words. They went out of Halliday's together. On the street, they parted. Curt and Chihuahua went toward the Palace, while Andy slipped between two buildings to head for the sheriff's corral.

The Palace was busy, tonight. But there was nothing unusual to be seen. Curt looked around, but restlessness had him. He grunted briefly to Chihuahua:

"I'll be wandering. You keep your eyes open, too, huh?"

"If anything, she's pop, I'm glad to help somebody to git sick," Chihuahua nodded, grinning. "Oh, Curt . . . Before you're go . . . Miss Shirley, she's *really* say w'at Andy's tell you she's say . . . Me, I'm think you're like to know. An', too, I'm think that she's one girl w'at's try ver' hard to keep from her face w'at she's have — *here . . .*"

He slapped his chest softly. His brown face was very grave. Curt frowned at him, then shrugged.

"She's certainly having lots of luck doing it, too!" he said grimly. "But — thanks, Chihuahua."

He went along the street until he came to the rising slope at the edge of town. Viewed from here, when he turned, Gurney appeared in the moonless darkness like a twinkling necklace flung carelessly down across the mesa on which the county seat had been built. On each side of the main street the lights of store and saloon and home shone yellow through the windows. Occasionally, while he watched, a light was dimmed as someone passed before a window, then gleamed again as the passer-by went on.

Curt leaned against Alarcon's big *bodega* and stared gloomily along the street, kicking the warehouse's 'dobe wall absently. Andy was already riding for Ancho. Curt hoped that the telegraph operator would be trustworthy; that there would be no leakage concerning the exchange of telegrams to such Ancho figures as Short Card Mann.

For the moment, he thought of nothing else that he could do. He wished that some action were possible, in his present mood. He would have welcomed a battle with his Trackless Bunch. But, to the best of his knowledge, Gurney held but one of them tonight — Tom Card. Bain was somewhere else — out at the Lazy B, possibly. None of his hard-case riders were in town, either.

Curt came back down the street and prowled about the rear of the buildings on the main street. Chihuahua, he knew, would be "riding herd" on the town, drifting from place to place, a smiling Bearer of the Winchester and Wearer of the Star. So he was free to wander as he liked. He was loafing in the shadow of a darkened store-porch on the main street when a lean horseman came *clop-clopping* into town. Curt, squatting against the front wall of the store, was invisible, but the rider was silhouetted against the light from a window on the other side of the street.

He showed as a tall cowboy, sitting easily in the saddle. There was a suggestion of youth about the erectness of his posture. His horse moved draggingly, as if Gurney marked the end of a long ride. The man went up on the street and halted before the Palace. Curt watched the lean figure swing down, tie his horse, then stretch luxuriously before he went at awkward horseman's gait inside the saloon.

Time passed. Curt saw Chihuahua sauntering up the opposite side of the street, moving, for all his high-heeled boots, as silently as a great cat. As Chihuahua disappeared into the Star Saloon, competitor of the Palace, a pistol-shot sounded dully. Curt turned his head to listen. After a perceptible interval of seconds, a second shot came.

Curt was on his feet with a single tigerish motion. As he leaped from the porch, Chihuahua came slipping out of the door of the Star. They met before the Palace and went inside together. The bar-tender jerked his head toward the door into the dance-hall. It was jammed with men who had been drinking, but not yet had any of these thoroughly informed citizens of the Territory gone rushing in where a third shot might sound with disastrous results to the over-curious.

Curt and Chihuahua pushed through them. The orchestra — at the far end of the dance-hall — sat with fiddles on their knees and the piano-player had turned to face down the room. The bartender, at the little bar just inside the door leading to the bar-room, turned a white face upon Curt and Chihuahua.

" 'Twas outside!" he gasped. "A .45 slug come tearin' through the window, gents. Right over my head! Looky!"

He indicated the little window high up in the 'dobe end wall of the building. The bullet had ranged through the sashless opening to go into the ceiling and the dirt-covered roof of the place.

Curt wasted no time in sympathizing with the shaken drink-vendor. He crossed the dance-floor quickly to the rear door which opened upon can-littered ground which bore, here and there, a small 'dobe house set to suit the builder's whim.

But before he reached the door, a man came through it with a Colt swinging in his hand. His face was white, but he looked steadily enough at Curt, who had stopped in his path. Curt frowned grimly at Zyler, that shiftless hanger-on of the Palace who had trailed him toward Los Alamos.

"What was the shooting, Zyler?" Curt demanded.

"Fellow took a shot at me and I put a hole in him!" Zyler replied calmy. "Long-coupled hairpin that came wandering into the saloon a half-hour ago an' had a bunch of drinks an' got hostile with me. I come on through the dance-hall. I was going over to see a girl when he come out the back door, here."

He stared steadily — almost *too* steadily — at Curt.

"I turned around, sort of without thinkin', an' there he was — with his hand filled! I moved on up in the dark right sudden. Well, he come prowlin' around ·an' I went the other way. Then he seen me an' whanged away an' bein' drunk, I reckon, he shot wide. *I* never! So I got him, instead of him gettin' me like he aimed to do."

"What made you stay so long? Robbing

the corpse, or something?"

Open disbelief was in Curt's face. Too, he had a sidelong view of Tom Card standing back of an encircling group and Zyler was a hanger-on of Card's. Curt found himself instinctively inclined to be unpleasant, tonight, to anybody or anything connected with Card.

The long Colt twitched in Zyler's hand as Curt's drawling remark brought subdued signs of amusement to the surface in the listeners. But Zyler, noting, perhaps, that Curt's arms were folded — managed to control himself without much apparent difficulty.

"You got no call to make talk like that!" he blustered. "I don't care if you *are* the sheriff I don't have to do no more'n tell you how I downed this trouble-huntin' stranger. You can look at him for yourself."

"You don't *have* to do a damn' thing, of course," Curt assured him unpleasantly. "I can make you, you know. All I *can* do is — make you wish you had! Let me have that gun."

Out of the corner of his eye, while seeming to watch only the manifestly reluctant Zyler, Curt seemed to see some sort of tiny head-motion by Card.

"Tell him out loud to hand it over, Card!"

301

he suggested, without turning. "That is, if he's really so valuable to you that you want to save him . . ."

Zyler stepped sullenly forward and passed over the Colt. Curt watched him closely to see that he attempted nothing like the old road-agent's spin. But Zyler handed his weapon over lying flat upon his palm, apparently thinking of no ruse.

Curt inspected the weapon. One shell had been fired, which gibed with Zyler's story thus far. But there was a detail which Curt found entirely unexplained. He lifted sardonic blue eyes to the killer. Zyler waited stiffly.

"You say you had got up on the roof, when this stranger slung his .45 at you?"

"Roof? Roof?" repeated Zyler, for the first time losing his rock-like calm. "What you talkin' about? 'Course I wasn't on no roof."

"No?" Curt cried amazedly. "No? Then — how-come his bullet ranged up so high that it carried through the window, there, and traveled on into the roof?"

"I reckon that's for the sheriff's office to figure out," Zyler snarled. "What you expect me to do, anyhow? Bust out cryin' because this *gunie* was so poor a shot he couldn't hit me, maybe?"

Curt stood staring at him, but watching

Card out of the corners of his eyes. He twitched the gun from palm into the air, so that it pinwheeled and came down with butt slapping into his hand. Zyler met his stare for a minute, but Curt's silent regard of him, accompanied by the pinwheeling Colt and the slap of the butt against hard palm, was wearing.

"Well! If you got any more to say, why the hell don't you say it?" he demanded blusteringly. "An' why don't you go out an' see the way he's lyin' an' all?"

"I will, but I had to see how you were lying, first," Curt grunted. "And don't worry about my saying what I have to say — anywhere, to anybody! That usually happens."

He looked thoughtfully at Card, but spoke to Chihuahua:

"Will you ride herd on Zyler awhile, Chihuahua? Know him? Or is he one of the bums who came in after you took off the star last time? I reckon he *wasn't* here during your other spell of deputying. Well, he's a ferocious customer, Zyler is — from behind a barrel or at your back. He admits his desperate disposition. So — if he should make a foot break and you have to down him, don't start crying about it unless you just feel that way. My notion is, there's just no telling what it'd save the county in the long run. He's just another of these lousy Palace bums."

He looked blankly at Tom Card and was rewarded by sight of the faint color his double-jointed insult brought to the gambler's inscrutable face. Zyler said nothing, only glared. Curt looked at Halliday, who had appeared in the crowd near him; and at Merle Sheehan of the hotel.

"Will you give me a hand to bring in this fellow?" he asked, and the two nodded, and followed him outside.

When he stood over the sprawling figure, to look around him moodily, studying the elements of the situation, he lifted a shoulder in impatient shrug. For he must admit, however grudgingly, and with no matter what feeling that Zyler had never been concerned in a fair fight, that a bullet from the dead man's pistol *could* — if fired very wildly — have gone through the window over the dance-hall's bar and penetrated the ceiling.

"I wish it was just absolutely impossible!" he said angrily. "I don't know of anything that I'd like better, tonight, than picking up one of Card's trained Fidos and slamming his south end into jail!"

"It could've happened like Zyler said,"

Merle Sheehan nodded. "Worse luck!"

"Well," Curt shrugged, "let's tote him inside and see if there's anything else to see. I know damn' well that, if Zyler did it, there was bushwhacking done!"

CHAPTER XI

Men came crowding officiously, in the manner of crowds everywhere, to help carry the long, limp body and put it upon two tables that others shoved together. Curt stared at Zyler's victim, and nodded grimly. It was the man whom he had seen ride past his seat on the store-porch hardly a half hour before, the tall cowboy who had got stiffly down before the Palace.

He was young, his face was lean and beard-stubbled and strong. A good face; a likable face. His clothing was nondescript; buttonless vest and flannel shirt and waist overalls and high-heeled boots like those worn by hundreds of range men. In his trousers pockets Curt found a heavy jackknife and a few silver dollars, a sack of Durham, book of brown papers and some loose matches. Nothing else. Nothing that tended to establish his identity.

"You don't know who he was, Zyler?" he asked the killer thoughtfully. "He was just a stranger to you?"

"Never seen him in my life until he come hellin' into the saloon tonight," shrugged Zyler. "But he took his whiskey like it was loco weed. Then he started pickin' on me — because I was handiest, I reckon."

"I thought maybe he was after you for something."

He twirled the dead man's gun around and inspected the cylinder. One shell fired . . . Again it seemed that he must admit the apparent hooking-up of the physical evidence and Zyler's story. He turned back the ancient vest over the flannel shirt and stared down in secret irritation. Oh! for a peg on which to hang the deadwood. Something to prove his instinctive suspicion of Card's man Zyler.

"Say, do I have to stand around all night, while you moon over him?" Zyler demanded sourly. "You know how she happened, now. That ought to be enough for you. Or is that the first dead man you ever saw?"

But Curt — who was now staring down at one side of the vest — let a tiny smile lift the corners of his mouth. Very thoughtfully, he turned to look at Zyler and something about his expression caused that worthy to change color suddenly. But Curt said no word to him. Instead, he stood up and beckoned to Chihuahua, whispered in the breed's ear, then glanced swiftly around at the puzzled faces of those surrounding him.

"Halliday!" he called, pleased to find the storekeeper still there. "Would you mind picking a couple of men that are well known — none of the Palace crowd; they are *too* well known — and going out with Chihuahua. Rest of you will *please* stay right here. That goes for you, Zyler — in particular."

Minutes passed. Curt spent them in staring alternately at Zyler and Tom Card. If only his guess proved to be right!

Feet scuffed in the doorway. Chihuahua came in, followed by Halliday, Powers the blacksmith — whom everyone knew and trusted — and Merle Sheehan. Chihuahua held out his palm. Upon it lay a silver deputy sheriff's star — which Curt had hoped for. But — and this brought a puzzled frown to his face — beside it lay an unexploded .45 cartridge.

"I'm find 'em under one tin can by them wall, ver' close by w'ere *he's* fall," Chihuahua grunted.

He nodded toward the dead man. Curt jiggled star and cartridge in his palm and whistled tunelessly.

"Together?" he demanded abruptly.

"*Si!* An' these Zyler's bootprints, she's go

right to them place. Me, I'm strike them match an' show Halliday an' Powers an' Sheehan . . ."

Curt stared at the unfired shell, then at the two Colts on the table beside the body. Both were of .45 caliber. Each had an exploded shell in it, besides four unexploded cartridges. Suddenly, he leaned to the table and held up the right flap of the dead man's vest.

"Folks," he drawled, "I saw these two holes here in the vest-lining and I've pinned my own star onto my vest that way enough to know what such holes mean. So — it sort of looked like this man was an officer of some kind — or had been pretty lately. You see, now, that he was a deputy sheriff — and that his star was taken off him, right — out — yonder."

Abruptly he turned the star over in his hand and looked at the back of it.

"R. W. Kerr — El Paso County!" he read aloud. Almost, his eyes jumped to Tom Card. But he caught himself in time: "Reckon Friend Zyler must've riled the El Paso folks, sometime . . . It certainly looks that way, anyhow."

The men crowded tensely about, to see for themselves the tiny holes, one above the other, where the star's pin had long pierced the lining of the vest; read the inscription on the back of the badge. Some turned to look at Zyler, who was having difficulty in maintaining his pose of indifference.

"But the bullet?" inquired Halliday. "What you reckon the bullet was alongside the star for, Curt?"

"Why —" Curt picked up the Colts from the table and selected the dead deputy's weapon. He pulled out the cylinder-pin, letting the cylinder drop into his palm. "Let's see . . . *Um-hmmm!* I was right . . . For he was a tidy man, this R. W. Kerr."

He held the Colt out to Halliday.

"Look at that barrel, then pass it to Powers and Sheehan. You look at it, too, Comanche. Do you see what I see? *That gun hasn't been fired tonight!* Look at the cylinder! This .45 shell that Chihuahua found with the star was pulled out of Kerr's gun. Then an empty shell from Zyler's gun was jammed in its place. Not a sniff of smoke about that cylinder, once you take the empty shell out!"

He faced the crowd:

"Folks — this skunk, here, Zyler, wanted to down this deputy for some reason or other. So he tolled him out of the Palace and shot him. Then he shot again and *that* was the bullet that came through the window. He shifted the empty shell, as I've

shown you; then he took off Kerr's star —
and probably took everything else Kerr
had."

"It's a pack of lies!" Zyler shouted, start-
ing forward. Beads of sweat burst through
the skin of his pallid forehead. "It happened
just like I told you. This damn' kid sheriff
—"

Chihuahua thrust out a foot very deftly
and Zyler sprawled his length on the floor.

"I reckon" — Curt faced in Tom Card's
general direction — "that I'll put Zyler
where the little doggies won't have a chance
to bite him. All of you who've seen these
things — I hope the honest ones of you will
remember what you've been shown tonight.
For we'll need you as witnesses when we
try Zyler for murder! Come on, Zyler. Your
days as a Palace Pup are over!"

Chihuahua gathered up the several exhib-
its — Zyler's Colt and the dead Kerr's, the
badge and the shell. Curt turned, where he
was pushing Zyler through a tight, mainly
hostile crowd. He caught Halliday's eyes.

"The body ought to go to Zink's," he said.
"We'll have an inquest early tomorrow. But
— do you mind taking that vest off him,
Halliday, and bringing it over to the office.
I'd hate for anything to be missing when
we're ready in the morning . . ."

Chihuahua trailed him down to the court-house. Shorty Wiggins got up from his cot at the stair's head and looked down. Curt prodded Zyler toward the stair.

"Got a skunk for you, Shorty! Zyler. Murdered an El Paso deputy sheriff behind the Palace."

"Them was the shots I heard," Shorty nodded. "Well — we maybe won't make him comfortable, Curt, but we'll certainly have him the next time somebody wants him. A deputy, huh? Zyler's gettin' up in the world. Last time, it was just a Mex' kid. Well . . ."

"This is the last time," Curt said grimly. "He stretches rope, this time."

"Yeh!" Zyler snarled. Somehow, now that he was away from that grim-faced crowd in the Palace, he seemed to have regained confidence. "You think so, huh? Well, wait an' see! An' see who's still around, laughin', when you're ready to push up the grass roots from the underside! We ain't both goin' to be around Gurney, long!"

"Take him, Shorty! Search him to the skin," Curt grunted.

He watched Zyler vanish into the jail. Chihuahua had followed Zyler up and gone in with Shorty and the prisoner. Curt drifted aimlessly to the door and leaned there for a while, looking at the lights along the street. It seemed to him that his telegram to El Paso would undoubtedly bring word of importance. He thought that the luckless Kerr had been recognized instantly upon his entry to the Palace — by Tom Card. It might be that he had come to Gurney for the sole purpose of collecting the gambler. That Card had suspected him. At any rate, it appeared fairly obvious that Card had given Zyler the job of killing Kerr.

He stepped outside and went slowly along the edge of the street until he came to the first sidewalk. He wandered absently and when he came to the Palace again looked in for a moment at the gambling in the Palace, standing in the street door where none inside saw him. Then he took a step forward and halted abruptly. He heard Shirley's voice from the window of the office, low and — it seemed to Curt — very tired. Cautiously, he edged down the wall until he stood almost beneath the window, his clothing merging with the drab 'dobe wall. Tom Card was speaking, now, in deep, even voice.

"— Unquestionably a case of self-defense," Card said. "But our young sheriff couldn't overlook even that slight opportunity to pose before an audience as the efficient peace officer. I'll arrange bail for

Zyler in the morning. He's not a particularly outstanding citizen, but he has always been devoted to me: I simply can't desert him when he's in trouble. Particularly when he's absolutely in the right."

"You *are* loyal, aren't you?" Shirley asked, with a warmth in her voice that made Curt grit his teeth.

"My dear! What sort of creature *is* a man who doesn't show loyalty to his own? The Lord knows that I can't pose as a saint. I have done many things — as I have admitted to you — that the law would consider punishable. But most of those "illegal" actions have been to correct injustices, to help friends. In this country, one often stands where the law is not; then, he must make his own laws, out of his own sense of right and wrong. I can't say that my conscience troubles me — and even a gambler can have a conscience."

"I know! I know!" she said softly, yet with a shadow of trouble in her tone.

"Shirley!" Card's voice deepened, slowed, a little. "I wonder if you can realize what it has meant to me — an exile from my own kind — to have you come into my life just at this time? I had been lonely beyond words; you came and —"

"Please!" she half-whispered. "Please!"

"No, you have to listen, Shirley. I have waited much longer than I thought I could. Listen to me, Shirley. You and I, alike, are exiles. We have managed to survive in this rough, savage environment. But it isn't our sort of life. We both are homesick for the cities."

He seemed to wait, but she made no answer and he went on.

"Soon — very soon, now — I will have my affairs here so arranged that I can draw out. One more big deal will accomplish that. Then — Shirley, I want to leave here. I want to take you with me. To the East, to Europe. There will be money to satisfy our every whim. In the beginning, I collected it only for my own spending. Now — I would care nothing for going if you weren't beside me. I have loved you from the first moment I saw you standing on Mrs. Sheehan's veranda and made bold to scrape acquaintance with you."

"Please!" she said again, almost whispering.

"We can settle all your difficulties. Send your mother and sister enough to support them luxuriously. We —"

"*You knew?* You knew where my money went?"

"From the first!" he told her indulgently.

"I cared too much, my dear, not to make it my business to learn everything. I knew, that first week, when you wanted to buck the faro game out there, that you desperately needed money, that you *had* to win —"

"Oh," she cried. "Oh! I see it now! You *let* me win. I saw you speak to the dealer. I thought you were only telling Newe I might play. You told him to see that I won!"

"What of it? You needed the money. You wouldn't have accepted it from me otherwise. It was easy for an old dealer like Newe to revert to tricks we don't countenance here."

"Oh!" she said gaspingly. "I'm ashamed! All this time. Hundreds and hundreds of dollars — and all from you!"

"Forget it! Everything I have in the world is yours, without the asking. Promise, Shirley! Promise that you'll come with me — soon. Three or four small deals; one big one — and we'll leave this forsaken desert and live! We —"

"I must go home!" she interrupted. "Please!"

"Of course! I'll see you to the door. No objections, now! I can't let you go alone."

Curt slid back the way he had come and stopped in the shadows. Two minutes later, he saw them come out of the Palace and turn toward Mrs. Sheehan's. He watched with such a fury, such a fear, as he had never known in his life. He leaned against the building in the darkness and his hands set like claws upon the butts of his Colts.

So it had gone this far between Tom Card and Shirley! The gambler could make love to her with no more than halfhearted objection on her side. But *he* was pushed away — told that she offered him no more than "casual friendliness." And she had not refused Tom Card's proposal.

Three or four small deals; one big one — then Tom Card would be ready to let the Trackless Bunch go its way alone. He would be rich; he would take Shirley . . . Three or four small deals only . . . Curt was cold with fear at thought that these might come so swiftly that he would not be in time. For he had no doubt, for all the guardedness of Tom Card's language, of what was meant by the word "deal."

"I'll wait till he comes back and pick a quarrel with him and kill him — tonight!" he decided. "I can't actually hang a damn' thing on him, yet. But I'll throw the Trackless Bunch in his face; get under his hide; make him pull. If he gets me — but he won't! I'll show Gurney the quickest draw and the straightest shooting it ever saw. I can't take a chance! One more big deal —"

Then, suddenly, he stopped short his incoherent mumbling.

"One more big deal, is it? All right, Tom Card! We'll see!"

He went fast across the street to Halliday's store. It was dark, but a window showed in the wall of the living-quarters behind. Curt went swiftly to the back door, knocked.

Came the squeak of a chair and footsteps. Halliday flung the door open — standing behind it, as a cautious man should. Curt stepped inside. His violet-blue eyes were shining; he was grinning, tight-lipped:

"Man! I have got an idea! I need your help, Halliday!"

"Sit down, Curt. Shoot!" commanded the storekeeper. As he looked at Curt, some of the younger man's barely suppressed excitement seemed conveyed to Halliday. He leaned forward in his chair. "What's on your mind, besides your cowlick, son?"

"Oh, just a little grief — for Tom Card," Curt said in elaborately casual drawl. Then he tensed. "Halliday, do you know anybody — know 'em well — real well — that is, up at The Points?"

"*Seguro!* I do that! Mike McCurdy — him

317

that owns the Glory Hole, you know? —
he's a real old desert rat. Well, Mike an' me
have known one another right promiscuous
for the last two-three hundred years."

"Anybody else? Anybody that'd be working for McCurdy, say? The owner of the
Hole wouldn't do for the job I'm thinking
about. Here's the layout, Halliday:

"Suppose it got to the ears of the Trackless Bunch — through Short Card Mann at
Ancho, say — that, because of the Bunch
sticking up the stages, the Glory Hole has
been letting the bulk of its bullion stack up,
for fear of having it stolen. And that Mike
McCurdy was going to sneak it out of The
Points — about ten-fifteen thousand dollars
worth of it —"

"A trap!" cried Halliday. His eyes were
beginning to glitter frostily. "Curt, I do
believe you've hit pay-dirt."

"It'll have to be a damn' good man that
gets the word to Short Card Mann!" Curt
reflected aloud. "He'll have to go rambling
down to Ancho and hang around the Coney
Island there, till he gets himself noticed by
Mann. Then, he'll have to sort of hint to
Mann that he knows where there's a
clean-up that he could make, if only he had
three-four men he could trust. He'll hum
and haw — we can trust Short Card Mann

318

to tell him that *he* knows the men who'll help! — and finally he'll come out and tell about Mike McCurdy's scheme . . ."

"By Gemini! She sounds like the real quill, Curt! She does that! We could get together enough of the folks to plumb massacre the Trackless Bunch. But we've got to fix it so's the whole Bunch is there, Curt! How'll we do that?"

"Easy! The fellow'll tell Mann that he'll need more than three-four men, that he'll need ten or twelve. He'll say that McCurdy's going to hide the stuff in a freight-wagon and send that wagon among a bunch of others — just as if it was a string of empties. We'll have to stick up the wagon-train at some place where part of our side can hole up."

"Ought to have plenty of our bunch in the wagons, though," Halliday counseled. He was grinning felinely. "That'll let us play safe. Man! We can get enough men together to outnumber the Trackless Bunch two to one. We can put half in the wagons, hidin' under tarp's. Half can be hid in the hills, ready to jump down an' take the Bunch behind!"

" *'Sta bueno!*" Curt nodded. "Well, who'll do the arranging with McCurdy, up at The Points?"

"Why, I reckon I better handle that end. Yeh, I'll take my foot in my hand, come mornin'. I can count on Mike knowin' somebody at The Points who can be trusted to play the part of a disgusted miner that's been fired, to slide down to Ancho an' carry the banner to this Short Card Mann. But — say! Can we count on Tom Card ridin' with the Bunch this time? Reckon he'll show hisself even that much, even on this big a crack?"

Curt shrugged a lean shoulder and grinned:

"*Quién sabe?* But I've got another ace in the hole, on that angle. I sent a telegram to El Paso —"

Halliday listened to the report of Chihuahua's recollections of Card in El Paso, and to Curt's account — if with reservations — of his eavesdropping. At the last he nodded pleasantly:

"I see! I — see! You figure that if we round up the gang and Card's not there and nobody squeals on him, there's still a good chance to take him in on an El Paso warrant!"

Curt's face was very quiet — and very hard. He made a flashing movement of the fingers that gripped his cigarette. Fragments of brown paper, powdered tobacco,

320

sifted down.

"I figure a little more than that," he said slowly. "I figure that, one way *or* another, I'm going to settle Tom Card." . . .

"What do you reckon's keeping Andy?" Curt asked Chihuahua with a scowl. They sat in the office on the fourth day after Andy's departure.

"W'y me, I'm reckon she's wait for them telegram from El Paso," Chihuahua shrugged. He blew a smoke ring daintily toward the ceiling. "You're say to Andy to wait. Maybe them El Paso sheriff an' marshal, she's busy, or maybe she's dead. In El Paso, Curt, she's one dam' fine men w'at will be them officer an' git fat. *Por Supuesto!*"

"And not a word from Halliday yet, either!" grumbled Curt. "Don't know as it makes any difference, now, but I'd *like* to make good on my bluff to Tom Card. I'd enjoy cutting loose on that Trackless Bunch — especially if Curt came riding up at the head — before my three weeks were up . . ."

"Me, I'm think I would go down to them Palace, now, an' kill me Tom Card," observed Chihuahua softly. "She's them girl, *amigo mio?* Me, I'm see plenty thing, Curt, w'en you're look at her. These Card, she's figure *she's* git them girl, hah?"

"I reckon he does, old-timer," Curt nodded. "I reckon he does . . . But he's going to bump into some lead with his address on it, first."

"Then, w'y will you have the worry?" Chihuahua asked bewilderedly. "We will kill these Tom Card any time w'en you're say. *Bueno!* Then how will she take them girl?"

"Sounds easy, huh?" Curt grinned twistedly. "But killing Tom Card will just save her from finding out, later on, what sort of prize scoundrel he is. It won't get her for me, Chihuahua. She's the sort that'd come to a man through hell and high water, if she loved him. If she didn't love him, he couldn't make her come by trying to run her affairs — even if she knew that was best for her . . ."

"Howdy!" Halliday said, from the door. They whirled quickly.

"Come on inside! Sit down and look shorter!" Curt said tensely.

For an instant, the storekeeper's cheerful red face altered as he stared at Curt, noting the muscles showing pale against the brown cheeks, the narrowing, the darkening to smoky violet, of the blue eyes, the thin gash-like line of a mouth.

"You're sort of honin' for a crack at 'em, now ain't you?" Halliday nodded. "Well —" he came on in and relaxed comfortably in a chair and fanned himself with his hatbrim. "She's all set! Like Mike McCurdy says, the fuse is laid an' we're standin' ready to light it — Mike was tickled stiff with your scheme, Curt, an' he had a man right there — an old desert rat of the real prospector breed. Scrutchett's workin' for Mike to git him a grubstake an' he was plumb tickled to take on this job instead of workin' at the mine."

"Has this Scrutchett gone to Ancho?" Curt asked quickly.

"Yeh. An' he took the word that the wagon-train would start next Thursday night. He's told Short Card Mann — I saw Scrutchett yesterday, late, outside Ancho — that some time Friday'll be the time to stick up the wagons. Him an' Mann discussed the best plan an' decided that the ford of Scalp Creek is where she ought to be — the wagons havin' to go slow down that steep bank to the ford an' then havin' all they can do to climb the far bank."

"Me, I'm think she's fine, them Scalp Creek!" nodded Chihuahua, sea-blue eyes alight. "She's have lots of cover, them Scalp Creek. Up and down, anyw'ere from these ford, she's easy for them army to hide!"

"Only thing Mike kicked about," Halliday grinned, "was lettin' Gurney handle the scrap on its lonesome. Mike says The Points has had about as much trouble with the Trackless Bunch as anybody. So the folks there are certainly due a crack at them hairpins. So, he's goin' to load up the wagons with a handpicked outfit, hidin' under the tarp's."

"I reckon that's the best way, at that," Curt nodded thoughtfully. "It would be sort of hard for us to get a bunch of Gurney men over to The Points in time to ride the wagons, without somebody here getting suspicious — and worried. If those wolves once sniff a trap in all this, we're going to have a hell of a time getting 'em at Scalp Creek — or ever getting 'em anywhere."

"Way I figured her, too," Halliday nodded.

"You reckon Scrutchett fooled Short Card — no doubt about it?"

"No doubt at all!" declared Halliday. "You see, he never went to Short Card at first. He hung around the Coney Island, drinkin' an' lookin' real sore-toed. Then he began to scrape up to first one, then another, of them hard cases. You know: sort of hintin' that he knew somethin' he could handle, if only he had a good bunch to help. One fellow tried

mighty hard to pump him, but old Scrutchett he just laughed at him. He told this fellow he'd lead him to the place, if he wanted
to come.

"Well, this fellow come to him after a bit.
He 'lowed that Short Card Mann'd like to
powwow with him. Scrutchett acted like he
was kind of suspicious of Mann. Yes, sir! He
played it like that until the tinhorn might'
nigh come clean with him. Then they got
together."

"That's fine!" Curt said. "Now, how many
of the Bunch do you reckon'll be at Scalp
Creek?"

"Plenty!" Halliday informed him grimly.
"Scrutchett tried to find that out, but all
Mann'd say was that he would get plenty
men to handle anything that came up. But,
shucks! We can get together enough guntot-
ers to mop 'em up like a wet spot!"

"Yeh. But getting our bunch out of town
without tipping our hand to Tom Card and
giving him a chance to send word to Bain is
the trouble . . . Halliday, I reckon you are
the one to pick the men we'll take out of
Gurney. Pick 'em with a fine-tooth comb!
We can't have a *gunie* in the crowd that
hasn't got more sand in his craw than a
creek-bed's got! And, too, we have to be sure
that nobody's going to whisper a word!"

"Can happen!" Halliday grinned. "Son, I know this town an' know it from the back. I can pick twenty-five men that'll raid hell with a bucket of water an'll talk more without sayin' a word than any outfit you ever heard of!"

"Chihuahua!" Curt drawled, grinning tightly, "Reckon you can round up the Wagon Wheel boys and Wolf Montague's Arrowhead outfit and some from Los Alamos?"

"*Por supuesto!* Me, I'm git them kind of boy w'at's *glad* to help these Trackless Bunch to git sick!"

"All right! Your bunch'll be the easiest to get on the ground without spreading the news. You have got to be up and down Scalp Creek by early Friday morning at the latest — before the wagons get there. Halliday, do you reckon the Trackless Bunch'll come up the road from Ancho?"

"Reckon they will. Chances are — most of 'em comin' from Ancho like they will — they'll just sneak out of town an' meet an' come foggin' it. Sam Bain'll come from the Lazy B, I figure. He'll naturally come up to Scalp Creek from the Ancho side of the ford, to keep from runnin' into the wagons if they should be a little bit ahead of time!"

Curt nodded, whistling softly.

"Sounds like sense! Chihuahua, you stay quite a way up and down the creek from the ford, so as to give 'em room to scatter for their bushwhacking without stepping on your feet. Then, when you hear the shooting at the ford, you can close in on 'em. Our outfit from Gurney will split and comb the road both ways, coming in from toward The Points and Ancho at the same time."

" 'Sta bueno!" Chihuahua nodded. "Me, I'm gone, Curt. Hah! We're give them Scalp Creek the name once more — for scalps of these Trackless Bunch w'at we're take."

He vanished like a shadow, leaving Halliday and Curt staring thoughtfully one at the other.

"If Tom Card'll only handle this job himself!" Curt said slowly. "If he only does . . ."

"I expect him to," Halliday reassured him. "Don't you worry." . . .

It was near noon of Thursday when Curt rode down into a deep arroyo well off the Ancho trail and found there thirteen citizens of Gurney, all of whom had left the county seat casually, as upon their regular businesses. Curt gave mental salute to Halliday, for the storekeeper had chosen men who normally moved in and out at trading or freighting or the like. Merle Sheehan was there, with Powers the blacksmith (Powers had discovered profanely that he had not a nail in his shop and had departed for Faith to murder the man who should have supplied him), old Comanche Smith, Bill Francis the cattle-buyer, Groody of the Square Deal Store, and others of like prominence.

"More's comin'," grunted Comanche Smith. "Halliday'll bring 'em. Maybe we'll sort of even up, son, for the time we was led by the nose up to Williams Creek."

"Hope so!" Curt shrugged, swinging down and unsaddling. "We ought to be moving inside two hours. Then we can take our time and still be ready by tomorrow morning."

An hour went by, while those old-timers sprawled comfortably in the shade of the arroyo walls and yarned of other battles or played cards. Presently Halliday came up, with three more men from the county seat. After his party's arrival they waited as before. Then old Joe Moore jogged into the arroyo with four happy-go-lucky young JM riders. Halliday turned to Curt:

"Reckon this is the smear! Twenty-three of us, in all . . . Everybody I tipped off."

"All right, men!" Curt drawled, standing up and speaking with an edge to his voice.

"You hereby are deputized to handle this Trackless Bunch. Now, I reckon it'll be the best idea to keep our eyes peeled right from the start. So, three of you'll ride point and one man'll ride a half-mile to the right and another'll do the same on the left. That way, if some curious hairpin comes fogging up to look us over, we'll have a chance to collect him."

He turned to the storekeeper:

"Halliday, let's ride a half-mile or so in the drag of the bunch. Maybe — *just* maybe — Tom Card'll be missing some of the town folk. He might slip out for a look. All right!"

So they saddled and rode out of the arroyo toward the ford of Scalp Creek, moving like a military column in enemy country. Curt and Halliday brought up the rear, riding very alertly, indeed, one keeping watch ahead to the left, the other staring alternately to the right and rear.

"What'll we do if Tom Card don't show up with the Bunch?" Halliday asked finally, in a low voice and with eyes weaving mechanically back and forth. "Make a bluff in Gurney?"

"I don't know," Curt confessed, in like tone. "I suppose we'll have to hope that Andy brings back a telegram from El Paso that means something. That is, if we can't

find somebody in the outfit who'll talk —
somebody like Bain or Short Card Mann.
They'd probably be the only ones who'd
know about Card. The others —"

He turned suddenly in the saddle and
listened, his head thrust tensely forward.
"Horse coming?" he whispered.

"Sounds like it." Halliday nodded.

They split and rode behind the loose-piled
boulders that here fenced in the trail left by
their main body. Each lifted his long gun
and waited strainedly. The soft thudding of
hoofs was unmistakable now.

Peeping cautiously through a crack between the boulders that sheltered him, Curt
saw approaching their ambush a Mexican
youth, who rode with eyes roving from the
trail floor to the boulders on right and left.
He was seemingly as suspicious of his sur-
roundings as would have been some wild
animal. He carried a Winchester across his
arm. They let him come abreast the boulders. Then their guns leaped to cover him:

"Hands up!" Curt cried.

But the Mexican snarled inarticulately and
fired without lifting the carbine from where
it lay across his arm. The bullet went wild
and the next moment he had whirled his
pony and was lying flat upon its neck while
it galloped, raking it with great rowels.

Curt's Winchester jerked up, but Halliday, old buffalo-hunter, was already on the ground with the Sharps resting in the saddle seat. The big rifle boomed and off his pony like a frog came the Mexican boy.

"Hell!" spat Halliday disgustedly, "I couldn't hit a barn a-wing! Shot at the pony, an' hit him!"

Curt was already spurring toward the fallen youth. He slid the buckskin to a halt, flung the reins over its head, and leaped down. And the Mexican moved convulsively like a stricken snake, and Curt leaped back in bare time to get his legs out of the path of the knife that flashed. He stamped upon the youth's hand and kicked the knife out of reach. Then — more cautiously — he stooped and turned the fallen one over.

The big bullet had torn through his lungs; that knife-stroke had been the last action he was capable of. He stared up steadily at Curt, with no fear in his black eyes.

"Where were you going? What'd you run for?" Curt demanded. "You work for Card. Come on, now! Tell us and we'll fix you up the best we can."

Defiantly the boy grinned up at him. He was still grinning when his eyes closed and the limpness of his body told Curt and Halliday that he was dead. Curt turned with defeated headshake to the storekeeper.

"Card surely has all the luck in picking 'em! This is the second one who just laughed and wouldn't talk. But I reckon he was coming to spy on us, or to take word to the Bunch. Let's scout the back trail a little bit, and see if he was by himself. If he was, the chances are we needn't worry about Card sending word. For we will be on the ground before a news-bringer could stop the Bunch."

So they rode back for a couple of miles, studying the trail. They found the Mexican youth's pony-tracks all the way, without sign of any companion.

"All right!" Curt nodded. "Let's hightail it back and tell the outfit. They likely heard that Sharps cannon of yours."

Chapter XII

From where he lay in scrub timber on the trail from Ancho to Scalp Creek Ford — a quarter-mile from the trail itself — Curt saw at dawn the tree-plumed crest of the creek valley. Around him lay ten of the Gurney men with their rifles beside them. Some were dozing, others were staring through the top of the scrub at the far bank of Scalp Creek — where Halliday and Comanche

Smith and the other Gurney men should be.

"Reckon we had better saddle up!" Curt grunted to Merle Sheehan, and the big ex-cavalryman nodded.

"If they haven't taken alarm, it's time for 'em to be coming."

They had saddled and were loafing beside their mounts, eating cold bacon and dried beef and bread, when one of the JM punchers came riding up from where he had been standing watch beside the trail.

"Comin'!" he grunted tensely. "From the dust they're kickin' up, there's a whole dam' herd, too!"

"Our move!" Curt said, with grim smile. "We sneak down to the trail and, the minute we hear a shot from the ford, we spread out like a fan and come down on the fight covering the trail and the brush on each side of it. Our play's to keep anybody from breaking through toward Ancho. Ready?"

They moved very silently, indeed, down toward the trail — not approaching it too closely, for they could hear the drumming hoofs from the direction of Ancho. They waited until the band passed on, going toward the ford. When the Mann party was at a safe distance, Curt lifted his hand. His men rode cautiously to the edge of the trail and, finding no sign of the riders, half of them crossed over and reined in among the brush on the other side.

The JM cowboy climbed a tree, from which he could see the far bank of Scalp Creek and — he said — the seemingly deserted ford. Minutes passed, then the cowboy grunted excitedly:

"Wagons are comin' over the ridge! Startin' down, now. Look like empties — all covered up with tarp's. Three, four, *five* wagons . . . All on the slope, now! First wagon's hit the creek, it's startin' up this side. Second wagon's splashin' water. Out! Third wagon's in an' —"

He came scrambling down, helter-skelter, landed on the ground with scratched hands and snagged shirt:

"Bunch was showin' in the brush, both sides of the creek!" he yelled. *"Listen to 'em shootin'!"*

Curt set spurs to his buckskin and jumped him onto the trail. The others followed, and they thundered down the trail to the beginning of the long slope that led to the creekbed. Here, for an instant, they reined in to look.

The firing below was a steady tattoo, now. Smoke wreathed upward from the wagons; from the brush at either end of the train.

There was yelling. While they sat there, from the brakes above the position of the Track-less Bunch and down the creek, came a shrill cowboy yell in which many voices blended. It was answered from up the creek almost instantly.

"Let's go!" Curt yelled, and spurred down the slope.

Over the crest of the other bank, now, came Comanche Smith and Halliday and their followers. So from four sides — as well as from the wagons — the Trackless Bunch was under fire.

The cowboys coming up the creek forced the outlaws down toward the trail. Here they were met by the steady firing from the wagons and by the hail of bullets from the other cowboy contingent, which was high enough to fire over the wagons. And from both ends of the trail the Gurney men har-ried them waspishly, firing from the ground, resting their Winchesters on their saddles. Curt swung up and raced the buckskin down toward the wagons, with bullets cut-ting dust around the horses' hoofs. He jerked back on the Spanish bit, and the buckskin, sitting down upon his stub-tail, slid to a dusty halt.

"Bain! Mann!" Curt yelled at the top of his voice, over and over. "All of you in the bushes, there! All you Ancho-men! You haven't got a chance! Throw down your guns and come on out! Throw 'em down and come out reaching high!"

"Come on out!" Curt yelled again. "But come reaching high!"

"Yeh! Come out an' git shot!" yelled an outlaw derisively. "You come on in after us!"

"We'll do that, if we have to!" Curt assured him. "But I'm sheriff and I'm giving you this chance."

"Go to hell!" the voice invited him.

"Hey, Curt!" came a familiar voice from just behind the outlaws. "Hey, Curt! She's me! We're have these Trackless Bunch covered. W'en they're shoot one time more, we're wipe 'em out!"

Dead silence fell, then from the bush that masked the Trackless Bunch came furious cries. Up over the wagon sides came seventeen or eighteen burly men, led by a squat, tremendously wide, and thick red-headed man. And into the trail swarmed mounted cowboys of Los Alamos and the Wagon Wheel outfits, those who had been firing at the outlaws over the wagons. Halliday and Comanche Smith pushed rapidly down the slope, as did Curt's men from the other side. So the men of the Trackless Bunch were narrowly hemmed in.

"Throw down them gun!" came Chihuahua's grim voice. "Them man w'at's wiggle
one finger, we're kill him dam' quick! You
will *please* move down by them wagon!"

Came a sudden splatter of shots and the
sound of galloping hoofs. Then into the trail
came a sullen-faced group with hands in
air, twelve or fourteen, Curt estimated
swiftly. But neither Bain nor Short Card
Mann was among them.

"Chihuahua!" Curt yelled. "Chihuahua!
Where's Bain? Where's Mann?"

"They're break through!" Chihuahua
roared, with a torrent of furious oaths.
"Come on, Curt! We're chase 'em! *We're*
help 'em to git sick!"

"Take care of these fellows!" Curt yelled
to Halliday. Then he set spurs to the buckskin and sent the animal scrambling into
the brush — that was studded pretty thickly
with bodies.

Chihuahua was pointing. Curt nodded
and rammed home the rowels. So they rode
hell-for-leather, regardless of the cactus, the
cat-claw, and the flailing branches of the
scrub.

"W'en them others, she's throw down
the gun," panted Chihuahua, "Bain an'
them Short Card Mann an' two more, she's
bust through us w'ere we're sneak up

337

behind 'em."

The fugitives' trail was not hard to follow, even at a pounding gallop. Chihuahua slipped into the lead and seemed to know intuitively where the quartet ahead would turn down an arroyo, where they would race up the bank and top out of it again.

"They're go for Gurney!" he yelled, after a halfhour. Curt nodded gravely. This had been apparent to him for minutes.

Their men had found a cow-trail and the going was a trifle easier and faster. Both the buckskin and Chihuahua's black were apt to be better than any horse ahead — save, perhaps, Sam Bain's tall bay. Three, at least, of the men, they should overhaul, given time.

"Yaaaiiiaah!" Chihuahua shrilled triumphantly, as from the crest of one hogback they saw dust upon the crest of the next, less than a mile away.

Harder they spurred. When next they saw the dust-cloud, it was nearer. Gradually, they cut down their quarry's lead. Then, mounting a hogback, they saw the four riders on the edge of an arroyo. And as they stared tensely, Sam Bain's tall bay stumbled and turned a somersault. Three horses only; three men — these were all that appeared on the other side of the arroyo . . .

One rider whirled his mount and seemed to wait. Up over the arroyo-lip crawled Bain. Curt and Chihuahua, pouring the leather into their mounts, were no more than four hundred yards, then three hundred, two hundred, yards away. Bain ran staggeringly forward and gripped the waiting one's leg. Then Chihuahua was on the ground, running beside the black till he had halted. His carbine had appeared from the saddle scabbard like a sleight-of-hand trick. And in all that Territory there was no rifle-shot so deadly . . .

The sound of his shots was like the rattle of a stick upon a paling-fence. Curt, riding ahead, but keeping well to one side, out of the line of fire, gaped incredulously as Bain crashed flat; as the rider, stiffening, suddenly slipped sideways from the saddle; as the horse itself crumpled like a tissue-paper animal.

Chihuahua was in the saddle again in a twinkling. He galloped up while Curt was staring down at the two dead men.

"Hah!" he grinned savagely. *"They* will say I'm not miss, *por Dios!"*

"Nope! But I'm sorry that Bain's not alive, though. I sort of figured that we might get something out of him . . . My fault, though: I should have told you to just nick him a couple of times."

Chihuahua swung down and studied the pair. Bain's companion was a hard-faced man of middle age, whom they had seen lounging about the Coney Island in Ancho. Curt, giving over for a moment thought of Mann and the other outlaw, who were galloping madly toward Gurney, eyed the dead figure of his enemy somberly. An exclamation from Chihuahua jerked his eyes sideways.

"Por Dios, Curt! She's not have them busted boot! *Mira!"*

And Curt, staring for the first time at Bain's feet, saw that they were shod in the smallest, most expensive pair of boots he had ever seen. He slipped from the saddle and gaped. Then he whirled, to the bootprints left by Bain as he scrambled out of the arroyo. He bent over and stared rigidly. Then suddenly he straightened and Chihuahua eyed him wonderingly. For Curt was grinning idiotically.

"It was *his* little bootprint I found, when the stage from The Points was stuck up!" Curt cried. "It was Bain's, Chihuahua!"

"Sí. But w'at will be the difference, w'en she's dead?"

"Difference? *Difference?* All the difference in the world! I — I — Oh, come on. Let's hightail after Mann and his friend. Man, Man! I'm so tickled I don't know what to do. I —"

He caught the saddle-horn and mounted without touching the stirrups. Chihuahua followed his example, but sedately, and shook his head bewilderedly as he roweled his black into the buckskin's frantic pace and came alongside.

"Me, I'm think you're loco," he yelled at Curt. " 'All the difference in these world,' hah? Now, *how* will she be them difference . . ."

But Curt ignored him and rode on grinning. Twenty minutes, almost, they were behind Short Card Mann and his companion. Curt wondered just why Mann should be heading for Gurney. To see Tom Card! It had been a disappointment not to find the gambler with the bunch at Scalp Creek. But the flight of Bain and Mann had given Curt little time to gloom over Card's absence. Now — much depended upon the telegram that Andy Allen should bring from Ancho. What if none of those familiar with the Trackless Bunch's organization would talk? Then, there would be no evidence whatever against Card. The only hope would lie in finding him a fugitive from El Paso justice.

Curt looked down thoughtfully at the buckskin. No thoroughbred, yet it was a grade-horse sired by a Kentucky stallion of wide note in that country. Curt had pushed him, before this, on near-incredible rides. He would probably be able, with a few breathing spells, to make Gurney without serious laboring. And Chihuahua's black was of much the same caliber. So he settled in the saddle and brought the buckskin to an even gallop.

Suddenly, well ahead, there sounded the flat report of a rifle, then the sharper, quicker staccato of pistol-shots — five of the last. Curt jerked his head around to stare frowningly at Chihuahua, who spurred alongside. So, together, they galloped on toward the jumble of arroyos and hogbacks from which the firing had come. "Hah!" Chihuahua grunted abruptly, gesturing toward a hogback. "She's them Andy, *por Dios!*"

Andy Allen sat his horse on the crest and stared at them for a considerable period, then jerked his arm in greeting and came sliding down on the cowtrail they were following.

"I just downed a hairpin!" he greeted them, when they pulled up before him. "I was comin' across country, hittin' for the mail trail, when these two polygamous *gunies* rounded a shoulder an' damn' near landed in my lap. Before a man could say 'Jack Robinson' — even if he was used to sayin' it — one jerked up his Winchester an' slung a .44 at me just as mathematical as you ever saw. I took that to mean commencement of downright peevish activities, so I answered back with the old hogleg an' down he flopped! The other fellow bit his horse's neck an' split the wind while I was clawin' for my Winchester."

"You must have had the old smoke wagon in front of you!" Curt remarked.

"Well, come to think about it, I reckon I did," Andy nodded grimly. "You see, I heard those *gunies* comin', a minute or so before they popped into sight. It looked sort of common-sensible to get His Honor facin' to the front . . ."

They followed him off the trail to where a horse grazed wearily. There lay one of the Cuchillo hard cases whom they had seen about the Coney Island in Ancho, the day that Curt had shot Quinn. He was very dead, with five bullet holes in breast and abdomen.

"Me, I'm think them dam' plowhandle w'at you're carryin' she's shoot w'ere you're hold him!" Chihuahua grunted to Andy, impressed by the five tokens of marksman-ship.

"Nothing on him," Curt shrugged after quick search. "Let's get going after Mann again. Oh! You get that telegram, Andy?"

HAVE YOU CHARGES AGAINST TOM CARD, GAMBLER, OR SAM BAIN HIS RIGHT BOWER? THEY COME GURNEY TWO YEARS BACK. CARD WAS SILENT PARTNER CRITERION SALOON. BAIN'S ABOUT SIX FOOT HIGH, SLENDER, RIGHT HANDSOME, WITH BLACK HAIR AN' EYES AN' DARK COMPLECTED. WALKS SHUFFLIN'.

That's what I sent.
An' the city marshal come back at you:

NO CHARGES AGAINST TOM CARD HERE. DON'T KNOW SAM BAIN. YOUR DESCRIPTION SOUNDS A LOT LIKE SLIM UPSON, EXCEPT FOR SHUFFLIN' WALK. UPSON VERY PROUD OF FEET LITTLE AS WOMAN'S. UPSON BADLY WANTED HERE, DEAD OR ALIVE. SEE REWARD NOTICE I SENT YOU ABOUT HIM.

"Sam Bain *is* 'Slim Upson,'" Curt told Andy. "Chihuahua Winchestered him awhile ago, back on the trail. The reward's to you,

Chihuahua. But if that's not hell! They don't want Card . . . Why couldn't he have been Slim Upson?"

"But what's it all about?" Andy Allen cried bewilderedly. "How-come Chihuahua cracked down on Bain? How-come these two hairpins were hightailin' in front of you? Who are they, anyhow? Say! If you've been glommin' off all the fun again, I'm free to state that this bein' a junior deputy's too damn' evolutionary for me. I —"

"Save it for a letter home!" Curt groaned. "Come on. We've got to make Gurney. No telling what Short Card Mann's up to. Chihuahua, you spill the news to our young trouble-hunter as we go!"

He swung up and whirled the buckskin; drove the rowels in and was off at a racing gallop, leaving Andy and Chihuahua to follow stirrup-to-stirrup. . . .

Gurney lay as silent, as deserted, as a ghost town, flooded with the white spring sunlight, the chalky dust of the main street ruffled only by vagrant gusts of wind from the Diablo cañons. Curt, with Chihuahua and Andy close behind him, halted on the county seat's outskirts. They stared ahead, for the trail of Short Card Mann had led straight here.

"Well?" Andy grunted, after a moment.

"What's what?"

"I don't know," Curt said very softly. "I just don't know. But — there's a tickle under my left shoulder. That's a sign of war in the Thompson family. There's maybe going to be hell popping around here, in short order."

He found a match in his hatband and struck it blindly. He relighted his dead cigarette and smiled gently.

"Short Card has got to Tom Card with the bag of news, by now. Question: What's Card going to elect to do? He may sit pat, figuring that there's nothing to connect *him* with any Trackless Bunch. On the other hand, he may figure that we got Bain alive and made him spill the beans. So —

"When I walk into the Palace, I don't know what I'm bucking. It's all blind. I count nearly a dozen horses at the Palace hitch-rack . . . Probably, most of the bunch belong to Tom Card's trained Fidos. So, you edge down the back of the buildings, while I ride on down the street. You cross over, Chihuahua and cover my back when I go in. Andy, you cover the Palace's back door. Wait a minute" — he checked Andy's protest with lifted hand — "I want it done my way. This is my day and my game. I'm going to call Tom Card's several bluffs. I'm going to call 'em and — there's not a reason in the world for me to give a hoot how it comes out!"

They stared at him blankly. He was looking grimly down the street. Then Andy pushed back his hat frowningly.

"What d'you mean? Why ain't there a reason for you to give a hoot how the callin' of Card's bluff comes out?"

Curt grunted impatiently and began to push his horse forward. And Chihuahua nodded, his lean face grim.

"You're not bother him," he said to Andy. "Me, I'm understand: Curt's give up them girl — Shirley. So — she's not give one small damn w'at's happen. But, we're see w'at's come in these life . . ."

Curt did not look back. He hardly heard Chihuahua, but kept his eyes on the Palace. When he came to the hitch-rack, there was nobody under the wooden awning before the big saloon. He swung down, tied the buckskin, then ducked under the rack's cross-bar and clumped across to bang the swing doors.

It was dusky in the big bar-room, after the almost incandescent glare of the sunlight on the white street. He stood blinking for a moment, seeing the men at the bar only as a dark and blurry mass, topped by whitish spots that were faces. It was foolish to stand so before *that* group of Palace loungers. At any time, he would have been the first to call it suicidal. But today he had the feeling of coming to the end of a trail. Not merely the end of the Trackless Bunch's course of the Territory, but the finish-line of some personal affairs, also. It was as he had told Andy and Chihuahua. He had come in here to face Tom Card, to have showdown with the big, sure gambler. And he expected to find Shirley at Card's side, the Card-partisan. He was beyond caution and when he reached that stage, his mood made him as dangerous to himself as to those he faced.

His eyes refocussed and no man at the long bar had moved more than was enough to let him face Curt. All were very quiet, very watchful. He looked from face to familiar face of the men whom he had been accustomed to call Card's "Fidos." He looked around the big room. The big gambler was not in sight. Curt moved down the room and it seemed to him that the drinkers tensed. He let his eyes shuttle away from them for an instant, to the door of the little office partitioned off saloon and gaming-room. That door was closed now.

"Where's the curly wolf?" Curt demanded of the men at the bar. A corner of his hard mouth lifted sardonically. "Where's Card?"

Nobody answered him. Still the line of them faced him with blank, watchful silence. He knew that he walked, just then, on the thinnest of thin ice. Let one of these barroom gladiators drop hand to gun and he would have to kill him. And that first shot would be the signal for action all down the line. It would mean red war in this now-quiet room.

In the heavy silence Curt looked around again. And he had the lift of spirit that came with a drink. Actually, he began to enjoy this moment, for its very foolhardiness. He laughed easily while he looked at the men, then at the door.

"Card!" he called loudly. "Oh, Card! This is Thompson! It's showdown, too! Come on out, Card. But come with your hand filled or with both of your hands up in the air!"

Suddenly, he heard a frantic drumming sound. It was as if someone pounded upon the thin partition of the office. Curt stared narrowly. He could not understand it. Some of the men at the bar began to shift position nervously. That hammering upon the thin planks of the office stopped abruptly. An instant later, the office door opened. Tom Card appeared in the widening crack. He faced Curt, pulling the door shut behind him. He walked across the barroom toward Curt.

His face was no more than usually pale, but it was hard of contour as if chiseled from grayish stone. And the blue eyes were not expressionless, now! Curt saw cold hatred in them and the glint of it made him wonder, then waked in him a savage sort of pleasure. It was pleasant to know that his hatred of Card was recognized and returned full-fold by the gambler. He began to smile. "You're — pretty noisy, aren't you?" Card drawled. "Is there some special reason for your yelling in my barroom?"

He had perfect control of his voice. Curt admitted that. But, then, he had never underestimated this man. Card was an enemy no man could afford to underrate.

"There's all the reason in the world," Curt nodded. "We dropped a loop over our gang of thieves and killers — the gang I named 'The Trackless Bunch.' At Scalp Creek, it was, and the creek's well-named now, if it never was before . . . We made it a pretty clean sweep. In fact, only Short Card Mann and —— But never mind that, it's Mann I want to talk about. And, too, being just a young sheriff who never lets a chance at glory-hunting get by him, I wanted to tell you that the promise I made, that day in the bank, is kept, now! I've settled the Trackless Bunch as I told you I would — and done it ahead of time. I — knew you'd be interested . . ."

"I suppose I'll have to offer you congratulations," Tom Card nodded. His mouth slid sardonically sideways in the smallest, tightest, of grins. "Perhaps we'll pass the hat and have a medal made for you to wear. Some small token of our regard for the Fearless Sheriff of Gurney. A sort of Saint George with foot on the dragon's neck — or do you know the story? — on a tin plaque about twelve inches across. But, now that you've notified me, is there something else I have to hear?"

"I wouldn't be surprised," Curt told him evenly. "The medal idea's interesting. When *you* suggest it, that makes it all the more interesting. And I've heard about Saint George, too. We had a book, or it may have been two, in the house when I was a boy. But it's Mann I want to talk about, right now. I want him. In fact, I can't count it a complete picnic without him. Bain hasn't talked enough, so far, to give me all the details about the higher-ups in this gang. So I sort of lean on Mann for the whole story."

He smiled unpleasantly at Card.

"All I need, now, is to find Mann. For,

when I find him, he'll sing his little song. He's that kind of bird — mightily little of the eagle to Mann, lots and lots of parrot blood in him. And we've got the persuasion to move him. I have a notion that when we *persuade* him the trouble will be shutting him off . . ."

"You said — *Bain!*" Card grunted. "You don't mean that Bain was riding with this outlaw gang? Not — Bain!"

"Oh, dear me, yes!" Curt nodded earnestly. "He was one of the straw-bosses. He was the man who murdered Ed Showalters that night of the bank robbery. Bain wasn't the simple cowman you took him for, Card. Goodness, no! That Lazy B iron of his — why, Card, you'd hardly believe it, but that was only a blind! Bain was a bad, bad man before ever he moved up here in our midst. I knew that, all along, but I wanted to give him more rope. So, when Chihuahua Joe gathered Bain in, at Scalp Creek, it was a three-thousand-dollar gather. El Paso wants 'Slim' Upson that much."

"Imagine that!" Card said, in a surprised voice.

"You don't have to imagine it! I'm telling you. But, now, about Short Card Mann —"

"You mentioned him, once before. Who *is*

this Mann?"

"Another straw-boss," Curt told him pleasantly. "Representing the Trackless Bunch in Ancho. And I want him, Card. Where is he?"

"Why ask me?" Card shrugged. His expression was almost absent, as if while talking he considered other things, more important things. "I wouldn't know about him. Why ask me?"

"Yeh!" a voice called from the dance-hall door. "Why not ask me? I have got our friend, Short Card Mann, right here. He was makin' a sneak out the back way when I come along. So I put a contemporary part in his scalp-lock with my pistol-barrel an' — here he is!"

The men at the bar — Tom Card — Curt — all stared at the lean, grinning figure of Andy Allen in the doorway. Andy held a Winchester comfortably across his arm, so that the muzzle was trained generally upon the room. His long Colt was not in its holster, but rammed into his waistband.

"I think you've lost this hand — and the game," Curt said drawlingly, to Card. "I knew, all the time, that it was you and Bain; you doing the head-work for the Trackless Bunch and Bain — and Short Card Mann, of course — carrying out your orders. The trouble was, getting hold of the right man, the man who'd know all the ins and outs when we began to — persuade him to spill what we needed for a jury."

Card said nothing. Without movement, without change of expression, he met Curt's eyes.

"I hoped that you'd come along today with your gang," Curt shrugged. "I wiggled that bullion from the Glory Hole in front of you, trying to get you, personally, on the ground. I knew that you were figuring on just one more big job, or two or three little ones, before skipping. For you didn't underrate me, Card, no matter what you pretended. You knew that I'd hang and I'd rattle until I got you. Well —"

He looked around, at the gaping men along the bar, who watched Tom Card and seemed to wait for a signal, then at Andy Allen and at Short Card Mann who lay on the floor behind Andy. Without turning back to Card, he said amusedly:

"But trying to stay in the back, clear of connection with your gang, didn't save you. For Mann will talk — if I have to ask Chihuahua to skin the soles off his feet —"

He whirled back, but the stubby derringer was already coming up in Card's hand. Curt's hands snapped up under his goatskin jacket. Gurney had never seen — not even in Frenchy Leonard's flaming days — the like of that two-handed draw. But before Card could level his .41, before Curt's twin Colts were clear of the jacket's flaps, a shot roared and another, from the rear of the dusky room. Card staggered.

There was movement at the bar. The men there, watching Card produce from coatsleeve the little derringer on its elastic band, had made their decision at last.

The room was thunderous with shots. Reeking powder smoke swirled toward the ceiling as Curt leveled his Colts on them, instead of Card — who sprawled, now, upon the floor at his feet.

From the rear, from the dance-hall, from Curt, lead was hurled into the last detachment of Tom Card's Trackless Bunch. And from the office, a thin, high overtone to the roar of the shooting, came frantic screaming.

Abruptly, the firing ceased. Curt looked dazedly about him, saw no more targets, and raced to the office door. He flung it open. Shirley lay flat upon the floor, her face pillowed upon outflung arm. Another woman, whom he saw but vaguely as a slender, garishly dressed figure of pale, pretty face and great, staring black eyes, half-sat, half-lay, in a corner. She was tied with silk neckerchiefs, hand and foot.

He heard the shouting in the bar-room and, sure that neither woman was hurt, turned back to the door. When he looked out the smoke still drifted, to canopy the low ceiling. Below it was a very shambles. And through all the doors came men of Gurney, not those whom Curt had led at Scalp Creek, but men whom Halliday for one reason or another had not included in his posse. They carried Winchesters and Sharpses, shotguns and pistols. Uniformly, they were very grim of face, and wearing an expression of quiet satisfaction.

"I think" — Curt said to Shirley, turning back — "that the Trackless Bunch is finished, as I promised Tom Card it would be before I stopped. Now — about this woman . . . Is she supposed to be tied up, or can I let her loose, now? Who is she?"

"That," she said, without looking at the other woman, "is the lady who should be Tom Card's wife. She came into Gurney from El Paso, at noon. She quarreled with Tom Card and he tied her that way, just a little while ago."

Curt nodded and crossed to the woman. He loosed the knots of the neckerchiefs and helped her to her feet. She was like a woman sleep-walking, he thought. He spoke to her gently.

"*Mi esposa?*" she said flatly. "My husband?"

"*Muerto,*" Curt shrugged. "He is dead."

"*Muerto?*" she repeated, staring at him. "*Madre de Dios!*"

And she whirled, darted past him and out. Curt shrugged, then turned with stony face to Shirley. Without a word, he put hand upon her arm and moved her to that front window — through which he had so often watched her working at Card's books. It seemed ages and ages past, now, as he thought of it. He hooked a chair to the window with his toe. He helped her step on it, then lifted her to the window-sill.

So, momentarily, her face was very close to his. The dark eyes were fixed levelly upon his own — questioningly. But he looked blankly at her. He virtually pushed her through the window, caught her hands and let her down. When her feet touched the planks of the sidewalk, he let go his grip.

In the bar-room, the woman from El Paso sat upon the floor with Tom Card's head upon her lap. She did not look at him, she did not make a sound. But the men moving about the grim business of separating the wounded from the dead went around her with pitying glances, while she stared with great black eyes at the wall.

Curt saw Andy and Chihuahua standing with Short Card Mann between them. The tinhorn was a shaken and draggled figure, now. Blood from his scalp-wound had dribbled down his face. His pale eyes roved nervously.

"Well, well!" Curt said, with a kind of genial savagery, "so here's our friend Quinn, the nester's man, again. That was pretty slick, Mann. But pretty slick is never slick. It's just almost. And that was your trouble all along, I reckon. You put the cuffs on him, did you, Andy? Good! Chouse him over to the jail and chain him up alongside of Zyler. We'll probably hang 'em with the two ends of the same rope."

"Ah, they won't hang Mann, will they?" Andy cried.

"Higher than Old Man Haman!" Curt assured him grimly. "He was riding point, today, wasn't he, when those teamsters were killed? Well, every one of the Bunch helped murder 'em. Every one of 'em is responsible, no matter who actually did the shooting. They're all murderers together!"

"You know, that's exactly what *we* figured," Halliday's booming voice announced, behind him. "The whole bunch was a passel of murderers. So it wouldn't have been nothin' but a nuisance, to bring 'em in an' have 'em eatin' their heads off while they was waitin' to be tried — an' then just bein' hanged, anyway. So —"

"So, what?" Curt said frowningly, but he knew.

"So we left the whole nine out there on Scalp Creek. There's a fine, big cottonwood out there, with a long, thick limb . . ."

"*Amor de Dios!* I might've known I didn't dare leave 'em with you!" Curt groaned. "The Governor will comb my hair! He'll just naturally give me hell!"

"Sure! He will that — officially. But, unofficially, he'll buy you a fine, tall drink. I *know* the Governor!" . . .

In a corner of the dance-hall, Curt and Andy and Chihuahua, with Halliday and others of the leading Gurney men, held a sort of preliminary investigation. Besides Short Card Mann, there were other prisoners, men slightly wounded by the blast of fire which had cut their side down at the bar.

He looked around, at last, a shade wearily. He was pale under bronzed skin, and his eyes were haggard. But if his voice was flat and dull, his questions were still very much to the point. And Short Card Mann, who listened to the examination of the lesser figures of Card's gang, suddenly leaned to Curt.

"Listen, Thompson," he said shakily, "I know when showdown comes. I'm the only one left that can give you the story, in a way to finish up your case. These men don't know anything, they just took orders. *I* was one of Card's three main bowers. I'll make a trade with you —"

"I don't know that I can make a trade," Curt shrugged. "Anyway, I don't know, either, that we haven't got plenty to round out the case against the bunch of you that's left."

"But you don't know where the unsold stock is. And you don't know, even, where the money and jewelry are — what was got in the various robberies. I'm not asking much, all I want is not to be charged with murder."

"That's not for me to say, of course," Curt said slowly, "but I'll do my best to talk the proper authorities into seeing it that way. I think we've had enough killings and I reckon they'll see it the same way."

"All right, then: Card was the Ramrod, as you figured. I handled odd jobs in Ancho. Bain was just a figurehead, of course. Card really owned the Lazy B. And that freckled-

360

face you-all downed at Tompkins's store — Nolan, his name was — was our expert cowthief. He was from Utah, a Green River man and as tough an egg as I ever ran into."

"That's about what I figured. But where's the stock you hadn't sold? Where's the loot from stage and bank robberies?"

"In Tom Card's safe — damn' near every nickel we got! He was more than careful about passing it out. He kept stalling the boys, telling 'em we'd have a big split when the country got too hot for us and we had to move on. I think he planned to cross everybody and skip with the most of it. But it did do one thing — his keeping it: nobody showed a lot of money and gave you a lead to us."

"Right!" Curt nodded. "I looked hard for that kind of thing and never saw it. But Card was slick enough. And you're right about his ideas: he was getting ready to hightail and leave the gang holding an empty sack."

"Look in the office, will you. There's a bare chance he left the safe open for something. If he didn't, we'll have to bring a man in from El Paso. Or blow her with giant."

Chihuahua came back, shrugging. The safe was locked. Curt nodded apathetically. He felt pretty sure that the loot was safely inside the heavy iron box. "Let's take the prisoners over. Take Mann back and chain him up again. I'll see that you don't hang, Mann. I may have trouble saving your neck, but I'll stick in Gurney until it is all settled."

They turned over to Shorty Wiggins the file of prisoners, then came downstairs again. The three of them stood at the office door. Andy stared upstreet, then looked furtively sidelong at Curt — who laughed. "Yeh, I think you're old enough, now," he said. "And you'll be heading for Los Alamos again, pretty soon. The manager's house, out there, is a nice place. And the way *she'd* fix it up, not the *casa principal* would be prettier. And I know Sudie-May likes her . . ."

"What —" Andy began, then grinned sheepishly. "I reckon you add mind readin' to your other talents, huh? That's exactly what I was thinkin'. I'm goin' to go ask her, now. I saw her in the door, just then."

They leaned, grinning, to watch him hurry toward Marie Young's door. They saw him stop and for a moment talk to her. Then he went inside the little store. Chihuahua laughed. He stretched long arms above his head and looked slantingly at Curt, who stared blankly out upon the street in the thickening dusk. Chihuahua yawned.

"Let's go clean up," he suggested. "Them Ortiz, she's have fi-ine hot baths an' she's shave us an' cut them hair. You're look like them young bear, Curt."

They got spare clothing from the office cupboards and drifted up the street. At Marie Young's door Andy Allen put out his head. He was grinning seraphically.

"She's all fixed!" he cried. "Come on in —"

"Congratulations," Curt smiled. "But we're headed for the barber's. See you tomorrow. Tell Marie I hope she carries on the good work with you."

At Ortiz's little shop in a 'dobe beyond Halliday's, they luxuriated in hot water, lying comfortably in Ortiz's big tin tubs, smoking. Then the fat little barber and his fatter son cut their hair and shaved them. Chihuahua, dressed, looked at himself approvingly and inspected Curt.

"*Por Dios!* except for them long face, you're look like one cowboy!" he said, grinning. "Now — supper, hah?"

They ate at the U-and-Me and here Halliday told them how the men of the town had come so opportunely to the Palace, to join the war against the last of Card's men.

"Mis' Sheehan told me," he said. "Seems this abandoned lady of Card's hit town at

363

noon an' she tore into Card plenty, for leavin' her flat in El Paso with their kid. Miss Shirley, as soon as she made out the straight of it, she walked out of the Palace. *After* tellin' Card ex-actly what she thought about him. She was through. But Card tolled her back with a yarn that the woman was awful sick, or somethin'. Mis' Sheehan, she guessed where Miss Shirley'd gone an' she come up an' listened under the office window. Short Card Mann had just come in with the Scalp Creek story an' Card told Miss Shirley he had to leave an' he was done with this other woman an' *she* had to go with him.

"Well — Mis' Sheehan never listened no more. She just loped up an' down an' gathered up the men-folks. They was right behind Andy an' Chihuahua, landin' at the Palace. Good thing, too!"

Curt nodded. He grinned twistedly at Chihuahua.

"I haven't thanked you, yet, for drilling Card when he snapped that derringer out of his sleeve."

"*De nada!* It's nothing. Me, I'm know you're pull faster an' kill him. But, w'y will I stop w'en I'm covering him? You are my witness that I kill them Bain w'at's Slim Upson. You will tell so that I'm git them three-thousand-dollar reward. Well! W'y will I take them chance that I'm lose my witness?"

On the street again, after supper, Chihuahua looked at Curt.

"You're tell them Short Card Mann you're stick around Gurney till she's tried," he said. "W'at will you mean? You're not stay more? You're not care for them sheriff job?"

"Oh, there's nothing to it. I never figured on making it a lifetime job. I wanted to see this Trackless Bunch wiped out. But now that's done. So when I'm free, I'll cinch the hull onto the buckskin and slide back to Texas to see my mother. Then —"

"But, now, I'm think that them blonde w'at I'm dance with one night in the Palace, she's wait for me," Chihuahua grinned. "She's not know it, but she's wait just the same. An' she's have other girls, Curt. Me, I'm think you're better, tonight, if you're dance an' drink an' not think about them one girl . . ."

"I'm not in the humor for floozeying. You go ahead."

When he had seen the tall figure vanish into darkness near the silent Palace, he drifted aimlessly back toward the office. But at a little *cantina* favored by Chihuahua, he stopped. He hesitated for a moment, then went in. Antonio, the *cantinero,* waved him

365

respectfully to a table in a dark corner. He brought the bottle that Curt demanded.

Curt sat with tin cup and uncorked bottle. He poured himself a drink and stared straight ahead. He was very tired, now. Of course, he had got no sleep the night before and this had been a full, hard day. But his weariness, dejection, were bone deep, far more than were justified by that. He lifted the bottle and poured a second big drink. Then quick, heavy feet in the *cantina's* doorway pulled his eyes that way.

"You young hellion!" Mrs. Sheehan said grimly. She came waddling back to the table and he got to his feet. "You — young — hellion! Nothin'll serve you but gettin' drunk, is it!"

"Why — Why, Mrs. Sheehan!" he began.

"Don't you be why-in' me! You'll never get drunk this night! You'll march, that's what you'll do! Come on, now! March! Shame on you — skulkin' here in this doggery an' makin' a decent woman search you out! Not a word out of you, now! Come along with me!"

"But, Mrs. Sheehan!" he protested. "What's it about?"

"Will it be by the ear that you'll come, then, like the child you are?"

There was nothing to do but go with her. He tossed a dollar to Antonio as he passed the *cantinero* and on the street fell in step beside his captor.

"Curt!" she said angrily, "I could be boxin' your ears, I could. What was it you told me about Shirley? You would be handin' over your last penny to her, you would be killin' Tom Card, so you would — all because you loved her so. An' what did you do, today, when she looked at you and waited? Shoved her through the window of that dirty office of the Palace! I saw that."

"She told me that *casual friendliness* was all I could expect from her," he said angrily. "She asked me to remember it, hereafter — and I have! I've got some pride, myself. Maybe she does come from a fine, nose-up family. I'm not ashamed of my family, either! And I'm not a bit ashamed of myself! When I'm in love with a girl, I tell her so. But — I don't get down on my knees like a swamper and tell her she's so much better than I am that — Well, that's the way I feel about it. If she feels that she's better than I am, she'll feel that way when I'm not there to be bothered. She led me to believe that she liked me, she let me kiss her, then she turned on me as if I was dirt —"

"Oh!" Mrs. Sheehan said softly. "So she

did let her feelin' show one time, did she! I wondered about that. For *I* knew how she was feelin' an' I thought maybe she'd not be able to keep that poker face on all the time! Curt . . . she's been in a hard place. She had to keep on at the Palace for the family's sake — she thought. An' she liked Card — many did! An' marryin' him — she thought of that, too — it would settle the money trouble. Then, on top of that —

"Do you remember a note you got, one day, warnin' you that Texas men was comin' with warrants?"

"I got two notes," Curt said contemptuously. "Tom Card thought he was being clever. He knew I was from Texas. He guessed that I'd been in trouble there. So he thought of warrants. But there was no warrant in Texas against me. He just over-played his hand."

"Two notes . . . I knew of but one. The one that Shirley sent you, on an envelope flap, it was. Card told her that he had heard of Texas officers comin' with warrants for you. An' though the charge fair made the girl sick, she sent you the note to give you the chance to run."

They had reached the steps of the hotel. Curt looked at her.

"What was I supposed to have done, to

earn the warrants?"

"Murdered your wife an' her father!"

"What? Murdered my — Why, I never was married in my life! I never wanted to *get* married — then! She believed that?"

"Of course not! What woman that loved a man would believe such a thing of him? She never believed it. She was just afraid it might be true."

"Wait a minute!" Curt snapped. "What are you trying to tell me? She didn't believe it, but she thought it might be true — what kind of tangle is that? Of course she believed it!"

"Ah, you nitwit! Can't you see the difference? Then take my word for it that there's all the difference in the world. Come upstairs with me."

He followed her scowlingly to the second floor. She took his arm in a red hand bigger than his own, but when she looked at him in the light of an oil lamp, the hard face had softened.

"That door!" she whispered. "Inside with you! An' if ever you tell that Teresa Sheehan traipsed the town over huntin' you an' lugged you out of a doggery —"

She pushed him gently and he turned the doorknob. The room was dusky, lit only by a shaded lamp on a narrow table by the window. On the bed were dresses and hats. A trunk stood open at the end of the bed. Shirley, with a dress in her hand, turned to face him. She was in a silk dressing-gown of dull crimson that somehow made paler the clear ivory of her face, made redder the line of her mouth, made duskier the mass of her hair. She stared at him.

"You're packing," he said slowly. "You're leaving us."

"I'm packing," she answered. "I'm leaving tomorrow."

He put up a hand to his hat, was surprised to find it on his head and took it off. He looked at it, then at her.

"I just found out about — your note," he said carefully. "I wanted to tell you that — that I never was married. And I never killed a woman, anywhere, so far as I can remember."

"I — didn't think you had. Won't you — sit down?"

He nodded stiffly and closed the door. The nearest chair was beside the trunk. He went toward it and stopped a yard from her. She seemed to have forgotten the dress she held. Watching her, he forgot the chair.

"I'm going away, too," he said. "Not tomorrow. But as soon as we can make out the cases against our prisoners. I am sort of sick of being the Sheriff of Gurney. I've been over a good deal of country, horseback and a little by train. I think I'll take the few thousands I've got and catch a train for the East and then get on a boat and — Oh, get over my restlessness."

"I'm just going back to New Orleans. My mother has discovered a few odds and ends of my father's estate. There's enough to make her and my sister comfortable. I'll find something to do there and — I'll try to forget some things."

"You haven't been very happy in Gurney," he nodded. "Neither have I. Especially, not of late. But I hope you have more luck at your forgetting than I'll have, at mine."

"*Curt!*" she said suddenly. The dress fell to the carpet and she stepped on it. "You make me feel — I did it! I did it to you. I hurt you, when you were being lovely to me. Partly, because you were such a swaggering, you-be-damned boy that you infuriated me. And I thought that — that he —"

"I'm not blaming you!" he cried. "It was my fault. I thought that I could make you love me — in fact, I was sure of it. I can't blame you because you didn't — don't —"

"But I *do!* I've loved you all the while! I — I loved you so much that, when you left me on the street and went marching toward Marie Young's, I came right after you! I was afraid you'd propose to her, so I called her! That — was unfair of her! To feed you apple pie, when you'd never eaten any of mine —"

He drew her arms up about his neck, tilted her chin so that parted lips were lifted and bent to them. She tightened her arms about him and lifted herself tiptoe to meet his mouth. A long while later he drew her to the window and held her, there, in the curve of his arm, his cheek against hers.

"See that light over there?" he said. "The yellowish one? Well — that's the justice of the peace. And if you were to put on some clothes and make yourself less scandalous — and a lot less beautiful — we could go over there and persuade him to take ten dollars of my money for marrying us. Odd, how things are . . ."

"I'll have a marrying dress on in about two minutes. *If* you'll stop kissing me," she added, in a muffled voice.

ABOUT THE AUTHOR

Eugene Cunningham grew up a Texan in Dallas and Fort Worth. He enlisted in the U.S. Navy in 1914 serving in the Mexican campaign and then the Great War until his discharge in 1919. He found work as a newspaper and magazine correspondent and toured Central America. He married Mary Emilstein in 1921 and they had two daughters, Mary Carolyn and Jean, and a son, Cleve. Although Cunningham's early fiction was preoccupied with the U.S. Navy and Central America, by the mid 1920s he came to be widely loved and recognized for his authentic Western stories which were showcased in *The Frontier* and *Lariat Story Magazine.* In fact, many of the serials he wrote for *Lariat* were later expanded to book-lengths when he joined the Houghton Mifflin stable of Western writers which included such luminaries as William MacLeod Raine and Eugene Manlove

Rhodes. His history of gunfighters — which he titled *Triggernometry* — has never been out of print and remains a staple book on the subject. Often his novels involve Texas Rangers as protagonists and among his most successful series of fictional adventures, yet to be collected into book form, are his tales of Ware's Kid and Bar-Nuthin' Red Ames, and ex-Ranger Shoutin' Shelley Raines. Among his most notable books are *Diamond River Man,* a retelling of Billy the Kid's part in the Lincoln County War, *Red Range* (which in its Pocket Books edition sold over a million copies), and his final novel, *Riding Gun.* Western historian W. H. Hutchinson once described Cunningham 'as fine a lapidary as ever polished an action Western for the market place.' At his best he wrote of a terrain in which he had grown up and in which he had lived much of his life and it provides his fiction with a vital center that has often proven elusive to authors who tried to write Western fiction without that life experience behind them. Yet, as Joseph Henry Jackson wrote of him, 'everywhere he went, he looked at life in terms of action, drama, romance, and danger. When you get a man that knows what men are like, what makes a story and how to write it, then you have the ideal writer in the Western field. Cunningham is precisely that.'